Seven Summers Later

Laila Rafi has dabbled in a few industries but realised that her real calling was putting pen to paper, or more accurately, fingers to keyboard and getting lost in the world of happily ever afters. So now that is exactly what she does. Her debut novel was shortlisted for the RNA Katie Fforde Debut Romantic Novel Award.

Laila lives in the heart of London with her boisterous family and when she's not writing or reading romance, she can be found watching almost any sport - preferably Formula 1 - or working on her latest crochet project.

Also by Laila Rafi

From Fake to Forever
First Comes Marriage

Seven Summers Later

LAILA RAFI

ORION

This paperback edition published in 2025
by Orion Fiction, an imprint of The Orion Publishing Group Ltd,
Carmelite House, 50 Victoria Embankment
London EC4Y 0DZ

An Hachette UK company

The authorised representative in the EEA is Hachette Ireland,
8 Castlecourt Centre, Dublin 15, D15 XTP3,
Ireland (email: info@hbgi.ie)

1   3   5   7   9   10   8   6   4   2

A CIP catalogue record for this book
is available from the British Library.

ISBN (Paperback) 978 1 3987 2105 0
ISBN (eBook) 978 1 3987 0996 6

Typeset by Born Group
Printed and bound in Great Britain by Clays Ltd, Elcograf S.p.A.

MIX
Paper | Supporting
responsible forestry
FSC® C104740

www.orionbooks.co.uk

For Zeina
Love you to the moon and back tot.
Keep smiling always X

1

Safiya

'Food for table eight ready.'
'Saf, table four are asking for the bill.'
'Excuse me, can we get some more of the—'

Two hours.

Just two more hours until I can go back to my tiny but quiet room and flop face down on the bed. It's been one of those days which I wish had ended at least six hours ago. Worst bit? I wasn't even supposed to be working today, but Flavio Sousa – our tyrannical acting manager – called me in. Why didn't I say no? Because I need this job and I could definitely do with the extra money.

My phone buzzes in my back pocket, and I know it's either Mum trying her best to not invade the boundaries I set up after I came back from Nairobi – and failing – or Vaneeza, my ever patient best-friend, awkwardly asking if I'll be able to transfer her the rent today. I really need to get that done.

I haul in what I hope is an energising breath, readjusting the plates of lamb tagine and a couscous salad on my arm before picking up a bowl of Moroccan lentil soup, and then I back out of the kitchen into the main restaurant, narrowly missing a little boy as he runs past me. He's been doing that since he came into the restaurant with his parents and it's driving me nuts.

He's just a child, I remind myself, *just a happy, if slightly wild child.*

A child, who should have his little backside firmly glued to a chair, but is instead running through the restaurant like it's his personal playground with nothing more than half-hearted protests from his parents, who are too busy in their own conversation. 'Georgie. Buddy, what did we say about running indoors?' Or, earlier, there had been, 'Georgieee. Honey, what did we say about sitting in the way where people need to pass?' *Honestly.* It didn't matter what they said, he obviously wasn't listening.

A much-welcome breeze washes over me and I look in the direction of the main door of the restaurant which opens to the bustling high street and suppress a groan when I find Haroon Saeed of all people standing there, giving me his signature grin when he spots me.

I deposit the plates I was holding on table eight and close the distance towards him. 'What are you doing here, Harry?' I hiss at my cousin, folding my arms across my chest for good measure to show him I mean business. Sadly, it doesn't make an iota of difference to him as he shrugs irreverently.

'Waiting to be seated. I've heard great things about this place.' His brow furrows in concern as he eyes the space around him, presumably taking in the cacophony of noise and customers.

'Really Harry? From who?' I narrow my eyes at him knowing perfectly well that he's not heard anything good or bad about this place and that's not why he's here.

He looks at me and after three seconds caves. 'Fine. I might have wanted to check in.'

'At my place of work?' I pick up a menu and walk Harry over to the table furthest away, giving Flavio an uneasy smile so he doesn't suspect anything, 'This isn't on, Harry. I wouldn't come to your workplace—'

'First things first, dear cousin-sister of mine, I don't have a workplace. And this was the only way I was guaranteed to find you. Kids these days are better at using their phone than you are. When the phone rings, you're supposed to swipe the screen and then hold the phone to your ear and—'

'I don't have time for your silliness right now, Haroon. Here, look at the menu. I have a job to do because I actually have a workplace.' I thrust the menu at him and, after giving him a glare that would make our grandmother proud, I make my way towards a table where the customers are ready to settle their bill.

I get shunted from behind and turn to see the same child give me a toothy grin before he zooms off again. *Please just sit down,* I pray silently, but my prayers go unanswered as he rushes around nearly knocking me over, his parents completely oblivious.

I can see Harry trying to wave at me from the corner of my eye, but I ignore him as I make my way towards the bar to get drinks.

'Saf,' Melissa flags me down. 'I just need to use the loo. Be a babe and take table six their drinks with yours please.' She bounces on the balls of her feet, a desperate look in her eye.

Reluctantly, I nod and load all eight drinks on the tray. I make my way through the tiny gaps between the tables, noticing Harry, who is still trying to wave me over, mouthing something as he does. My eyes narrow as I try to lip-read and make sense of it and then—

Crash.

In life, there are sometimes those dreams . . . nightmares, actually. The ones which make the small hairs on the back of your neck stand up and wake you up at 3 a.m. with a pounding heart and beads of sweat on your upper lip. This is one of them. My hair is standing on end, my heart is pounding and sweat has not only beaded on my upper lip, a droplet of it slides down my spine. Except this is no dream. It's a very real nightmare.

Georgie, who had plonked himself right in between the tables, was hitting the tiled floor, using a spoon as a makeshift drumstick. With my attention on Harry, I spotted him a little too late and lunged to the side to avoid falling on top of him and went down – with the drinks and my dignity – like a sack of potatoes. The resounding crash sends a shiver down my spine. It'll probably hound me in the afterlife – it was that bad.

My elbow hits the floor and pain shoots through my limbs. 'Ow,' I whisper. And then, for a moment – just *one* peaceful moment – everything is quiet, like the restaurant has frozen in time. I stare at the mahogany brown walls, the lights hanging from the ceilings, the dated artwork, until my eyes land on Harry's face. I wince as I manage to sit upright, glancing to my side. Thankfully, Georgie seems unharmed. He stares back at me with wide eyes for a whole five seconds until his bottom lip protrudes, trembles and then he lets out an ear-splitting wail, as though all those glasses have crashed on his head, making me wince again.

'Georgie,' I bargain, softly, like I used to with my younger cousins before one of them complained to our parents after we'd been play-fighting with each other. 'It's OK. You're OK. Look I'm the one with all the drink on me.' I hope to get him to quieten down whilst inside I'm ready to bawl my eyes out along with him.

Flavio – the complete pain in my neck that he is – bustles over and starts flapping around Georgie and his parents, while Harry swiftly makes his way towards me. 'Saf. Are you hurt?'

The other waitstaff on the floor give me sympathetic looks, quietly relieved it wasn't them I'm sure, and stand frozen as Harry helps me up.

'Yeah, I'm fine. I just bumped my knees and elbow.' I rub my aching elbow as I look at the carnage around me. It's a mess. Smashed glass and liquid everywhere.

Flavio brings a yellow cone which says CAUTION and sticks it next to me. He apologises to the parents, all of them ignoring me and focusing on Georgie before Flavio turns towards me and then speaks through gritted teeth in a voice loud enough that only Harry and I hear him. 'Go home, Safiya. You've done enough.'

Harry offers to drop me off at my flat and the car ride is unusually quiet. Every so often, I sigh, reliving the last embarrassing – and painful – hour of my life, while Harry clears his throat.

I drag myself to the flat I share with Vaneeza, my best friend since before either of us could string a sentence together, and pour myself a glass of water. I've only taken a few sips when Vaz walks in, her Pomeranian, Biscuit, following closely behind her.

'Heyyy,' Vaz says, in a voice she reserves for Serious Chats. 'Did you make the transfer? Because nothing's come through on my side.' She leans against the small table under the window, waving her phone in the air.

I groan at the question. 'Shit, no. I meant to but—'

Vaz frowns as she massages her temples. Guilt begins to grow in my stomach, wishing things were different – that

I was different. 'We spoke about this, Saf. I can't afford to cover our rent for the next month and you said you'd take care of it. You know I would if I could, but—'

'I know and I will. Let me do it now. I was going to do it while on my break, but then I got asked to cover for an extra ten minutes and it slipped my mind.' I pull my phone out of my back pocket and see all the notifications lined up – the top, most recent one an email from Flavio.

To: Safiya Saeed
From: Flavio Sousa
Subject: Notice of Dismissal

Dear Safiya,
I am sorry to inform you that you will no longer be employed at this restaurant effective immediately—

My stomach drops as I scroll through the email. 'Oh no.'

'What is it? Is everything OK?' I hear Vaz ask in the background, but I don't respond as my eyes flit over the email.

Biscuit comes and sits in front of me, her shiny eyes on me when I look down at her. She barks and then whines softly before lowering her head to the ground.

'I've been fired.' I hear myself whisper the words and a wave of nausea washes over me. 'Apparently, Georgie's parents complained – adding to the list of mounting complaints against me. Whatever those might be.'

'What?' I block out Vaz's shrieked question but feel her take the phone out of my limp fingers. 'Let me see. Oh, Saf.'

I pull out a chair on autopilot and lower myself into it, dropping my head into my hands. What on earth am I going to do? I needed that job and without it . . . I close my eyes as a sense of defeat and fatigue washes over me.

You've got a false sense of superiority, Safiya. No actual substance, just a bucketload of pride. Do you think anyone else would want you?

Ejaz's words reverberate through my head, drowning out the noise around me. My ex-husband never spared a moment in which he could point out my flaws. I thought I had brushed them off, but they're always there at the edge of my subconscious, poking and prodding, and now I wonder if perhaps he wasn't as much off the mark as I keep trying to convince myself he was. My family try to reassure me that he was talking rubbish, the little I shared with them, but I'm beginning to find it hard to believe that. All I have to show for myself is one failure after the next. Failed marriage? Tick. Unsuccessful professional career? Tick. Fractured relationships with family? Tick, tick, tick. And now I've just been fired from my waitressing job before I could complete the probation period. How abysmal is that?

I need to pay Vaz and with no job, how am I going to manage that? She's already helped me for the past three months to take care of my share of the rent – given that I couldn't afford the full amount and have anything left to actually feed myself. She was quite clear that this month she would need more of a contribution from me – as was only right. At the grand old age of thirty-three, I should absolutely be taking care of my own share of the rent and rates, except I have no idea how I can afford it now.

The doorbell rings and Vaz goes to answer it, leaving me with my thoughts.

I know I could go home. My parents would be happy to have me back in a heartbeat – in fact they'd be over the moon, as would Daadi, my paternal grandmother – but just the thought of that has me feeling like I can't breathe. I can't go home. Not like this.

But with no job, no money and nothing to fall back on, what the hell am I going to do? And I can't cause Vaz any more trouble than I already have, I love her too much to do that to her. I could ask my parents or even my brother for financial support, but the very thought makes my toes curl.

I can't take a step backwards like that, not after everything I've had to fight through. All it will do is confirm everyone's belief that I need taking care of. I see the way they look at me. *Poor Safiya.* And I don't want to be that anymore. I want to be more like how I used to be. I just need a bloody break.

I feel my shoulder being squeezed and I glance up to find a remorseful Harry looking down at me. 'Vaz told me what happened. I'm sorry, Saf.' He frowns. 'It's my fault. I didn't mean for any of that to happen.'

I heave a tired sigh. 'Yeah. Me too. And it's not your fault.' I drop my head into my hands once more and I feel Biscuit's paws on my knees as she stands on her hind legs, whining softly. I give her a scratch behind the ears and she barks joyfully, making the corners of my mouth twitch upwards into a slight smile.

'Right.' Vaz clasps her hands together with a determined look in her eye. 'Here is what we're going to do. I'm going to put the kettle on. You are going to change out of those clothes.' She points at me and swings her finger over at Harry. 'And you're going to open those chocolate-flavoured goodies you've just brought back with you and we're going to come up with a plan.'

If there's anything Vaz can do, it's rouse motivation. Or fear. I showered, and had a little therapeutic cry, before changing into comfy pyjamas. Harry is sitting next to me on the sofa, his brief guilt having worn off as he dips his third chocolate digestive into my tea.

I shoot him a glare. 'Get your own.' I scoot away from him, while Vaz sips her tea from her precious cup and saucer.

The anxiety after receiving Flavio's email hasn't quite dissipated. I still don't know quite what I'm going to do, but I need to come up with something, that's for sure. And if there is anyone I can do it with, it's Vaz and Harry.

'Hey. Cheer up. It was a shit job. So, blessing in disguise, really.' Harry quirks his brow.

I know he feels bad but it's really not his fault and he's not wrong – it was a pretty crap deal. I did it because both the restaurant manager – the actual manager – and I were desperate and it satisfied both our needs at the time. Besides, I wasn't sure what I really wanted to do. In fact, I'm still not.

Biscuit, who had been snoozing in Harry's lap, jumps down, clearly annoyed at the lack of attention, and makes her way to her dog bed, while Harry moves closer and throws his arm around me, giving me both a sense of comfort and familiarity. 'I'll make it up to you, Saf. I promise. I know you said it's not my fault, but still. By the way, I like what you've done with this place. It could do with a lick of paint, but the touches you both have added are nice.'

I groan as Vaz gets her chance to jump onto the same old topic. 'And guess who's behind it all?' Vaz says, pride in her eyes. 'That wall hanging? Saf. Those gorgeous coloured cushions and the throw? Saf. This rug? Saf. Those pieces decorating the mantel piece?'

'Let me guess. Saf?' Harry says with a cheeky grin and I elbow him. His comforting presence moving into annoying territory as it inevitably does with my six brothers. Well, technically I've got one brother and five cousins, of whom Haroon Saeed is the youngest.

'I know what you're doing and it won't work. I don't do that stuff anymore. I only did it here to spruce this place up. The walls are literally grey, for God's sake. It's quite obvious I can't do it on a professional level. Any suggestions I made to Flavio about making changes to the interior of the restaurant were met with a firm refusal. After he had scoffed at the idea, of course.'

'And since when is Flavio's unwanted opinion any authority on the subject? You're Safiya bloody Saeed. Of course you can do it,' Vaz retorts.

'I said no, Vaz.' My voice is harsh and I regret it as soon as I say it. The guilt instantly claws at my insides. 'Sorry, hun. I'm just . . .' I can't even justify myself, and sensing the state of my mind, Vaz comes and sits on my other side, while Harry scoots closer again, laying a reassuring hand on my knee.

Vaz puts her arms around me. 'Don't be sorry. I shouldn't have pushed, knowing how you're feeling this evening, no thanks to Foul Flavio.'

I snort out a laugh, unable to stop. Soon, Harry and Vaz are too, thinking up other names for Flavio. An annoying man who had nothing better to do than constantly pick holes in anything I did because he had taken an instant dislike to me. All I did was tell him that the capital of Morocco was Rabat and not Marrakech. Maybe I should have left him in blessed ignorance.

We put on the TV, watching the next episode of *Love Island* with frequent breaks for commentary. I try to ignore my problems and put them aside for tomorrow, but anxiety stirs in my belly.

Do you think anyone else would want you? The words echo in my head. The self-doubt, the heartbreak, the regret – it all comes rushing back, until Harry's raucous laugh snaps me out of it and I decide I need to stop feeling sorry for myself.

Seven summers ago, I didn't think I'd be back here. I definitely didn't think I'd be living with Vaz and watching reality TV with Harry. I'm surrounded by people I love. People who gave me a second chance without batting an eyelid and would probably give me a hundred more, and I owe it to myself to do the same.

I am Safiya bloody Saeed after all.

2

Murad

'It's just not the same anymore,' Antonella sighs, holding onto the stem of her wine glass. We're sitting in a small, darkly lit wine bar – one of Antonella's favourites. 'You used to hire someone and not worry that they weren't going to do the job. Or – what's the word? – half-arse it.' Her rich Italian accent comes through and I cover my mouth to hide the smile. Antonella's in her mid-sixties and hearing her say words like *half-arse* will never not make me laugh. 'It's not funny, Murad.'

'I know. It's not,' I say, genuinely, and lean in. 'But it's not the end of the world, Antonella. The skeleton of the place is sound, and it'd be a dream for someone to design. Now we just need to find that *someone*. And that's on me. Not for you to worry about.'

'Hmm.' She pouts, taking a sip of her white wine, clearly sceptical.

'I tell you what. I'll speak to my friend, Zaf Saeed. He's also in the property business, so he might have some contacts we could use.'

She nods. 'Fine. I trust you, I do. But I really want this one to go through, Murad. We've made a loss on the last two properties we've sold. We don't need this one to break even. We need to make a profit.'

I nod. While I know she doesn't hold me personally responsible for the losses, it doesn't stop me from feeling personally responsible for them. I need to do better for this project, otherwise she'd be well within her rights to refuse to work with me altogether.

'You have my word, Antonella. I'll bring in a cracking deal for this flat. But before that, we need to get it finished, so let me get that done. Try not to let it worry you – at least not yet.' I grin at her and throw in a wink for good measure and she shakes her head.

'Always the charmer, ready to pour oil over troubled waters.' She takes another sip of her wine and starts talking about an impending visit to her home town in Southern Italy. I have my ears on our conversation, but my mind is trying to figure out how to get our current project done satisfactorily because failure is not an option – not for a third time.

It's bad enough that we made losses on our previous two projects, but for her to raise it as a concern . . . it makes me feel a sense of inadequacy – a feeling I thought I had shaken off a long time ago. I could have done better, but I failed both her and myself. Sure, the property market fluctuates, I know that, and as a property developer I make allowances for such fluctuations. But my skill is in trying to beat these market trends. To offer buyers something that transcends what the market dictates as valuable or economically viable.

I can't mess this up. Not again.

'Hey Mum.' I answer the phone as I switch the engine off and get out of my car.

'Murad. How are you? I've not spoken to you in what feels like forever,' Mum says, trying to invoke guilt.

'Really? My phone records will probably show your *forever* to be three days in my universe. We spoke on Tuesday, Ma.'

'That was hardly anything. Are you coming up this weekend?' I hear clanging in the background, suggesting my mother has probably got her phone pressed between her ear and her shoulder and is pottering about in the kitchen. Mum considers it a waste of time not to multi-task.

'No. I've got some work that needs my attention and if I come to Birmingham, you, your daughter and your grand-daughter will make it impossible for me to manage anything.'

'It's called love, Murad. We all love you. And Sumi's only three. She doesn't understand the concept of work being more important than her.'

I sigh as she mentions my niece, twisting her little knife of guilt between my ribs. 'I never said work was more important than her. I'm just saying—'

'I know, darling. I'm pulling your leg.' I can hear the smile in her voice and the concern that laces it with her next sentence. 'You sound stressed. Everything OK?'

I haul in a deep breath as I take in the fresh autumn air and turn my collar up against the slight breeze that's picked up since this afternoon as I make my way towards Zaf's office building. 'I'm fine, it's just work stuff. How are things at your end? How's Meerab and the new little man doing?'

'They're fine, as is everyone else. Except Sumaira, of course. She's still put out that Irfan was supposed to be a sister, not a brother. She insists we take him back with the receipt.' Mum chuckles as I hear the tap go on in the background. My poor little niece is having trouble adjusting to the advent of a little brother in her life. She's trying her best to have someone take him off her pudgy little hands.

'Poor Sumi. I might come up next weekend and take her out for some quality uncle-niece time.'

'That would be lovely. In fact, you can meet my friend's niece who's come from Singapore while you're here. Sumi really liked her.'

'No, Mum.' I hold back a sigh.

'Can you at least hear me out?'

'Not really. You've got nothing to say that I've not heard – and soundly rejected – before. I've said countless times that I'm a grown up thirty-four-year-old man and I don't need you to set me up with every single woman in your orbit. Something you've not ceased doing for the past five years.'

'I don't do it with every single woman. Only the unattached and romantically available ones.'

'Very funny. Dad's humour is clearly starting to rub off on you. I can take care of my relationships all by myself, thank you.' It was a completely different matter that they didn't go the distance.

'There's no harm in me introducing you to someone. It doesn't mean you have to announce your engagement that very same weekend.'

'This is it with you. You go off like a rocket when it comes to this topic. I don't want to rush into anything.'

'Murad, my darling, you've been saying that for the last few years.'

If I don't put an end to this, I'll keep going around in circles with my mother and that's the last thing I need. She's a champion of this sport and I can feel a headache coming on after my meeting with Antonella and I still need to have a catch-up with Zafar. Thankfully, I'm right outside the entrance to his office building.

'I've got to go, Mum. I'll catch up with you soon, OK?' I walk through the revolving door, instantly surrounded by warmth.

15

'I know what a cut-off sounds like, sweetheart. I'm your mother.'

'That's the only reason I put up with you.' I grin as I say it and she laughs in response.

'Fine. Take care of yourself. Speak soon, OK?'

'Yeah.'

'Love you.'

'I love you too.' I end the call and, shaking my head, I push the button to call the lift and make my way towards Zaf's floor, where his assistant gives me a nod and points towards his office. It's time to get a solution to my problem.

'Good timing.' Zafar leans back in his chair as I close the door behind me. 'I was just about to head home.'

'Since when do you leave before five? Even if it is a Friday,' I say, amused, taking the seat opposite him as I theatrically check the time on my watch.

'Since I've discovered the joys of being married. You should try it.' Zafar shrugs, 'What happened to that anyway?'

'What happened to what?'

'Your dating life, slowcoach. How are things with Evie? Or was it Aisha?'

I shift from leaning on my left side to my right and Zafar raises an eyebrow in question. If it's not my mother, it's Zaf who's determined to interrogate me on this. 'It's Evie. Or was. We parted ways week before last. I've not met an Aisha yet.'

He hangs his head, as though I've failed us both.

'Sorry to disappoint you, Dad.' I pair my sarcasm with a grin. 'But we did part on good terms.'

He appears more bothered than I feel, which doesn't reflect well on my commitment to the relationship.

Zafar scoffs. 'Don't you always?! What happened this time? I thought things were going well.'

'They were. But she wanted more and I wasn't ready for it.' What he doesn't need to know is that I don't think I'll ever be ready for it and that's not something I can explain to myself fully, let alone share with anyone else, so I move on swiftly. 'I need to pick your brain on something.'

He nods, leaning forward. 'Sure. What's up?' Thankfully, he accepts my subject change.

'The flat I'm working on with Antonella has come to a standstill.'

'Again?' he asks incredulously. 'That place is like the gift that keeps on giving.'

I let out a sigh. 'The interior designer has bogged off and left us with nothing more than a mist coat on the walls.'

'Had you paid up?'

'Give me some credit, Zaf.' I lean forward and pick up a pen, flicking it through my fingers.

He grunts in response as he steeples his fingers together, leaning back. 'Is the building work sound or does it need clearance from a surveyor?'

'It's sound. The one silver lining on this thunder cloud, but that's not what I need your help with.'

'Well, that's something. I—'

The door swings open and Harry, Zafar's youngest brother, swaggers in without a care in the world. 'Perfect. I was hoping you hadn't already left.' He fist-bumps me and then his brother. 'How's it going?'

'*Me?*' I ask incredulously.

'No. Him.' He grins as he points at Zafar. 'I was in the city. Need a lift home.' He shrugs as he throws himself down on the small sectional sofa against the wall.

'You'll have to wait. We've got something to work out and then we can be on our way shortly,' Zafar says as he opens his laptop again.

17

Harry shrugs again, clearly used to listening to instructions from his older brother, and pulls out his phone.

I turn back to look at Zafar. 'It's fine, Zaf. We can do this next week. I'm in on Monday, so we can see what to do then. It's not like we'll find an interior designer right now. Besides, I want to be absolutely sure about the person we work with now. I can't afford any more glitches with this project.'

Zafar nods. 'I know you're worr—'

'Are you talking about interior designers? I have an idea.' Harry strides over with a grin. 'One that's going to fix your problem and, more importantly, mine.'

'Go on,' I say, intrigued.

'Safiya. She's an interior designer. You need one and she needs work aaand, most importantly, I kind of owe her one.' Harry enumerates his points on his fingers, oblivious of the impact they've just had on me.

Icy tendrils snake down my spine at the mention of *that* name, but with an iron will, I don't let so much as a flicker of an eyelash give me away. I haven't for seven years. And don't intend to start today.

Safiya. Saf. *My Fiya.* Or, at least, I had once been naïve to think she was, but I had fast enough been dispelled of that notion.

'I've already suggested she come and work with us and she refused,' Zafar says, momentarily taking his eyes off his screen. 'I'm not going to keep harassing her to do something she's made clear she doesn't want to do. Not until she says otherwise herself.'

I swallow down the dryness in my throat as the brothers talk to each other. Both of them oblivious to the fact that the mention of Safiya – even after all these years and countless attempts on my part for it not to be the case – has my heart stuttering in its rhythm and my breath hitching.

'I think you'll find things have changed since yesterday. Saf lost her job at the restaurant and she's going to need to find something else. She's desperate, Zaf, and I hate to see her like that,' Harry explains.

'How do you know?' Zafar frowns, the concern on his face probably visible from Mars.

'Because I saw her last night. When it all hit the fan.'

I clench and unclench my fist against my thigh a couple of times before mentally shaking myself out of my thoughts and clearing my throat, breaking into the conversation. 'I need this project resumed sooner rather than later, so let's see what we can come up with and we'll reconvene on Monday. Yeah?' I stand up, completely overlooking Harry's suggestion and keeping my eyes on Zafar until he nods in assent.

'I'll put a shortlist together over the weekend and then we'll take it from there. I'm sure we'll get it sorted.' He says it with more confidence than I'm feeling right now.

'Yeah. I'll see you on Monday.'

We say our byes and, with a sudden leaden feeling in my limbs and chest, I make my way out of there, grateful that I only had to deal with the mention of her rather than come face-to-face with Safiya.

Only God knows how I would have dealt with that!

3

Safiya

Is it possible to be sick if you haven't had anything to eat?

My palms are cold and clammy and I feel like curling up in bed and sleeping the entire week away, but that's not an option. Not when you're wearing big girl knickers on a Monday morning. It's the time for action.

I push the button on the panel and the lift doors silently close before the lift begins its ascent. Had things worked out differently, I likely would have been doing this journey on a daily basis, or at least as often as I came into the office.

This is the building where my much-esteemed paternal grandfather set up the headquarters for his family business as property developers, which moved to the eldest sons in the family. When I was younger, I had always thought that my elder brother Qais, Zafar and I would work for the business in some capacity, gradually joined by the rest of our brothers. It is the family business after all. But I hadn't factored in that my grandfather had favourites and a strict hierarchy.

But I can't let my aversion for what this place represents and the man who set it up affect my decision-making in the present. I can't let my pride do the talking for me. I've spent the whole weekend trying to come up with some other option – *any* other option – to try to meet my financial obligations without becoming more of a burden on Vaz – or any of my family members for that matter. But London is expensive and I took that for granted when my parents were taking care of me. Now, I have no choice. I can't leave the flat, because, firstly, it would mean staying with my parents, which I don't think I'm ready for and, secondly, it would leave Vaz in the lurch and I can't do that to her, not when she opened her arms and door to me when I needed it most.

So here I am, cap in hand, hoping that the offer Zafar made me when I first got back might still be on the table.

The lift doors open and, wiping my palms on my washed-out jeans, I step over the threshold for the first time in over seven years.

I stare at the sign on the glass doors in front of me.

Saeed & Sons – Property Developers

Sons. It leaves a bitter taste in my mouth, and I haul in a shaky breath, nearly coughing as dry air hits the back of my throat and makes my head pound. I really should have eaten something before coming, a banana at the very least.

Being here makes my skin feel too tight, but I make my way to the reception desk anyway, where a man in a suit and glasses is giving the keyboard a run for its money.

'Good morning,' the man says, politely. His brow quirks as he gives my favourite, and perhaps overworn, hoodie a once-over. 'How can I help you?'

'Hi. Morning.' I'm not sure why I've offered him two greetings, but it's probably a window into the state of my mind right now. 'I was wondering if I could see Zafar Saeed, please. I'm Safiya Saeed.'

'Of course. If you just take a seat in the waiting area, I'll see if he's free.' I pretend not to notice the slight straightening of the guy's back when I say who I am before he picks up the handset beside his keyboard. He speaks softly and, barely thirty seconds after he's put the handset down, I see Zafar striding down the corridor towards me, a broad smile on his handsome face.

'Saf! What a lovely surprise.' Zafar just about comes to a standstill before I'm being held close against him, his arms secure around me. I allow myself a moment of self-indulgence as I burrow against his big frame, letting my ever-present sense of stress take a back seat while I soak in some comfort, until Zafar eases back, keeping his hands on my shoulders as he looks at me. 'Come on. Fancy some breakfast? I was just about to order some for myself.'

He leads me into what I assume is a meeting room and within thirty minutes – while he catches me up on the latest goings-on about the extended Saeed family – he has a small breakfast spread before us, along with a pot of tea for me and coffee for him. My stomach gives an inelegant rumble and my cheeks go warm as he chuckles.

'Here, dig in.' He pushes a plate towards me which is piled high with an authentic Pakistani breakfast – a potato and chickpea curry, kebabs, parathas and a creamy semolina pudding.

'Bit much for a Monday morning, don't you think?'

'That's the best part about being an adult, Saf. We can actually do whatever we want, whenever we want. If that means a big desi breakfast on a Monday morning, then so be it.'

I love how he's become more carefree and less highly strung than he used to be before I got married, but I can't help but scoff at what he's said. 'If only that were true.'

I break off a bit of the flaky paratha and scoop up some potato and chickpea curry with it, closing my eyes as the herbs and spices explode in a burst of flavour on my tongue. It tastes like home.

It doesn't take me long to do justice to the food on my plate. I finish my meal off with the sweet semolina pudding with crushed nuts on top and my tea, a feeling of satiation making me feel pretty content for the moment. At least, until I have to tell Zafar why I'm here.

'How are things?' He cuts straight to it as he pushes his empty plate away and picks up his mug.

'If you tell me how much Harry's told you, I can fill in the gaps.'

He shakes his head with an indulgent smile as he takes a sip of his coffee, his cheek dimpling.

'There's no way he's not said anything to you. He might hide a lot of things from a lot of people, but he sings like a canary for you. I know I've been away for a while, but there are certain things I know haven't changed.' I allow a genuine smile to make an appearance and his broadens.

'OK. Fine. He told me you left the restaurant.'

A snort leaves my mouth. 'More like was let go.' I swallow hard as I lower my cup in its saucer and top up my tea from the pot, taking my time as I spoon in some sugar and stir it slowly. Zafar doesn't rush me, sitting there calmly as I muster up the courage to ask him the one thing I had hoped not to have to. 'I was wondering . . .'

'Hmm.'

I swallow once more. 'How's Reshma?' My voice is more high-pitched than I intended for it to be.

'She's fine, Saf. And you asked me this while we were waiting for breakfast to arrive.' He covers my fidgeting fingers with his warm palm and I let them go still. 'What's up?'

I try to find the courage to let go of my pride and to ask for a job in a place which has never welcomed me before. 'I need . . .' My voice drops to little more than a whisper, so I clear my throat and try again. 'I need a job,

Zaf. I was . . . Is your offer of one still open? It's just temporary. Once I figure things out, I'll leave. I promise, I just—' I look at him, partly in hope and partly in dread. This isn't what I wanted, but it's what I need. I think back to what he said about being an adult and doing whatever we wanted, whenever we wanted. I can't even begin to articulate how much I wish that were true and how far I feel from a sense of such autonomy and freedom. I feel like a puppet on strings being pulled one way and then the other.

'Hey, hey.' Zafar squeezes my hand and I realise I'm breathing heavily, as though I've just sprinted here. 'Relax, Saf. Everything will be OK. We'll fix it together. You don't have to do this by yourself, we're all here with you every step of the way, whenever you need us. Or don't. I'll admit I've found it hard to give you space. It makes me feel like I'm failing you as an older brother. Again.'

I shake my head. 'You've never failed me, Zaf. I just . . . There are things I need to do for myself, by myself. And I do appreciate how much you're doing for me . . . or not.' I smile at him and he huffs out a short laugh.

When I came back from Nairobi four months ago, after the divorce, I asked every member of my family to back off and give me space. I know they all love me and want to help me, but I just felt suffocated by that at the time, when I needed to build a life for myself. Not one that was handed to me, and not one that was expected of me. A life for me, chosen by me, earned by me. And, right now, the fact that I'm having to ask Zafar to help me with work rankles because it's at the very place where my prejudiced grandfather used to sit and reign. The man who caused me so much damage and loss that I can't even begin to undo it. But, damn it, I need to.

24

I look at Zafar, trying to see the similarities between him and our grandfather. He smiles at me gently, his eyes full of love and compassion. It doesn't matter how hard I look, aside from having the same name as him, I can't find any similarity between them. I feel a sense of reassurance at the realisation, only now accepting that a small part of me had feared I might.

'What sort of work would you like to do? I know you're not keen to venture back towards interior design, even though I've got something I think could be right up your street. We could find something administrative, legal, financial, or I could even speak to other business contacts about—'

'Actually, I've changed my mind on the interior work front. If you're up for giving me a chance, I'd like to dip my toes back into that pool.' *See if I've still got it,* I add silently.

'Really?' He holds his hands up in surrender. 'Have I just forced you?' He looks adorably puzzled and I can't help but giggle.

'Zaf! You haven't done anything of the sort. Now, what design job have you got?'

'It's a period conversion flat, some original features, some modern ones and a complete blank canvas to do whatever you want – within budget of course – and it'll then most likely be sold on.'

'You have a team of workpeople I can use once designs are finalised.?' I narrow my eyes, making a to-do list in my head already, feeling the tiniest flicker of interest slowly begin to unfurl inside me.

'It can be arranged by the end of the week. I just need to—'

'Here you are. I've been wondering where you were. I thought we were supposed to catch up in your office.'

25

I freeze. His voice stops me in my tracks, even though I wasn't moving. Deep, assured, familiar. Though it has been seven years since I last heard it, I would always recognise it. *Always.* My blood feels like it has turned to ice and my jaw locks. Thank God I've got my back to the door.

'Ah, just the man I needed.' Zafar, oblivious to my immediate rigidity, cheerfully gets up and moves out of my line of sight. 'I was just telling Saf here about the period conversion.' I hear back thumping and then Zafar comes back towards his chair, waving his arm towards the chair on his other side. 'Come and take a seat. I've got some good news for you.'

There's a stillness in the air, only a sense of tension permeating it, which Zaf seems immune to as he picks up his phone which just buzzed, smiles at it and then taps at the screen.

Time seems to have frozen, as I wait with a sick sense of dread in the pit of my stomach for the man standing behind me to come into my line of sight.

I close my eyes as darkness creeps in around the edges because I'm holding my breath. I take in some much-needed oxygen and will my heart rate to drop from its punishing pace, because right now it feels like it's going to beat right out of my chest. And when I open my eyes, there he is.

Murad.

I take one look at him and instantly feel adrift. His tall frame, certainly broader than I remember and with a hardness about it that wasn't there before, the softness gone. His clean-shaved jaw is clenched, and he is frowning with creases around his big brown eyes. Clearly not happy to see me, but what else should I expect? There is something else different too. A presence which I don't think was there before. He walks with purpose, but casually like he doesn't care I'm here. It stings, though I hate to admit it.

He unbuttons his suit jacket and takes it off, placing it, neatly folded, on the chair beside his before sitting opposite me, as though he has all the time in the world. His expression gives nothing away as his eyes rove over my face, from the top of my messy bun, down to where my hoodie disappears under the mahogany conference desk.

He doesn't care, I think. And I should be happy about that, but I'm not.

I unclasp my fingers that are tangled together tightly under the table as I try to find my own sense of control and make an effort to look at least somewhat relaxed, as though Murad's sudden appearance – after seven long years – hasn't affected me in the slightest.

'This is perfect.' Zafar puts his phone down, looking between me and his childhood friend. 'The period conversion is Murad's project, so he can tell you all about it himself.' He faces Murad. 'Didn't I tell you we'd work something out on Monday? Meet your new interior designer.' He waves his hand my way in presentation. 'Saf's interested in taking on the project.'

'Is that right?' Murad murmurs, as if he is completely disinterested. The deep cadence of his voice skates along my dead nerve endings, my pulse quickens and I try to pace my breathing. I don't remember the last time I felt this way.

I raise my chin as a corner of his mouth turns up like he's become sparing with his smiles. Smiles which used to light up my entire day at one time. I mentally try to shake off the thoughts that are bouncing around in my head like a rubber ball.

I need to focus.

I need to not be near Murad. I need to find another way to work things out for myself because there's no way I can take this job now, is there?

'I was just asking Zaf what he needed. Nothing's confirmed yet.' My voice doesn't come out as strong as I'd have liked, but at least it's not shaky.

'Pfft. Those are just formalities, Saf. Murad was on the lookout for someone to take over the design of the flat and you walked in this morning. Perfect serendipity.'

Murad's slight smile turns wide as he glances Zafar's way. 'You sound like Reshma,' he says, which makes Zafar's face light up with an infectious joy. Out of all of the cousins, Zafar was the one who was raised directly under our grandfather's shadow. And seeing how different he is from him and how he has managed to come out from under it and found true love with Reshma fills me with joy. And if I feel a small stab of sadness at what I could have had but don't, I ignore it.

'Why don't you both go check out the period conversion now?' Zafar suggests, standing up. 'I have a meeting to get to, so I'll leave you both to it.'

I glance over to Murad, whose steely gaze is firmly on me and the twitch in his jaw has returned. I know I need this job. God knows, I have no other option. But working on a project with the only man I've ever loved? Being in close proximity to the man who showed me nothing but love and expected nothing in return?

That's impossible.

Because the last time I saw him, I broke not only his heart but mine too and his expression tells me that he remembers that fact, crystal clear.

4

Murad

I deserve an award for the performance I've just put on. My neck and shoulders are screaming with the amount of tension I'm holding in them, but my punishment isn't quite over. In fact, it seems as though it's only just begun.

The crazy thing is, I knew Safiya was in the room the second I opened the door. I don't know how I knew, I just did. My body and soul knew she was there. It was my brain that took a few seconds too long to catch up and by then I had made Zaf aware of my presence.

I should have just told Zaf when things ended with Safiya seven years ago. Or told him I was dating his cousin. Sure, he would have found it awkward for his best friend and cousin to date, but at least I'd be spared the hell of all this lying. This pretending. We would probably have been spared having to work together on this period conversion, too.

The only upside is that Safiya is brilliant at her job. I know she's more than capable of doing a great job of designing and finishing the interior. She's probably only got better at her job over time. But just because I'd accept her working the project doesn't mean that I have to have anything more to do with her. She can take care of the design project with Zaf and then I can take over its management again once it's complete, *if* she agrees to doing it in the first place.

'I'm ready.' I turn and find her standing a few metres away, her sleeves pulled over her hands like she used to before . . . I take a shuddering breath and move away from the wall I was leaning against while I waited for her, waving towards the glass doors that will lead us to the lifts.

It's a silent ride down and when we get to the underground car park, she quietly follows behind me towards my car. It's only when we get close to it that I hear her gasp softly. She speeds up as I slow down and then she's standing in front of it, her eyes bright and sparkling as she takes in the bodywork of my Ferrari. She always was a petrolhead, influenced by her brother and cousins, though her penchant for fast cars outdid theirs.

She looks towards me and her smile dims slightly, though it doesn't quite vanish. 'You bought it.' Her voice is so soft, it barely reaches my ears.

I unlock the car, but neither of us make a move to get in. She stares at me, as though wanting me to confirm something she thinks she already knows. It's her favourite car. She always used to say that one day, we would get ourselves one, when we'd both made it. And when I could afford it, that's what I did. We just didn't do it together.

But for me, it's nothing more than a status symbol – a clear-cut sign to anyone who looks that I'm financially better off than I used to be – by miles. There might have been no sentimental reason behind my purchase, but as I look at her, a wave of memories hits me and I feel like that naïve young boy who fell for a girl who was too good for him.

I clear my throat. 'We need to get going. There're temporary traffic lights causing tailbacks and I need to get back to work.' I open the passenger-side door and pause long enough to see her make her way towards it and then I move towards the driver's side while she settles in.

The silence during the drive to the flat is the most awkward I've ever endured. I have no idea what to say or if I even want to say anything. There's so much history between us that I wouldn't know where to begin, and yet, ignoring it makes me feel like I'm pretending nothing really happened, and there's no way I'm going to do that. I'm not sure what the best way forward with this situation is just yet.

I pull up outside the flat and lead the way towards it. She precedes me into the ground-floor conversion, pulling out a notebook from the large pocket on the front of her hoodie, a slim pen pushed through the spiral binding. She slowly makes her way around the place, chewing her lower lip as she goes, stopping every now and then to jot something down or take pictures with her phone.

We've said nothing to each other, but the tension is palpable. I move towards the French doors that overlook the small garden at the back of the flat and lean against the frame after opening the door a bit to let some air in, hoping that steady breathing might calm both my pulse and my thoughts. I turn my head when I hear her voice.

'I can't see any radiators,' she says softly. 'Do they need to be installed or is there underfloor heating?'

I turn and face her, standing in shafts of muted daylight coming in from the overcast day outside. There was a time when I could sit and watch her for hours and memories of that flash through my mind. How her eyes were sometimes the colour of polished jade and at other times a deep forest green. How I used to trace the smattering of freckles across her face with my thumb. How it felt the first time we kissed, when her soft lips touched mine under an impossibly blue sky. Back then, I thought anything was possible. Especially with Safiya by my side.

'Murad?' Her voice snaps me out of my memories. Memories I have no place thinking about. The way she said my name has a thousand feelings rush through me at the speed of light and the only one that pauses long enough for me to feel the full impact of it is the pain I felt when she broke up with me, breaking my heart in the process.

I exhale deeply. 'Underfloor heating runs throughout, except in the bedrooms. They're to be carpeted and both have radiators.'

Safiya nods after a moment and makes her way towards the rooms, her expression inscrutable.

This is what we've been reduced to. After everything we've shared, we're left talking about bloody radiators. The tension in the flat is thick enough to choke me.

My phone buzzes and, shaking my head, I pull it out of my pocket.

Evie: I'll be dropping by to collect the stuff I left behind later. Will I see you? X

I stare at the message, hoping, willing myself to feel something – anything – like I did when I *felt* Safiya's presence in that conference room. Or like I did when she sat beside me in my car. Or like I did just now when she said my name.

But I feel nothing as I fire off a reply to tell her I'm busy today. Not even the slightest pang of loss or sorrow at seeing my now ex-girlfriend's message on my phone. And yet, after seven years of nothing from Safiya, there's a storm of sensations within me, why?

I chalk it up to the fact that Safiya was the first woman I ever loved. And I hope that once the shock of being in her presence fades, these feelings will slither back into the box I had stuffed them in all those years ago and die a quick death.

Maybe then, I'll finally be able to move on.

'So,' Safiya begins, casually looking ahead at the standstill traffic due to those godforsaken temporary traffic lights. 'How are your parents?'

The flat viewing finished in silence and I wasn't expecting her to speak now either, so when she does, I look her way in surprise before I eventually respond. 'They're fine,' I say, looking back towards the blasted red light a dozen cars ahead of us as we lapse into silence once more, until a few moments later, she speaks again.

'That's good. What's Meerab up to these days?'

Tension builds between my eyebrows as I let the car roll forward. From the corner of my eye, I can see her. See how intently Safiya is watching me and I stare straight ahead. 'Why?'

'Er, what do you mean "why"?'

I shrug. 'Why do you want to know how my family is or what Meerab's doing? What's with the third degree?'

Safiya wipes her hands on her jeans before clasping them together. I notice her nails, short and devoid of colour. She used to love painting them all sorts of colours before . . . I close my eyes in frustration and tighten my grip on the steering wheel.

'I'm just being friendly, Murad,' Safiya says, with a sigh. 'It's the polite thing to do.'

I can't help but give a short huff of bitter laughter at that. 'Yeah, it is. But *we* don't have to do that. We're here to do a job and that's it. I needed to show you the flat and, if you agree, you'll be working on it. None of that requires

33

friendship. We tried that and more once before and we both know how that turned out, so . . . Let's just keep it to the bare minimum. We can handle this professionally like we would with any other third party. Nothing more.'

Safiya sucks in an audible breath and when I look at her, she's looking the other way, out of the window. I feel a stab of guilt that I might have upset her with my words. There was a time when I would have rather walked over hot coals than upset Safiya. Just the thought of it used to make me restless. But that was before. Now it's less about upsetting and offending her and more about self-preservation.

I've never been able to get back to my old self, despite the passage of seven years, but at least I've managed to keep going. If I let her in again – even if it's just as a friend – how am I going to stop the eventual crumbling of the little that's left of me? She's one woman who has the potential to completely destroy me.

The light turns green, but the car ahead doesn't move, not until drivers begin honking, and then it does so slowly. Once again, we are stuck at the red light. 'Oh for Christ's sake,' I mutter, groaning.

'You're right.' Safiya shuffles in the seat, tucking her hands under her legs to gain some warmth. I turn on the heating for the seats. 'If we're going to be working on this together, then I think it's best that we navigate it professionally.'

'We're not going to be working together as such. You'll have access to the flat while you work and Zafar can handle anything that needs taking care of. Once it's done, I can take over again and manage the sale.'

She turns and looks my way, a small furrow between her eyebrows. 'But you know more about the place than Zaf does. He said as much. You can give me an initial spec of what you want of course, but there's always some back and forth on things like this. Besides, how will you explain why you're handing the project over to him? Unless we come clean.'

She's not wrong. Zaf knows the bare minimum about the conversion and while I can fill him in on the details, he's bound to ask why I'm not taking care of it myself. To be fair to him, he's got enough on his plate. As for coming clean . . . What's the point? It's all water under the bridge.

And, most importantly for me, it's crucial that this project is a success and for that, I need to keep my head in the right place and my finger on the pulse. Even if that pulse happens to be one that I'd rather avoid. I owe it to Antonella.

'Fine. We can communicate via email and I can make visits to the flat when necessary.'

Safiya nods, scrunching her nose, deep in thought. 'We can set some basic ground rules. Be professional, of course. Talk only when we have to for work and—' She pauses when I look her way. Her lips tilt downwards momentarily and she tears her gaze away. 'We don't talk about the past. At all. *Ever.*'

Rules are a good idea and being professional is a basic one. Not talking about the past is a smart one, for sure, but, for some reason, it doesn't feel right. Not saying anything to Zafar is one thing, but to ignore it between me and her?

A car horn blares from behind. I glance at the empty space in front of me and the traffic light goes from green to amber before I look in my rear-view mirror to see an outraged driver. I raise my hand to apologise and move forward, the red light staring at me as though giving me a sign.

'I think it'll be best going forward if we stick to that. At least it'll make seeing each other and working together easier for us and it'll save us from having to provide any explanations to anyone,' she says primly. 'It's the sensible thing to do.'

'Is that how life works for you then? Follow a set of rules sensibly and everything will work out and go according to plan.' I shake my head, my thoughts battling with my emotions right now. 'Life doesn't work that way. Sometimes a bolt out of the blue strikes when you're least expecting it and it can change the course of your life. All your plans and rules mean nothing then, Fi—'

Thankfully – *thankfully* – I manage to stop myself. The traffic lights change, and I step on the accelerator as though my life depends on it, the engine roaring so loud, pedestrians turn and look.

And there's another rule I add to the list for the sake of self-preservation: do not – *under any circumstances* – make the mistake of falling in love with Safiya Saeed.

Not again.

5

To: Murad Aziz
From: Safiya Saeed
Subject: 19 Tempington Crescent

Murad
Please find attached the preliminary designs. Let me know
if there are any changes you'd like made in a separate
document. Is the team that's been hired for the job ready
to go? Also, can I have any lists of suppliers you've used
before, please? Thanks.
Safiya

To: Safiya Saeed
From: Murad Aziz
Subject: Re: 19 Tempington Crescent

Attached.

To: Murad Aziz
From: Safiya Saeed
Subject: Re: 19 Tempington Crescent

Murad
Please find attached the revised designs. These should be
the final ones. I'm hoping to meet the work team leader
tomorrow and discuss materials and purchasing – that
way I'll know what things I need to get and when.

Ideally, the work should start next week. Will you be there?
Safiya

To: Safiya Saeed
From: Murad Aziz
Subject: Re: 19 Tempington Crescent

All fine. Unlikely.

To: Murad Aziz
From: Safiya Saeed
Subject: Re: 19 Tempington Crescent

Murad
Can you arrange for another electrician to come by? Some of the wiring doesn't appear to have been earthed.
Safiya

To: Safiya Saeed
From: Murad Aziz
Subject: Re: 19 Tempington Crescent

I'll check with Baz.

To: Murad Aziz
From: Safiya Saeed
Subject: Re: 19 Tempington Crescent

Isn't he the electrician who completed the initial installation without the earthing?! If so, then I'd rather we didn't call him. I'm not very pleased with his finish on some of the fixtures. Is there anyone else on the books we can use?
Safiya

To: Safiya Saeed
From: Murad Aziz
Subject: Re: 19 Tempington Crescent

Baz is the only guy we trust and use. I've seen his work and it's fine.

To: Murad Aziz
From: Safiya Saeed
Subject: Re: 19 Tempington Crescent

Maybe if Baz's workmanship had been better than just fine, we wouldn't be having this discussion. Any builder, plumber or electrician worth their salt knows that you need to go to the right places to get supplies. If you get substandard workers with their substandard supplies doing the work for you, then the chances are — brace yourself — you'll get substandard results!
Safiya

To: Safiya Saeed
From: Murad Aziz
Subject: Re: 19 Tempington Crescent

Is there a point in there somewhere? Baz will be there tomorrow.

To: Safiya Saeed
From: Murad Aziz
Subject: Re: 19 Tempington Crescent

I stopped by today. You weren't there. When was the pink approved?

To: Murad Aziz
From: Safiya Saeed
Subject: Re: 19 Tempington Crescent

You didn't say you were coming. This is why we have those rules — you're supposed to communicate things like that. And you approved the pink yourself. I sent you all the paint choices and you said they were fine.
Safiya
P.S. Your electrician is a prickly and miserable man!

To: Safiya Saeed
From: Murad Aziz
Subject: Re: 19 Tempington Crescent

I would never have approved the pink. Baz has always been fine with me. Maybe if you didn't tell him how to do his job, he'd be fine with you too.

To: Murad Aziz
From: Safiya Saeed
Subject: Re: 19 Tempington Crescent

Please see attached re the paint and your approval of it.
Safiya

To: Safiya Saeed
From: Murad Aziz
Subject: Re: 19 Tempington Crescent

How am I supposed to know what Pistachio Frost, Subtle Elderflower, Spring Shimmer or Blueberry Mist mean. What's wrong with saying green, blue or yellow?

To: Murad Aziz
From: Safiya Saeed
Subject: Re: 19 Tempington Crescent

*I'm not decorating a classroom! None of the colours I
suggested are green, blue or yellow. The list I sent was of
different shades of colours of which I sent you samples.
It's not my fault if you didn't check them! And I'm not
responsible for the names of the colours. The team are
wrapping up today. I'll do a final check this weekend.
When are you or Antonella coming?*
Safiya

To: Safiya Saeed
From: Murad Aziz
Subject: Re: 19 Tempington Crescent

I'll be there on Monday afternoon with Antonella.

6

Safiya

I remember it so clearly.

One evening, Daadi was babysitting us and she had bought me a new paint set. I splashed the canvas with bright colours. Oranges, yellows, reds. Qais had walked into our playroom and started being his mischievous self and I decided to chase him with my paintbrush, swinging it around.

Daadi came in to see what we were up to. It wasn't until she gasped and I turned around to see that the previously white walls were covered with splatters of colours, like a rainbow. All three of us had sat sheepishly, waiting for our parents to come home. My mother had walked in, saw the terrified look on my face, and started laughing. *My little artist*, Dad had said, scooping me into his arms and swinging me around so that I was giggling and shrieking.

That was the first time I had ever 'designed' something and it had sparked something in me – something I hadn't been able to let go. Not until now. That childlike confidence – that burst of light – seems lost. Extinguished. Now I cannot help but second-guess everything.

'I think I've chosen the wrong colours.' I stride into the kitchen, my brow furrowed. 'I shouldn't have chosen these.'

'What? Why not?' Vaz asks without taking her eyes off her laptop screen from the little dining table in the kitchen.

She works for an events company and she's managing an exclusive bridal shower for a very famous influencer this weekend – her first solo gig and she's planning it to the nth degree.

Samples and photographs of the flat are all spread out on my side of the table. I pushed Vaneeza onto one side and decided to use this as my office. It used to be part of my process, to take pictures and keep track of the progress of whichever project I was working on, and I've done the same with this period conversion too, not that I have a great deal of experience to fall back on. After university, I had worked for about eighteen months doing various internships and short-term projects, but then I got married.

At first, my in-laws suggested that I didn't work so I could settle in with Ejaz in Nairobi, get to know the family and my new home. It made sense. Every now and then, I helped a family-friend with a new home or office space. But it wasn't enough, and each time I brought the subject up with Ejaz, he would talk me out of it, telling me that it wasn't a great idea. *Things are different in Nairobi*, he said, though I wasn't sure they were. *I can take care of you. Why do you even need to work?* Work became a dirty word. Whenever I mentioned it, we fought. He questioned and doubted my abilities so much and so often that his words became stuck in my head. No matter how hard I try, they are still there. *Not good enough.*

'You spent hours shortlisting the colours for the rooms and asked me what I thought. Twice. And we agreed that your choices are perfect. So why are you second-guessing yourself?' Vaz takes her eyes off her work and pins them on me.

'I don't know. Murad wasn't too impressed.'

'Er, didn't you send him samples to approve?' I nod. 'So, then what's he whinging about? The colour choices

43

are perfect, Saf. Stop doubting yourself and stop letting someone who has no idea about light, colour and ambience get inside that beautiful head of yours. You know what you're doing, you just need to brush away the dust that's gathered over the past seven years and flex those muscles a bit. The foundation is likely just as strong as it was. Give yourself some grace. And from what I've seen from the progress pictures you've taken, it looks stunning.'

I smile and scrunch my nose at my best friend. 'You're the best.'

Vaz rolls her eyes playfully. 'Tell me something I don't know. Right, put your stuff away and go and get ready, otherwise you'll be late for tea with your parents. I need to make a move and get this show on the road too.'

'All the best. I'm positive it'll be an absolute blast.'

She scrunches her nose at me just like I did and closes her laptop.

I flick through my samples once more. Vaz is right. I took my time choosing the colours so they complemented the space, taking into account the amount of natural light in each room. I sent Murad the shortlist and if he didn't check it properly, then that's on him, not me. The amount of attitude he's giving me through emails is crazy and I've been hard-pressed not to respond in kind, though I have let some sass through. He never used to be like that.

My thoughts go back to that day I saw him at the office and our subsequent first visit to the period conversion. I had thought that we might be able to leave the past in the past and move forward as friends. God knows I could never expect anything more, not after how I ended things with him the first time, even though that's not what I had wanted. He doesn't know that. I thought that if we could be friendly, it would make working together easier for both of us and we'd be able to move on from what had happened seven years ago. But Murad obviously didn't agree.

His reaction surprised me at the time. Heck, it had hurt, and it was only through sheer willpower that I hadn't let any of my true thoughts and feelings come through in that moment. But now, when I think about it, I can see that it shouldn't have come as a surprise. When I burnt that particular bridge, I lost the right to claim any friendship with him thereafter, and that's something I'll have to learn to live with. Our paths are bound to cross given that he's best friends with Zaf and the family, and that he also works on a part-time basis as a consultant for the business. The best I can hope for is that we can maintain a professional and civil relationship and that, over time, I get used to the feeling of seeing him and knowing that he was the one that got away.

My phone buzzes and I check the new message.

Mum: I've got all your favourites. Daddy and I can't wait to see you later. You sure you don't want to stay over for the weekend? Xx

I stare at the spread on the table with wide eyes while Mum beams at me. 'Sit down, darling. Daddy's bringing the pot of tea.' She pulls a chair out for me and I lower myself onto it as the doorbell rings

It has been almost a month since I've seen my parents, so I thought I'd pop by this afternoon, and while I was here, I could sort through some of my things which are still in boxes in the spare room after all these years. The room Mum and Dad insist is mine for whenever I want to *come back home.*

I've never actually lived in this house. My parents bought it after I married Ejaz and moved to Nairobi. That one decision of my grandfather's fractured our whole family. My parents moved out of the family home and bought this place, Qais moved out and lives separately and, at the time, Zafar had moved out too. Except, when our grandfather got really ill towards the end, Zafar moved back into the family home and took the place our grandfather had always wanted him to take.

'Look who's here, Saf,' Mum calls out as she walks back into the dining room, closely followed by my older brother, Qais. His stoic expression softens as he sees me, a small smile teasing the corners of his lips as he closes the distance between us.

I get up and move towards him, but before I can put my arms around his middle, he grabs my head in a headlock and pulls the scrunchie out of my hair.

'Argh! Mum stop him.'

'You're so easy, Saf.' He flings the scrunchie across the room and, after messing my hair up, he pulls back and grins, clearly impressed with his handiwork. 'You look great.' He bodily moves me out of the way and then takes the chair I was sitting on, loading a plate up with the snacks laid out before him.

'You're such a child.' I huff as I flick his ear and then retrieve my scrunchie before retying my hair and sitting down opposite him, Mum smiling indulgently as she sits adjacent to the pair of us, leaving the seat opposite hers for my dad, who comes in with the promised pot of tea.

'It's good to see you, son. It's nice having both our children home like this, together.' Dad gives me a tentative smile and I do the same. After the breakdown in our family and my time away, it's been hard for us to get back to where we were – especially between Dad and me and Qais. To be honest, I don't think we'll ever get back to what we had before, too much has happened and changed for that. But it'd be nice if we could be a bit more comfortable with each other. At least it's not as difficult with Mum.

We all dig into the mini feast of sandwiches, pies, scones, cakes, biscuits and copious amounts of tea, while Mum fills our plates repeatedly and the silence with her chatter about the neighbourhood and the school where she works as a teaching assistant.

'How's work, Qais?' Dad asks when there's a slight lull.

'Fine. Busy,' Qais says with a shrug.

'What are you doing these days?' I ask him as I top up the cups with more tea. I hardly spoke to my family while I was in Nairobi, I was hurting too much and then guilt got the better of me, stopping me from reaching out to them. Since I've been back, we've gradually started opening up to each other again but it's not been easy and there's so much I've missed out on. I know before I left that Qais was at university but that's it.

Mum and Dad look between us, but Qais says nothing, shrugging instead and keeping his eyes on his now empty plate.

Dad answers my question. 'He works in two different hospitals. Your brother's become a heart specialist.'

I stare at him wide-eyed. I knew I was out of the loop, but this is crazy. 'You're a what?'

'It's nothing, don't make a thing of it. And don't say anything to anyone either. I don't want anyone outside this room to know.' Qais says somewhat belligerently, as though he doesn't care but I can hear the insecurity in his tone.

'Erm, it's not nothing. It's a mahoosive something. Why would you hide that about yourself?' Guilt claws at my insides at missing out on what was important to my brother all these years. I had no idea that he might have wanted to pursue a career in medicine.

47

'It's my secret to share, Saf, and I'll do it in my own time. End of story.'

I should listen to him, but I'm not his annoying little sister for nothing. 'For now. Though I want the full story at some point and a strong incentive for keeping your secret.'

He gives me an evil grin. 'How about your rag doll, Rosie's safety?'

I gasp in outrage. 'You wouldn't.'

He shrugs and Dad tuts. 'Qais, stop teasing your sister. Rosie is safe, sweetheart. She's in the box with all your other belongings.'

'Is she, though?' Qais stage whispers and then slides his finger across his throat.

I bound out of my chair. 'Mum, I'm going up to sort out those boxes.'

I hear Qais laughing and Mum futilely trying to tell him off as I make my way upstairs and into the bedroom with my tea, though I can't help the smile from widening on my face at seeing my family looking happy, smiling and messing around – even if it is at my darling Rosie's expense.

I open the first box and peer inside to find books and folders full of random things. There's a suitcase full of old clothes and another box labelled 'Miscellaneous Items'. The third box has my old toys and stuffed animals in them and I find Rosie in the corner, the stuffed doll smelling of lavender. I'm inspecting her for damage when the door swings open and Qais walks in.

'Oh, you found her.' I scowl at him and he grins. 'You should keep your face like that. You look marginally less ugly than usual.'

'Says the king of monkeys.'

He lowers himself to the floor opposite me and peers into the boxes. 'You taking all this stuff with you.'

'Probably not. I need to go through it and then either donate stuff or throw it away. I've done without it all for seven years, so I obviously don't need it.'

He's silent for a few minutes, going through the books in one of the boxes while I check out the miscellaneous items in the other box.

'You said Captain Zaf allowed you on board last time we spoke. How's that working out for you?' Thanks to our grandfather treating Qais and Zafar the way he did, there's a distance between them which has only increased over time. They're not sworn enemies as such, but Qais makes no effort to breach the gap, no matter how much Zafar tries. And yet, when we were children, they got along like a house on fire, a younger Zafar looking up to Qais and following his lead in whatever they did.

I shake my head in a bid to rid myself of thoughts of the past. 'Zaf's been great about everything. His support meant being able to pay my rent, clear my debts and sort myself out to be more financially stable going forward. All within the space of six weeks.'

'I would have taken care of all of that, Saf. But good old Cap. Riding in to your rescue, right on cue.' His tone oozes sarcasm and resentment, but there's pain and sadness there too.

'I know, Qais, but that's not what I needed. And none of what happened was his fault. In fact, he's making a conscious effort to be different and do things differently. If that wasn't the case, I wouldn't have got the opportunity I did. He could have easily turned me away, but he didn't. I was the one who rebuffed any effort he made when I came back and, despite that, when I went to him, he did nothing except ask what *I* wanted.'

'Hmm. I'm glad things have worked out for you.'

'I'd love for you to work things out too, Bhai.' I don't often give him the title of older brother, but when I do, he and I both know I don't do it lightly. 'They're our brothers. We should be together. Don't let one man's prejudice and medieval thinking affect our relationships in the here and now.' My own words immediately echo in my ears and I silently note how much easier it is to say the words than actually believe them and follow through with that belief. We're both struggling with the same thing, but just in different ways.

He looks at me closely, though I know his mind is mulling over my words. He speaks after a few minutes of silently sorting the boxed items. 'All right, smarty-pants. How's the work itself?'

'Uh-uh, that's nothing compared to your bombshell, Dr Qais Saeed. Heart specialist, huh?'

He smiles shyly, a completely incongruous look on my brother, before his stoic expression is very much back into place. 'Do you remember when he used to tell me that I won't amount to anything?' He doesn't need to spell it out for me. I know he's talking about our grandfather. 'The irony of the whole thing is that he died before I could tell him what I had done. Since then, I've just not told anyone except Mum and Dad, and now you, and I'd rather it stayed that way.'

The only thing Qais ever sought in life was approval from the patriarch of our family, and after all his hard work, he was denied the opportunity. I swipe at the tear that's rolled down my cheek, my heart going out to him. I'm sure there's more to it than just that, but I'll let him tell me in his own time.

'So, what does everyone think you do? When I left, you were studying and working at the dealership and you had said you wanted to continue working with bikes in some capacity. All this time I assumed that's what you were doing. I'm a terrible sister, I should have known—'

'You knew what I wanted you to know, Saf. I was quiet about it all very deliberately and kept up some shifts at the dealership, so you weren't far off the mark. Like I said, only Mum and Dad and now you know about what I do. I'm not really bothered what anyone else thinks about what I do but I guess they probably still think I work for a motorbike dealership.' He grins mischievously, but his statement breaks my heart. Our grandfather always considered Qais' interest in motorbikes a waste of time. He often told him that he'd not amount to much if he didn't follow his younger cousin, Zafar's example.

We resume sorting boxes, chatting about the period conversion when his phone rings and he says he has to go. I decide to call it a day on sorting stuff and I'm about to close the lid of the box when I spot a small notebook with a lock on it in a clear plastic wallet.

I pull it out and rub my thumb across the writing on the cover. *Safiya's little book of dreams.*

7

Murad

'If I had to take a punt, I'd say Pistachio Frost is a shade of green,' my brother-in-law, Zubair, says thoughtfully through the speaker. 'The *Frost* part suggests that it might be on the lighter side. I feel like the Spring Shimmer might be pinkish in colour perhaps. Am I right?'

'Uh, I'm not sure I care.' I hold back a smile.

'Hey, you're the one who was complaining about paint names to me not five minutes ago,' he says, defensively.

I'm outside the period conversion, waiting for Antonella to turn up, 'Actually, I was complaining about Safiya's attitude regarding the paint. But thanks for not listening. Haven't you got any appointments this afternoon or is your practice failing?'

'I'm a very sought-after dentist, I'll have you know. But even genius people like me need a lunch break and I couldn't message you back and forth. This is much more efficient. In fact, I was telling your sister the other day that messaging has killed the pleasure of having a conversation. You know, once upon a time, phone conversations used to be a pastime?'

'Riveting stuff. Did she keep up or fall asleep?'

He barks out a laugh. 'Beats discussing paint colours, mate.'

'It's work, Zubair,' I remind him.

'Hmm. And that's all, is it?'

'Yes. That's it. Nothing less and absolutely *nothing* more,' I emphasise, slowly, so he gets the point. I've got a set of rules to prove it.

'Oh-kay. If you say so. But just to remind you that Safiya is enemy number one as far as Meerab is concerned. If she hears you're working with her, she'll go ballistic.'

'I'll tell her it was all your idea. Right, Antonella's here. I've got to go. Bye.' I end the call on him spluttering, unable to stop myself from smiling. Winding Zubair up is a particularly favourite *pastime* of mine.

I step out of my car as Antonella comes towards me.

'You look radiant.' I kiss her on both cheeks and step back and she smiles broadly at me. 'Italy makes you glow.'

'Charmer. Have you already seen it?' She looks in the direction of the flat.

I shake my head. 'No. I was waiting for you. Thought we'd see it together.' I don't tell her that I'm also trying to avoid my exposure to a certain woman who I know is in the flat as we speak. I look in the flat's direction and spot her standing at the window, her eyes shooting daggers my way. God knows what I've done to earn that glare, but whatever it is, we're well past the point of me caring what she thinks, and vice versa, I'm sure.

Be professional. The golden rule goes through my head.

I lock my car and follow after Antonella as we make our way towards the entrance.

When we get there, Safiya's standing outside the front door of the flat, the door closed behind her. I have not seen her in eight weeks. Whenever I needed to come by, I made sure it was when I knew she wasn't there. It was hard enough being caught off guard the first time I came face-to-face with her, so it's better to limit our interactions to only the necessary ones.

When I see her, I stop in my tracks. She looks so different. Two months ago, Safiya looked broken. Tired. Like she was carrying the weight of the world on her shoulders. Now, with her bright T-shirt and floaty skirt, there is a lightness about her, though she's obviously nervous, chewing on her lower lip.

Antonella walks over, holding her hand out. 'You must be Safiya. My name is Antonella and I'm so delighted to finally meet you. I can't tell you how excited I am to see the place. Murad's been very secretive.' She feigns a pout and then looks back at me. 'Murad? Coming?' she says and I realise I had frozen.

I put on a smile and walk over.

'It's lovely to meet you, Antonella. I won't keep you to waiting any longer. Please.' Safiya steps aside and gestures to Antonella to open the front door and head inside, before she looks my way. I give her an acknowledging nod and she reciprocates, blinking furiously.

Without any thought, I put my hand on her upper arm. 'Relax. I'm sure she'll love it.' *So much for not caring.*

Safiya softens, her sparkling green eyes wide. I have no idea why I felt the need to reassure her, but I did, the feeling coming from somewhere deep inside me.

I pull my arm back and wave it in the direction of the door, but she shakes her head. 'You go first. I want you to see it properly without me bouncing on the balls of my feet nearby.' She gives me a tentative smile.

I nod briskly, stopping myself from offering any further reassurance. It's only the second time I'm seeing her since she's been back and I'm already responding to her despite all my assertions about needing to keep my distance.

I walk over the threshold, trying to get my mind back to where it needs to be. *Rules. Remember the rules.* Funny how they fly out of my head as soon as I see her.

The lights in the hallway are switched on, filling the small space with a sense of openness. I follow behind Antonella as she heads towards the reception room and her gasp is audible. 'Oh Murad. It's completely transformed.'

I look around me in wonder, taking in the aforementioned transformation. The wooden floor is gleaming where it's not covered by plush rugs. The walls are a combination of exposed brickwork, paint and papering, making the space feel longer than it actually is. The furniture and upholstery fit perfectly, functional yet comfortable, making a person feel like they can sit down and feel at home.

The room then opens up into the kitchen-diner, which looks over the garden through French doors. The frame is painted black and looks incredible, like its framing a collection of moving photographs of the garden. The kitchen is across one wall, with a dining table, two chairs and two benches set against the opposite wall. Again, functional and comfortable. I can just picture someone using the kitchen or sitting at the table chatting under the low-hanging overhead light.

'All the furniture is easily taken apart and moved. I know you're planning on selling the place, so I didn't blow the budget on it.' Standing just inside the doorway, with her hands clasped behind her back, Safiya gives Antonella a nervous smile and then turns to me, unease crystal clear on her face.

Since when does Safiya get nervous like this? She was always gutsy and forthright, sure of herself, no matter where she was or what she was doing. And when it came to design work – the little I had seen while we were together – she was damn good at it and she knew it. So where has this apprehension come from? Perhaps it's because this is her first project after coming back to London? Maybe she's just been out of the saddle, so to speak, for a while? Not that I care, I remind myself. This is all professional.

'Can I see the rooms?' Antonella asks, her voice full of awe and excitement. I can tell she loves what she's seen so far. Heck, I'm loving what I've seen so far. But then I should have known that Safiya would wave her magic wand in here and turn the place around.

'Of course. This way.' She gestures back towards the hallway and Antonella goes towards one bedroom and I go towards the other before we swap. The second bedroom I go into is the pink one, and yet it doesn't look anything like I thought it might. The carpet is a dark dusky rose colour and the ceiling, woodwork and windows are all white. It looks like the perfect place to leave your stresses at the door and come and rest.

I look Safiya's way, only to find her looking at me. 'Spring Shimmer,' she says with a half-smile on her lips. There's that sass. She never could help herself from handing out sassy quips and inexplicably, it pleases me after the show of nerves not moments earlier.

'And it's perfect. Sì, Murad?' Antonella stands in the doorway, her hands clasped under her chin. 'Safiya, cara, I'm in love. Come, let's go back to the other room.'

Antonella moves towards the reception room and Safiya and I follow after her. We sit at the table; Antonella takes a chair and Safiya and I sit on the benches, opposite each other.

'Tell me, Safiya, how did you manage this, both in the timescale and budget?'

'You really like it?' Safiya asks sceptically.

'Like it?' Antonella sounds shocked at the question as she looks between me and Safiya. 'It's wonderful. I wouldn't change a thing and I think we will definitely have interest from buyers in this property. The location and property themselves were great, but with the finish you've given this place . . . I'm speechless. Murad?'

I stare back at Antonella before glancing at Safiya's once more apprehensive expression, taking a moment before responding, my words coming out unfiltered. 'Antonella's right. You've done a remarkable job, but there was never any question in my mind. I knew you'd do this place justice.'

Safiya stares at me as she bites the inside of her cheek, sucking it in, her eyes bright. Is she about to cry?

Antonella's phone rings and she excuses herself, but I don't take my eyes off Safiya. A lone tear rolls down her cheek and I feel an immediate sense of panic.

'Hey.' Instinctively, I cover her hand resting on the table between us with mine. 'What's happened? Are you OK?'

She sniffles and nods, sliding her hand out from under mine and swiping both hands under her eyes. 'I'm fine. I just . . . I . . . .' She swallows and looks up at the ceiling.

So much has happened between us. So much so that it wouldn't be outside the realms of possibility if we never spoke to each other again. But, for some reason, the sight of her upset still has my stomach plummeting like I'm in a lift that's free falling. How and why are questions I definitely need to analyse, but right now, the only thing I want to do is change that expression on her face. Vanquish whichever demon is troubling her. A siren heralding trouble goes off in my head, but I pay it no heed.

'You've done a fantastic job. You always were an incredible designer. I've not seen anyone with an artistic eye like yours.' I keep my voice low but try to infuse it with as much emphasis as I can. 'I'm certain that this property will be snapped up.'

She has a surprised look on her face, as though I've said something unexpected and her words confirm it. 'I didn't think I could do it.' Her voice is barely above a whisper.

I look at her in confusion. Why would she think she couldn't do a job she's both qualified to do and has experience of doing? Of course, she might have had a bit of a break, but I'd have thought getting back to it would be a bit like riding a bike – a bit rusty to begin with, but once you find your rhythm, you're good to go.

I watch her as she dries her tears and takes in a shuddering breath, rolling her lips in on themselves. The corners of her eyes and mouth show signs of strain which I hadn't noticed before. It's like I'm looking at a completely different Safiya and I can't help but wonder what brought about these changes.

But why should I wonder? I should be focused on maintaining nothing more than a professional – a very distant and professional – relationship with her. It's no concern of mine what has put that slightly haunted look in her eyes. It certainly wasn't me.

'Sorry about that. It was Giancarlo, my brother. He's nothing but a fount of bad news for me these last few days.'

I welcome Antonella's return, turning to face her. 'Is everything OK?'

'Yes and no. They're all fine, but you know the villa in Perla Rosa I told you about? The one Nonna left my mama? We're trying to get it restored and sold and its presenting one obstacle after another. Today, he's found the source of the leak upstairs and has discovered that the roof needs replacing. The place is from the early twentieth century, so we can't really sell it for more than peanuts unless we spruce it up. Much like this place.' She looks around us, her eyes sparkling with joy. 'Safiya, sorry for the interruption. You were going to tell me about it.'

She gives Safiya all her attention and, haltingly, Safiya begins to tell Antonella about the project and her thoughts behind some of the decisions she's made. Gradually, her voice gets stronger and she becomes more animated. 'I thought black frames would make the French doors stand out and it breaks up the softness in here. Also, the lighting had to be completely changed from what had been fitted initially.'

She goes on to discuss her woes with Baz's work and I bite the inside of my cheek to stop myself from laughing or smiling. Her issues with him did crack me up, I can't lie. For his part, Baz wasn't too pleased with Safiya either. She gives me an arch look as she discusses the lack of earthing before turning to Antonella again and talking about her colour choices. By the time she's finished, her cheeks are rosy and her eyes have some of their sparkle back.

'I'm so impressed. Tell me, Safiya, what project are you moving onto next?' Antonella's question gives her pause.

She tucks a few errant strands of hair behind her ear, glancing my way before facing Antonella. 'I'm not sure yet. I'll have a chat with Zafar and see what he's got going on.'

Antonella nods and faces me. 'Well, Murad. It's all yours now. Hopefully we can do Safiya's hard work justice by bringing in a good sale.'

'Of course.' I smile at her and am about to get up when she smacks her hand on top of mine, stopping me in my tracks. I look at Safiya, who's staring at Antonella with wide eyes.

'I've got it!' I stare at Antonella in confusion. She looks a bit wild as she eyes me and then Safiya. 'Why don't you both work on the villa in Perla Rosa?!'

'What?'

'Erm . . .' Both Safiya and I speak at the same time, while Antonella takes off like a runaway train.

'Yes! You don't have a project to move onto immediately.' She looks at Safiya. 'I'm in love with your work and

I'm quite happy to give you free rein on the villa. Having heard you speak about this period conversion, I'm keen to see what you can do on a bigger scale. Murad's been there before and is familiar with it. He can help manage the project with you and once it's done, we can sell it.' She looks at a dumbstruck Safiya and then at me. 'What do you say?'

I swallow the lump in my throat, nothing more than a single thought going through my mind. We're going to need a lot more rules.

8

Safiya

'I think it sounds very exciting. Have you spoken to anyone else about it?' I pick up a cucumber stick, shaking my head to Mum's question as she kneads dough. She covers the bowl with a tea towel and puts it to the side. 'What are your concerns?' She walks to the sink.

Since coming back, I've found it difficult to fully open myself up to my parents. Six years of silence will do that to you, I suppose, but we're all trying. I've made gradual progress with Mum at least. We talk on the phone more often these days and today I decided to pop in and fill her in on Antonella's latest idea. Not least because it's been going round in my head and while I can acknowledge how great an opportunity it is, there's the teeny tiny consideration of Murad.

I sigh and lean back, resting my head against the wall unit from my perch on the kitchen worktop, staring at the ceiling. 'My main concern is that Antonella was caught up in the moment and offered me the project on a whim. I'm nowhere near ready to take on a project of that magnitude. My experience can fit on the back of a postcard and still have space for the address and a drawing.'

Mum dries her hands and then comes and leans against the worktop beside my swinging legs. 'From what you've described, Antonella doesn't strike me as someone who would do something on a whim, but let's assume she has. So what?'

I frown and wrinkle my nose. 'What do you mean, "so what"?'

'Just that, Saf. It doesn't matter why she's offered you the project, the important fact is that she *has* offered it to you and I think this is a shiny, sparkly, golden opportunity for you to take and run with.' She pats my cheek and then gets her loaf tin out of the cupboard.

'Muuum. Can you take your maternal cap off for once and look at this from my perspective? Working on someone's ancestral villa isn't the same as decorating a two-bedroom flat. And did you miss the part where I said it's in Italy?'

'I didn't miss any of it, I heard everything you said. I still can't see what your reservations are.'

'Reservations about what?' Dad walks in holding three used mugs in each hand.

'Where did you find those?' Mum has her hand on her hip as she regards the mugs Dad's trying to hide behind him.

'That's not what's important. What's important is that I found them and I'm about to wash them. Myself.' He gives her a sheepish look and then winks at me when she rolls her eyes. I can't help but giggle at them and I catch the look of slight surprise on my dad's face, though he tries to hide it as he goes to the sink. 'Who has reservations and about what?' he asks again.

'I do. About a design project I've been offered. It's an ancestral villa in Italy.'

Dad whistles, clearly impressed. 'Tell me about it.'

And so I do. We move from the kitchen to the front room, Dad carrying in tea in his freshly washed mugs for all of us as I tell him about the period conversion, Antonella's praise and subsequent offer and my reservations.

When I finish, he and Mum look at each other, an indulgent smile on my mum's face.

Dad turns to me. 'I think it's perfectly natural for you to have doubts; it is indeed a big project. I can understand why you're feeling apprehensive, but I don't think those are reasons to decline the opportunity, especially if this lady has seen your work and liked it already. I'm sure she knew what she was doing when she made the offer.' He pauses. 'I know I've not been as supportive of you and Qais and your choices as I should have been. I was blinkered by guilt, too busy trying to make it up to my own father, instead of focusing on being a better father myself.'

It's the first time my father's ever openly acknowledged as much which surprises me. 'Daddy, you don't have to—'

'Yes, I do, sweetheart. It's a statement of fact. I supported my father's decision instead of standing by my children and encouraging them to make choices of their own and which they wanted, and I'll carry the guilt of that. But that doesn't mean we can't make that effort now. For what it's worth, I think you should go and see the villa at the very least. See what's required and see if you genuinely think you can't do it. If you believe that, then decline the offer and come back home. But if even a small part of you feels a sense of excitement at the prospect of a challenge, then take it with two hands. Besides, we all know Murad, so at least you won't be out there by yourself. You'll have someone to work with. Not that I don't think you can manage by yourself. It's just reassuring to know you won't be alone.'

Mum gives Dad's knee a squeeze, smiling at me as she does. 'Just promise us you'll think about it.'

I nod. 'I will.' While their words are encouraging, I'm still feeling a keen sense of apprehension. It's not as easy as they're saying, is it? Especially with Murad being there.

Unsure about what more to say to them, I finish my tea and head upstairs to continue sorting through some of my things since I'm here, my dad's words weighing heavily on my mind and heart.

The time he was referring to was difficult for each and every one of us and we all carry a burden of some kind since then. Maybe I was wrong in trying to stop my dad from sharing his thoughts earlier and to minimise his involvement — or lack thereof — at the time; if I feel entitled to carry the jumble of emotions and feelings I do, then surely he does too. Just as Qais carries his.

I get to the room and open the window for some fresh air. I locate the box of miscellaneous items, finding my old diary sitting on top, exactly where I had left it when I found it last time. Taking it out of the plastic wallet, along with the keys, I unlock the little padlock on the front.

God, this must be at least fifteen years old, if not older. I used to write all sorts of rubbish in it.

I open it, flicking through the pages. There's a list of films and books, with some crossed out and others not.

- Harry Potter series (Books 1–4)
- Harry Potter and the Order of the Phoenix
- Star Wars Trilogy
- Legally Blonde
- Lord of the Rings — books 1–3
- Back to the Future series
- Goosebumps Retro Collection

I was obviously keeping a list of things to watch and read, crossing them out as I went. I still love the feeling of ticking an item off a list — it's so satisfying.

I flick through a few more pages, finding a mind map of design ideas for my old bedroom and another one with a cringeworthy ode to a certain vampire series which I found the books for in another box. When I find some magazine cuttings of some dated style of clothing and make-up – heavy black eyeliner and all – I shake my head at the questionable taste my younger self had in some things.

I flick to the back of the diary and find a list with neater handwriting, suggesting I was a bit older.

- Home game at Wembley Stadium
- Grand Prix at Silverstone
- Edinburgh Castle – preferably Hogmanay.
- London Eye
- The Lion King in theatre
- Gelato at a gelateria in Italy
- Macarons in Paris
- Dip my toes in the Indian Ocean off Mombasa
- Stargaze in the countryside

I can't help but smile at the list. I had completely forgotten about it.

I pull the box back towards me and riffle through it until I find my old pencil case, pulling out a pencil and putting a line through: Dip my toes in the Indian Ocean off Mombasa. I did manage that while I was in Kenya, and while I don't have fond memories of my time there, it doesn't take away from the fact that it's a gorgeous place I had wanted to explore.

Young me was so much more dynamic than I am now. Look at all these little dreams she had, listed down and then crossed off as she went about doing what she had set out to do. And look at me now. Unsure of myself, afraid to move forward and scared of going back – stuck in the middle. Second-guessing myself and uncertain of who I even am anymore.

'And why? Where is the old Safiya and how can I get even a small part of her back?'

I look at item number six: Gelato at a gelateria in Italy. Coincidence?

'You know it's a sign of madness to talk to yourself? I know. I'm a doctor.'

I roll my eyes. 'How long have you been waiting to use that one?'

'Longer than I care to admit.' Qais grins at me as he swaggers into the room. 'Still sorting through everything?' He drops down on the bed, turning my way and leaning on his elbow.

'Yeah. I just found an old bucket list.'

'The one you dragged me to Edinburgh for?' He shudders theatrically. It wasn't the best trip for poor Qais, who ended up catching a cold while we were there and was miserable throughout our trip.

'Mmhmm.' I run my finger across 'Italy'. 'I got offered a project in Italy, Bhai.'

'Yeah. The folks told me. You going?' Qais sits up and regards me closely, his hazel eyes missing nothing.

'I don't know. What if I'm rubbish?' Similar doubt had assailed me during the period conversion too, though Antonella's obvious joy and praise for my work had boosted my confidence. Murad had also praised it and gone so far as to say that he had known I'd do the place justice, making me feel a spark of warmth because the praise had come from him. But it didn't take long for my doubts to creep up on me again after Antonella suggested I work on her ancestral villa in Italy and since then, they've only snowballed.

'You are rubbish. You always have been. But that's never stopped you before,' Qais says drily.

'Ha ha ha, so funny.'

'You don't need me to tell you how bad you are at your job. But this sounds like a decent opportunity for you, so I reckon you should go out there and have fun. Paint some walls, assemble a bookcase, eat some pizza. Isn't Italy one of the places on this bucket list?' I nod as I close the little diary, but keep a hold of it, looking up at my brother and choosing to ignore his deliberately inaccurate summation of my job. I know he's just winding me up. 'You should go, Saf. I think you could do with both the challenge and the shake-up. Stop looking to set a comfort zone up for yourself. Be spontaneous and give into that curiosity of yours which seems to be hiding under a rock. Let it out and give it air. And if you think the opportunity's not for you, then tell the person you'll agree once you've scoped the place out, but don't dismiss it out of hand.'

I think back to what Dad and Mum said about the opportunity. I look at the little book of dreams in my hand, where the younger me had had faith and confidence that she would build a life for herself that she would be proud of. That thought strengthens my resolve and I decide that, if nothing else, I'm going to do this for the Safiya of then, who deserved so much better than what she got.

I look back up at Qais. 'I'm going to go for it.'

He smiles broadly at that. 'Attagirl. You deserve a chance to show the Italian population what extreme feral looks like.'

I roll my eyes again. 'You were doing really well until then.'

He grins at me as he gets up, holding a hand out to help me up. I'm about to put my hand in his when he moves his out of the way. 'Too slow. Last one down's a loser.' He strides out of the room, switching the light off and closing the door behind him, his laughter fading as he goes downstairs. You wouldn't think he's a thirty-five-year-old grown man, a cardiologist even, but it makes me smile. I've missed my brother, missed having this relationship with him, even if his main aim in life is to annoy me.

I get up and switch the light back on before putting away what I've not sorted and taking one of the bags for the charity shop downstairs, along with the little diary to take back with me as a reminder and a lucky charm. Who knows, maybe some of the old Safiya's flair and zest for life might come through and colour the life of today's Safiya.

9

To: Safiya Saeed
From: Murad Aziz
Subject: Perla Rosa Villa Project

I'm making the travel arrangements and doing the
paperwork for Perla Rosa. I need your passport details.

> To: Murad Aziz
> From: Safiya Saeed
> Subject: Re: Perla Rosa Villa Project
>
> Murad
> Please find copy of passport attached. When are we going
> to be heading out to Italy? Also, has the period
> conversion been sold?
> Safiya

To: Safiya Saeed
From: Murad Aziz
Subject: Re: Perla Rosa Villa Project

Once the paperwork goes through. Shouldn't take more
than a couple of weeks. Yes.

To: Safiya Saeed
From: Murad Aziz
Subject: Re: Perla Rosa Villa Project

Your travel paperwork is attached. We leave on Tuesday next week.

To: Murad Aziz
From: Safiya Saeed
Subject: Re: Perla Rosa Villa Project

So quickly? That barely gives me time to prepare. How are we getting to the airport and where from – will you come here?
Safiya

To: Safiya Saeed
From: Murad Aziz
Subject: Re: Perla Rosa Villa Project

You've known about this for long enough to have been prepared. I'll see you at the airport. It's a three-hour flight and then a half-hour drive to the villa. Don't be late!

To: Murad Aziz
From: Safiya Saeed
Subject: Re: Perla Rosa Villa Project

Are we staying at the villa? I thought Antonella said we'd be staying in a smaller cottage near the villa.
Safiya

70

10

Murad

'How long are you going to be out there for?' Mum's frown tells me she's not pleased about my impending visit to Italy.

'Hang on a second.' Meerab comes on the screen, plonking herself beside our mother. 'Did you know you were going when you were here last weekend?' She narrows her eyes at me in a way she's mastered since our childhood.

'Yes, I did.' Mum looks betrayed as Meerab's mouth drops open. 'I also knew that if I told you both, you'd ask me a hundred and one questions and not let me leave in peace. I'm not going for weeks on end, just long enough to get the project off the ground. I'll be back after that and perhaps make short trips there occasionally. I told Dad and Zubair.'

As I expected, the pair of them narrow their eyes on their respective husbands and I use the moment to end the video call with a promise to call them soon, catching Zubair's sarcastic thanks as the call ends.

I take my earphones out and scan the airport, trying to spot the thorn that is going to be in my side for the next few weeks in Italy. No sign. Still, there's time before we need to check-in.

I lean back against the pillar behind the chair I'm sitting on. I can't believe this is happening. It was bad enough trying to avoid Safiya while we both lived in the same city, but to work on a project in the small town of Perla Rosa together is the stuff of nightmares for me. And the icing on this cake of horrors? We have to share living space.

I tried my best to get out of this strategically, both the project to begin with and then having to share the cottage with Safiya but it was almost impossible to do so without giving anything away and raising unwanted questions. Antonella insisted I manage the project and help Safiya because I've been to Perla Rosa before and she trusts me. And of course, there was no question about me staying anywhere except at the cottage on the same estate. She even offered to take care of any outstanding properties I was working on in the UK while I'm in Perla Rosa. I tried to use my consultation service with Zafar as a reason to get out of it, but she said she'd speak to him herself and I didn't want that. To add to that, Zafar expressed his satisfaction that I was going to be there with Safiya, so he had nothing to worry about. Even the reclusive Qais checked in with me separately, rendering me speechless with his out of the blue call. The pair of them *reminding* me to take care of their sister. As though I've got nothing better to do with my time.

Little do either of them know that their sister made it crystal clear to me seven years ago that she wanted nothing to do with me. Once again, I curse the moment when I agreed with Safiya to keep our relationship a secret from her family. If we hadn't, I wouldn't have had to keep the break-up a secret and, right now, I wouldn't be in this bloody situation.

'Hey.' I'm pulled from my thoughts by the person herself. She takes the seat next to mine, rolling her two suitcases to sit in front of us. She looks at her watch. 'Have you been waiting long?'

'No.' I stand up abruptly. 'We should check-in.' I pull up the handles of my suitcases and she follows suit. The best thing, in the circumstances, would be to maintain strict professionalism because I can't see any other way of making it through to the other side of this as painlessly as possible.

We make our way to the check-in desk and once we're through to the departure lounge, I head towards a row of chairs, taking the one at the end of the row. Safiya takes the chair next to mine and before she can say anything, I pull out my laptop and stick in my earphones.

She waits all of two minutes before she taps my arm. 'I'm getting a coffee? Fancy one?'

'No.'

She shrugs and, leaving her small holdall on the chair beside me, goes off in search of coffee. I wonder again how I'm going to get through the coming weeks in Safiya's company. My usual MO is to be easy-going and friendly with whoever I work with but doing that with Safiya is far too risky, it's like navigating a slippery downward slope wearing roller skates. But I can hardly spend the next several weeks barking at her and being abrupt.

She comes back twenty minutes later, during which time I've been through my emails and messages. I pull up listings of upcoming auctions which might be of interest, only to have Safiya tap my arm again, my momentary calm vanishing in a puff of smoke. 'You never said how the sale of the period conversion went. Did it go for what you and Antonella hoped?'

I'm about to ignore her question when I remember that since she worked on it, it's only right that I answer her question. It's hardly a state secret and, despite my humble beginnings, my parents raised me to be honourable and fair. 'It was sold in a week. We made a twelve per cent profit, which is more than either of us anticipated. We were cautiously optimistic, but the sale exceeded our expectations. We nearly had a bidding war on our hands.'

'Really? I'm so glad to hear that.' She smiles at me brightly and throws me back in time to when a smile like that would fill me with pride because I had done or said something to put it there. It used to light up my entire day.

I look away, trying to focus on my laptop screen once more.

'So, what's Perla Rosa like? Antonella was saying great things about it, but she's hardly impartial.'

'We'll be there soon enough. You can find out for yourself.' I highlight a few of the auctions I think may be of interest and add the dates to my calendar.

'What about this vill—'

'Like I said, Safiya, we'll be there soon enough for you to discover whatever it is you'd like to know for yourself. Let me also remind you that we don't need to pursue this pretence of a friendship. We're not friends. We haven't been for seven years after you decided to end what we had and we seem to have managed just fine.'

She stares at me for a few loaded seconds before blinking rapidly and nodding. 'Yes. You're right. Of course.' She gets up and walks towards the glass that overlooks the planes and the runway, her large coffee cup clutched in her hands. Her shoulders are hiked up and I can feel her tension all the way here.

I close my eyes as I'm swamped with a sense of guilt for snapping at her like that. Why do I react to her? Why can't I just respond to her questions with simple answers and leave it at that? All I can think about is that this is the same woman who I thought the world of and who

74

thought nothing of me. Talking to her, seeing her, brings all those feelings back to the forefront of my heart and mind and I can't stand it. It makes me feel that same sense of inadequacy and abandonment and I hate it. At least if I keep my distance from her, and remember those rules whenever we have to be around each other, I can try to prevent those feelings from consuming me like they nearly did once before.

'*Ciao. Benvenuti a Perla Rosa.* Welcome to Perla Rosa.' A young man in his early twenties gives me a cursory glance before beaming at Safiya as we get out of the taxi. 'I hope you had a pleasant journey, Signorina. My name is Amadeo. I am Bianca's nephew, Signora Antonella's housekeeper.'

'*Ciao*, Amadeo. And thank you.' Safiya beams right back, looking like a bright-eyed tourist as she takes in the sight before her.

The taxi driver gets out and makes his way towards the boot, pulling out our luggage. After handing me his card, he gets back into his car and drives off.

I grab my suitcases, leaving Safiya to get her own, and wheel them towards the small cottage near the main villa. Bianca is waiting by the door, a look of disapproval on her face, and fires off rapid Italian at her nephew, most of which I don't understand despite trying to pick up the language on Duolingo since I first came here. He scrambles to grab Safiya's things and makes his way past us and into the cottage.

'*Ciao*, Bianca. Good to see you again,' I smile.

'*Benvenuto*, Signor Murad. Nice to see you too. How was your journey?'

'Tiring, but I'm glad it's over.'

She tries to take my luggage, but I stop her. She shakes her head and then she's smiling at Safiya.

'*Benvenuta*, Signorina. My name is Bianca.'

'Nice to meet you, Bianca. Please, call me Safiya.'

'I have prepared rooms upstairs for you, and once you feel ready, come back downstairs for something to eat, yes?'

'That sounds perfect. *Grazie mille*, Bianca,' Safiya says sweetly and I grit my teeth. The past several hours have been nothing short of torture for me. I thought her questions and chatter were difficult to manage, but they've got nothing on her injured and sad vibe after I had snapped at her at the airport. What's worse is that it bothers me, and that fact in itself bothers me. It makes my head spin.

'*Prego*.' Bianca leads the way inside and ushers us upstairs before making her way towards the kitchen.

The cottage is just how I remember it. Beautiful, spacious and airy, with plenty of light coming through the wide windows. It opens into a large main living area, off which is a kitchen and a small dining area. There are paintings on the wall – of a sparkling sea, beautiful Italian architecture, of a woman with an austere look. Towards the back, there is a set of stairs that leads to the first floor, where there are the bedrooms and two bathrooms. It would have been an absolute pleasure to stay here for the duration of this project if I didn't have the added complication of Safiya's presence.

We head upstairs and two of the bedrooms have open doors, while the rest of the doors are closed. I turn when I hear Bianca speak as she makes her way upstairs, stopping before reaching the last step. 'I have cleaned those two rooms because they both face the lake and the sea in the distance. If you prefer a mountain view, I can open up one of the other rooms for you?' She looks between us. 'Also, I'm afraid only one bathroom is in use at the moment. The second one has some plumbing issues, which

76

I'm hoping Amadeo can look at, but, in the meantime, you'll have to use one,' she says, apologetically.

'That's fine, Bianca. We'll use these rooms.' I smile at her reassuringly.

She gives me a nod and then turns to make her way back downstairs.

When I turn back, I see that Safiya has already wheeled her suitcases and moved into the room on the left, leaving the room on the right – in pinks, lavenders and lace – for me.

I'm sure she's done that deliberately. I ought to challenge her on it, but that's probably what she's expecting me to do and I refuse to give her the satisfaction.

I drag my suitcases into the room and push them against the wall, taking in the room around me. There's a four-poster bed in white wood with white bedding and matching bedside drawers. A small white wood desk is set against the opposite wall beside a cupboard. A patio door makes up the third wall of the room, overlooking the lake, just as Bianca said.

The evening sun glints off the surface of the water and the sight has an almost immediate calming effect on me. I slide open the doors and step outside onto the balcony, inhaling the warm air. The view is mesmerising, overlooking hills and vineyards in the distance. It's glorious and just a fraction of the views that can be seen from inside the villa, which isn't too far from the cottage but faces the same direction.

The balcony is a large wraparound one with garden furniture arranged on it, patio doors leading into the bedrooms, which means I share it with—

'Stunning view, isn't it?' Safiya has her elbows resting against the balcony railing, her chin on the palm of her hand as she takes in the view I was admiring mere seconds ago from the other end of the balcony. She glances my way and smiles, her earlier sadness gone, and I feel my irritation at the situation morph into anger; thoughts, memories and emotions clamouring in my head with no escape. There is just no getting away from her, and I'm expected to spend an as yet unspecified number of weeks here while we get this project underway. I've barely taken in a moment of calm when it's been snatched away by my reality.

I'm tempted to lash out again, but I hold onto my anger by the skin of my teeth, ignoring her instead and making my way back inside the room, before I grab some essentials and go into the bathroom. I stand under the blast of the shower, hoping it'll help settle my taut nerves so that I can see the rest of the day through, though the tightness in my temples suggests it'll be a struggle.

I just need to keep my head straight. Not get sucked in by her beguiling smile or her bright eyes or her glossy lips . . . I need to remember the rules – ours and, more importantly, my own. With that resolve, I turn off the tap and, after getting changed, I make my way downstairs.

The smell of Bianca's cooking wafts through the cottage, making my stomach rumble as I approach her at the dining table.

'You look well, Signor Murad. How's the family?'

I smile at her, grateful that my frustration isn't stamped on my face for all to see. 'They're all fine. My sister recently had a baby boy and he's keeping everyone busy and entertained. How have you been?'

The last time I came to Perla Rosa had been for a short break. I was working in Abu Dhabi when Antonella invited me over for dinner with her now late husband. She told me of the town where she grew up – of the food, of the scenery, of the people. It was the perfect place to cure a broken heart, Antonella had said, as if she could read minds. That was six years ago and now I'm here again with the very person whose memories I've spent so long running away from. I stayed in this same cottage, where Bianca spent the duration of my stay feeding me and making sure I was well looked after.

I had feared that being alone would deepen my anguish – remind me of what I had lost – but I had braved that fear and come out anyway and being here had been cathartic in some ways. It had helped calm my thoughts and feelings. To accept the fact that my life had done a one hundred and eighty after the break-up with Safiya and didn't resemble anything I might have thought or hoped it might. It was a new version of life but still my own and one that I could mould to become what I wanted it to. I was in charge, and maybe up until that point, I hadn't been – or I hadn't accepted ownership at least.

'Here.' Bianca places a basket of fresh warm bread in front of me next to a dish with olive oil.

I can't help myself and break off a piece and dip it in, savouring the flavour as it bursts on my tongue.

'Oh, that's good, Bianca. I see you haven't lost your touch.'

She grins and the apples of her plump cheeks go pink.

'Can I put a request in for some cannoli, please?' I ask her, trying to mimic Sumi as best as I can, and she shakes her head indulgently.

'I had a feeling that request would be coming my way. So, I thought I'd beat you to it,' she says proudly as she goes back to the kitchen and lifts a tea towel off a tray on which she's laid out the confection, making my mouth water.

'You're the best.'

'*Sì*. I won't argue with that.' Bianca nods.

'Something smells delicious,' I hear Safiya say from the top of the stairs and I stiffen.

Bianca eyes me, curiously, and lifts her brow, but before she can say anything, I give her a smile and take another bite of the bread.

The magic of Perla Rosa helped me once before. Now with Safiya back in my life, I wonder if it will help me again.

11

Safiya

I pick my way through the villa the next morning, Amadeo a few steps ahead of me as he plays the role of guide, pointing out the various features to me as though I'm a potential buyer rather than the person hired to make changes to most of the interior as I carry out my preliminary walk-through. It's endearing really and makes a nice change from being snapped at and treated like a necessary burden that he can barely tolerate being around. There's only so much a girl can take of that kind of treatment, so Amadeo's puppyish adoration is actually very much welcome.

I don't recognise this Murad at all. There's no part of what I've seen and what I remember that I can reconcile. I understand – a lot more than he gives me credit for – that what happened seven years ago changed so much for both of us. But I'm trying to find my old self, while he seems to be making a conscious effort to be the polar opposite of who he used to be. And to me, he had been perfect in every way.

'Look at this Signorina Saf.' Amadeo spreads his arms wide as we step into a conservatory-like room. 'The glass in this room gives lots of natural light. You can see all the different colours in the sky from morning till evening. Sunsets, sunrises.'

I glance up at the glass ceiling and let out a soft gasp. In fact, it's more than just a glass ceiling. Half of the room is made of glass and, instantly, I wonder what options could be explored in this room. I close my eyes and visualise them – maybe a beautiful chaise in one corner, or a wooden dining table in the middle of the room for special events, pots of large plants at each corner. The conservatory is on the ground floor, an extension of the house which has been forgotten. Clearly there was an abundance of glass left over, but not bricks. It is beautiful, but it could be so much more. The possibilities are endless. I make some notes in my notebook and take some pictures and then Amadeo leads the way through the rest of the villa, which has a hidden magical energy about it which I hope will unveil itself as it's restored.

Murad was supposed to come and view the villa too, but he decided that he'd check it out himself later. Apparently, he had other work to get on with, which was news to me because *this* was work we were supposed to get started today. It feels like an excuse. Since we arrived at Perla Rosa, he's been nothing but monosyllabic, ill-tempered and distant. We have history, I get it. I can't help but keep thinking that he never used to be like this, my mind continuously running comparisons between *my* Murad and this version of him. My Murad was always gentle, soft. The only one who could soften my rough edges when we were younger, talk me off a ledge. If I burned hot, he ran cold. Not that he didn't get angry or annoyed, of course he did. But he would always talk it through, never let his annoyance or impatience show. He seems restless now. Different. Not just to the guy I knew seven years ago, but to the Murad in London too.

Yesterday, Murad ignored me for practically the whole

day and then, after dinner, he left without a word. I found myself spending the rest of the evening alone, sitting on the balcony and looking over towards his room to see if he might come out. As I waited, the sun set. Hues of yellows, oranges, pinks painted the sky until night fell. Stars sparkled like diamonds. Nothing like London. As I watched it, I thought of my list: Stargaze in the countryside. I had to do it properly to cross it off the list, and I made a mental note to ask Bianca or Amadeo where the best spot might be.

I laid my head against the headrest, watching the sky. Like a slideshow, memories of the past flashed through my head, but, for a change, I didn't fight them and it felt surprisingly cathartic. Fighting it always left me exhausted, like I'd gone through a wringer. My eyes grew heavy and I fell asleep out in the cold. But when I woke up, there was a blanket on my lap.

If I thought a new day might bring a new Murad, I was wrong. He was the same in the morning. One look at him had told me that he'd had a rough night because when he'd come down this morning after I had been halfway through my breakfast, his eyes had been tired and sunken; he'd not bothered shaving, leaving dark stubble coating his jaw. He'd barely glanced my way before he'd sat down and had his breakfast in record time before getting up to head back upstairs. He'd not even glanced my way.

Rather than ruminate over pointless matters, like Murad's mood, I need to remember to focus on the job at hand. If he wants to enact the role of a bear with a sore head, all the best to him. I've got more important things to concentrate on.

'*Un gatto così stupido.* This silly cat. Get down you greedy boy.' I turn and find Amadeo glaring at a cat, who's sitting on a shelf as though surveying his subjects while I blink up at him.

'How did he get in?' I ask, pointlessly it turns out, after I see the small gap in the wall beside the door frame which clearly needs a builder's attention.

'He goes to one house for a meal and then moves onto the next as though he's been starving for days. He's been at the business end of Bianca's broom many times.' The cat practically glares at Amadeo before moving in a circle and then settling down ready to nap. 'He's stubborn. Doesn't listen to anyone.'

'Well, he's not harming anyone up on that shelf. Let's leave him alone for a bit and see the rest of the villa. When the time comes, we'll move him out.' I smile reassuringly at Amadeo and he grins back before we complete the tour of the villa, at the end of which both my notebook and brain are bursting with ideas which I want to convert into plans on paper. I feel energised, much like I did when I saw the blank canvas of the period conversion and it lends a spring in my step as I go back to the cottage, my doubts momentarily taking a back seat.

Bianca's at the kitchen worktop, preparing something that smells mouth-wateringly good. She gives me a warm smile when I tell her I'm starving and promises me a hearty lunch shortly. 'By then Signor Murad should also be back.'

That's news to me. 'He's out?'

'Yes. He said he was meeting with some prospective contractors or something. Some business meeting. What did you think of the villa? It's lovely, isn't it?' Bianca comments, her hands on her hips.

'It most certainly is. The bare bones are there and they seem to be strong. We just need to dress it all up and bring it back to its former glory. It'll look stunning, I'm sure.' Something I'm determined to make happen, with or without Murad's help.

★

I knock on the door and wait. Nothing.

I knock again and, after a short pause, I open the door slowly, taking my time in case Murad decides to finally respond. He doesn't, so I push the door open all the way and peer inside his room, only to find it empty.

I spot some of his clothes strewn over the light pink duvet looking completely incongruous and can't help but smile as I remember seeing both rooms and deliberately making a beeline for the one decorated in greens and blues, leaving the pinks and purples for him. I had thought he would object vociferously – he had always had a thing against pink, thanks to his older sister, Meerab practically living in the colour – but he did no such thing. There wasn't a single sound of objection from him about the room.

That thought makes the smile slip from my face. Are we really that far gone that he wants absolutely nothing to do with me?

I slowly pull the door closed but jump when I hear his deep rumble behind me as he approaches the bedroom. 'What are you doing?'

I hold my hand against my racing heart as I face him. 'You scared me.'

He raises his brow. 'Only people with a guilty conscience get scared like that. What have you got to be scared about?'

'What? Nothing. Your sudden appearance scared me,' I explain, defensively.

'That's because you're lurking where you shouldn't be.' He takes a few steps towards me. We're closer than we have been in a while.

I blink, then move my hand from my chest to my hip.

'I wasn't lurking. I was looking for you. I'm working on the preliminary designs and I thought I'd—'

'Email them to me.' He moves to walk past me and into his bedroom, but I sidestep and stop him, standing in front of the open door.

'Why on earth would I email them to you when you're right here?'

'I can't deal with this right now.' He takes half a step forward towards his bedroom door, but I don't move.

'Pfft. You've not had the patience for anything since we went to see the period conversion. You don't have patience for simple questions about your family's well-being. You don't have any patience for the offer of a coffee. You don't have patience for being warm and friendly given we're the only people here and how new this all is for me.'

'And whose fault is that?' If Murad had shouted the words, they wouldn't have had as much of an impact as his quietly voiced question did. 'You decided that you didn't want anything to do with me for something that was completely out of my control and decided to cut off any connection we had. And now you stand here, berating me for not responding to your friendly gestures and not wanting to spend more time than I absolutely have to in your company.' He scoffs and shakes his head.

My breath quivers. 'So, is that it then, Murad?' I ask. 'This is how you plan to move forward? By bringing the past with us?'

'You want me to forget?'

'Not forget—'

'Then what?' he asks, standing so close that I can feel the warmth of his breath on my face. 'What do you want, Safiya?'

I break his gaze, looking down at my hands. 'For things

to be the same again. Like when we were kids. Before . . .'
I pause.

Murad lets out a bitter laugh. 'Things can never be the
same again. You broke us. You don't get to decide how
I feel – how I react. So, no, Safiya, I don't want to be
friends or talk to you about my family. Or share a coffee,'
he says. 'You might be OK with pretending. Used to it.
But I'm not.'

My breaths are short and sharp, feeling as though I'm
swallowing shards of ice, his accusations hitting me like
stones. His words shouldn't bother me because, really,
they're not true, not in the sense he believes at least.
There's so much more to it than he knows, but at the
time, I did exactly what he's accusing me of. I had to
make him believe me and it turns out that I did a bloody
fantastic job of it.

Murad opens his mouth as if he has something else
to say before pursing his lips again. He walks past me,
leaving me standing there as he goes downstairs and then
I hear the front door slam shut. I let out a painful breath
on a whimper, my eyes filling with tears which I have no
strength to stop from pouring down my cheeks.

12

Murad

My gut churns, a burning sensation climbing up my chest and past my throat, leaving a bitter taste in my mouth.

For the last seven years, I thought about what I might say if I saw Safiya again. I thought when I did, I'd feel better – things would feel resolved. But they don't. I rub my fist against my sternum, but it does nothing to ease the restlessness that has taken centre stage since I saw Safiya outside my bedroom. Hell, it's been there a long time before that. And instead of diminishing, lately, it is gathering speed and momentum, as though heading towards something unknown.

I know I shouldn't have lashed out at her like that, and I feel like absolute crap for having done so. But I had just got off the phone with Meerab, who wasn't happy to find out I was in Perla Rosa with Safiya. 'I can't believe you lied to me, Murad,' Meerab said, sounding disappointed.

'I didn't lie. I just didn't tell you who I was with and, it turns out, I was right. Look at your reaction! Give me some credit, Meerab. I'm a thirty-four-year-old adult for God's sake, you think I can't handle being in the same room as my ex-girlfriend?' Maybe telling her about me and Safiya after we broke up hadn't been my best idea.

'She's not just your ex-girlfriend, Murad,' Meerab had said through gritted teeth, her rage coming through the phone crystal clear. 'She broke your heart. She made you fundamentally change who you are. She's the reason you've never been able to find peace, or slow down for long enough to actually enjoy what you've earnt because you're too busy trying to reach the next level and it's a never-ending race. If it hadn't been for her, you would have been happy to pursue your career but also make more time for family. You might have had a partner of your own with whom you could have built the family I know you've always wanted. Someone who cherished you – unlike her.'

'It wasn't just her, Meerab. I know she broke my heart, but I'm not just this broken-hearted guy who can't move on. I wanted to focus on my work and career,' I said, weakly.

I could hear the concern and sadness mingled with anger in my older sister's voice and I spent the next half-hour trying to calm her down. In the end, she huffed and handed the phone to a bewildered Zubair, but with my own stress levels being sky-high, I had told him I'd speak to him later and ended the call. I had thought I'd go for a run, only to find Safiya outside my bedroom pulling the door closed and I snapped and I hate that I did that. Again. It's not me and it's certainly not how I was raised.

My upbringing, despite our economic struggles as a family, had been in a happy, supportive and loving environment. My father was a bus driver before he retired and my mum still works as a seamstress. Even now, you can see the affection they have for each other. How my dad will watch movies he doesn't like with my mum if only to spend time with her. How my mother will reluctantly listen to his infamously bad music. Their affection has only deepened over time and it was no secret that both Meerab and I aspired to having relationships that mirrored that of our parents'.

Meerab found that. She fell in love with Zubair in university, then moved to Birmingham where he was based. They got married, had Sumaira and my parents moved to be closer to them, while I stayed in London, deciding to split my time between the two cities.

Safiya and I had broken up shortly before Meerab's wedding. Talk about bad timing. Since we were close, Meerab knew all about it. After moving to Birmingham, she had often tried to convince me to do the same and cut ties with London, but I had never been able to bring myself to. My work was in London and I still thought of it as home, though I did take some time away from it when, after Meerab's wedding, I met Antonella and her husband, Filippo, and accepted their offer to work for their property development firm in their Abu Dhabi office. The property market in the Middle East was booming and I made the most of working there and building my experience and profile in the industry.

Fast-forward six years and I now work as a consultant with a sizeable investment in Antonella's business after Filippo passed and I also work as a consultant with Zafar. My time in the Middle East proved a financially successful one because I'm now in a position where I don't have to work if I don't want to and I can still live very comfortably. For now at least. But, as Meerab said, I can't seem to stop myself from pushing for more. It's not the money I'm after, though I'd be lying if I said it wasn't nice not having that to worry about. I had felt a great sense of satisfaction when I had paid off my parents' debts and helped my brother-in-law establish his dental practice – though he's since paid me back.

No, it's not the money. It's the thrill of doing what I do. Scoping the market, finding hidden treasures and giving them the shine they need before striking deals and pushing the boundaries to see how much better I can do with each project. Pride surges inside me when I accomplish that because I prove, time and time again, that I'm more than my humble beginnings. Beginnings which weren't good enough for someone and led to me being rejected. Beginnings which I had no control over and which I had never thought defined me. But I had obviously been wrong.

Acid climbs up my throat as I remember the sense of inadequacy and vulnerability I had felt seven years ago, as though I had been stripped bare. Something that had never really been an insecurity of mine, only an awareness, became one and I've not been able to be rid of it since then, no matter how many deals I secure or how much money I make.

The restlessness inside me threatens to bubble over and I decide to go for a walk in lieu of a run. Anything to burn off this excess energy coursing through me. I make my way towards the gate leading away from the grounds of the villa and the cottage, only to see a car trundling up the driveway. It comes closer, pulling up just in front of me, and Antonella's brother, Giancarlo, steps out and makes his way towards me.

'Murad. So good to see you. How are you?'

I wipe my face of all expression and smile as I step forward to shake his hand. We exchange pleasantries and then he points towards the car, where a man I didn't see is standing.

'I've brought a surveyor in to check the structural integrity and roof. Antonella insisted we make sure all the paperwork is taken care of properly before we start the work.'

'Of course. Yes, she mentioned as much to me when I spoke to her yesterday. I didn't realise you'd have a surveyor round so soon. I'll let you carry on.'

'Actually, I think you should come with us. That way, if there are any questions or issues, you're in the know. I'm only here as the middleman.' He grins and then speaks to the surveyor in Italian before leading the way towards the villa.

With little choice, I follow after the pair of them, the need to apologise to Safiya for snapping at her lodging itself in the back of my mind.

It takes me two days to gather the courage to make my apology and, unfortunately, it doesn't go to plan.

I've just ended a call with Antonella, discussing an upcoming auction with her, when a large truck bearing building supplies comes up the driveway. Amadeo comes out to deal with it and it doesn't take long for the delivery men to start unloading the supplies, carrying them into the villa.

Safiya walks out of the villa, expressing her delight to Amadeo. 'This is brilliant and well before time too.' She claps her hands before clasping them together as the men continue unloading the truck.

I watch Safiya as she in turn watches the supplies being unloaded. Her hair is up in a messy bun with tendrils framing her face, which is bare of any make-up but has a slight sheen, presumably from her exertion inside the villa. To be fair, it is quite warm and she'd been helping the recently hired clean-up team with some of the clearing out of the place. Her jeans are folded up to just above her ankles, an anklet sitting on her right pink Converse. She's wearing a light green T-shirt with a printed sun donning sunglasses and she looks as gorgeous as I've ever seen. The witch.

We haven't spoken since that day. Safiya has either been working on the designs or out of the villa with Amadeo or Bianca. She seems to be enjoying what she's doing, approaching each day with a keen energy. Yesterday, we had a video call with Antonella and watching Safiya talk about her vision for the villa had me in awe. It's like I thought after seeing the period conversion, she's got a real knack for bringing out the best in a property. Of course, she kept things strictly professional whilst we were on the call, and as soon as the call ended, she proceeded to ignore me. It's what I wanted, so why it bothers me is baffling.

The shrill ringing of my phone jars me out of my thoughts and I catch Safiya glance my way before she resumes watching the unloading as I answer the call. 'Hello?'

'Mumu?' My less than pleasant mood instantly shifts to give way to joy at the sound of my niece's voice.

'Hi, sweetheart. How's my favourite baby girl?'

'I'm not a baby. I'm going to be four soon.'

I don't tell her she's got many months to go before her next birthday. 'You're right. You're not a baby, Irfan is.'

'Yes,' she says emphatically. 'He can't even hold his own milk bottle.' Like it's a huge failure on the newborn's part.

I spend a few minutes listening to her entertaining chatter before Meerab comes on the phone. I'm still not quite over the blistering from two days ago, so after ascertaining that all is well at her end, I promise to call her soon and get off the phone. Thankfully, she's preoccupied enough with the children to not rake me over the coals.

I pocket my phone in time to see the truck reversing away and Safiya and Amadeo heading back inside the villa. I really need to speak to her and apologise. The longer I leave it, the harder it'll be . . . Not that it's not nearly impossible anyway.

Telling myself it's now or never, I call out to her. 'Safiya.' She turns a surprised glance my way before stopping and

93

raising an eyebrow at me. Amadeo stops too. 'Can I have a word?' Her second eyebrow goes up too. 'Please?'

There's painful silence for a few seconds. Safiya turns to Amadeo, saying something too softly for me to catch at this distance, and once he heads into the villa, she turns to look at me, her arms folded across her chest.

She's obviously not going to come this way, so I take a breath and close the distance between us. She's curious, I can tell by the sparkle in her eyes, but she stands silently, waiting for me to make clear why I've stopped her. Well, I don't need to drag this out.

I stuff my hands in the pockets of my jeans, wondering how I should say what I need to say. I used to be better at this. 'I wanted to apologise to you.'

Silence.

'For the way I behaved.'

More silence.

'Two days ago.'

Safiya lowers her brows, her expression is one of confusion for a split second. Then it clears like she has found the solution to a complex puzzle. '*Oh.* You mean when you bit my head off? Is that what you're referring to?' She feigns confusion, but I know I need to eat humble pie today, so I'll let her have her jab.

'Yes. I was rude and it was unacceptable. I'm sorry.'

There's a smile on her face, but it looks forced. 'You don't have to apologise for telling me your true feelings, Murad. In fact, I wouldn't be surprised if you thought I should fall off the face of the earth.'

My heart swoops something nasty at the image her words conjure. 'I would never . . .' I scrub a hand through my hair. 'Look, I was frustrated and I let my emotions do the talking. I flew off the handle without watching what

I was saying.' Some of that frustration threatens to bubble up now, but I grit my teeth and focus on the moment. 'I shouldn't have reacted that way. I'm sorry.'

Surprise washes over her face and then Safiya is quiet, studying me. Like she knows something I don't. 'The thing is, Murad, it wasn't just a momentary reaction. It feels like whiplash. Sometimes you're warm, friendly. Then it's coldness, abruptness and the crystal-clear feeling that you'd rather be anywhere else. It's obviously because of me.'

My forehead throbs as I think about walking away, but I'm frozen. *Frozen* in time. I'm still there, right where Safiya left me, her bitter words etched in my head. It's clear now. Clear that all my attempts of getting over her were futile, and it's frustrating. 'That much is true and I'm pretty sure, had the shoe been on the other foot, you would feel the same way about me,' I say, a heavy sigh leaving my mouth. 'I might not want you to fall off the face of the earth, Safiya, but I don't want to be anywhere near you. That shouldn't surprise you. It's what you wanted, right? What did you say again?'

Safiya's jaw twitches. 'Don't . . .'

'*It was never meant to be a forever kind of thing, just for now,*' I say, the words bitter on my tongue. 'We were too different. Our backgrounds, our families, *us*. How could it be anything more when my dad was just a bus driver, and my mum a seamstress?' Tears well in my eyes, but I blink them away. 'Where would we live, after all? On your family's estate or on my council estate?'

Her lips are pressed together as she watches me wide-eyed, her chest rising and falling with each ragged breath she takes. 'Stop.' Her voice is barely above a croak, but I'm on a roll.

'What else was there?' I pretend to scratch my head in thought. 'You covered differences in wealth, connections and family backgrounds. You said that "love" – that filthy four-lettered word – wasn't enough to keep us together in the long term. How would I manage if my family became dependent on me, which, inevitably, they would because their prospects weren't exactly great. How would I compare with your brothers and—'

'I did it for you,' Safiya says. 'Everything. It was all for you.'

13

Safiya

Pillowy clouds drift in and out of the impossibly blue sky. Murad's eyes are glassy as waves of emotions wash over his face. Shock, curiosity, pain. *I shouldn't have said that,* I think, and wish I could take it away.

My insides feel like they're trembling with the intensity of my feelings. It's too much. I can't be here. I get the feeling he's got the capacity of going into full shark mode if he smells even a drop of blood and I can't let him do that. Besides, all that's gone between us is ancient history and digging up those old fossils won't serve either of us. He's moved on and I need to move on. If circumstances – and my desperate need – hadn't thrust us together for work, we'd be on our separate paths doing our own thing, never having to rake over old ground.

'Forget I said anything. It's done. Over. There's no point going over ancient history and what was said or done. It's over, in the past so just . . . leave it.' I plead. The words are on repeat, but I don't know what more to say.

He shakes his head, whether in denial or confusion, I don't know. A humourless huff of laughter escapes his lips. 'If you think you can say something like that and say nothing more, then you're mistaken, Safiya. You have to explain what you mean. Even if we stand here until tomorrow morning's sunrise.'

I can't believe I blurted those words out. Murad's words were cutting me to the quick and I couldn't hold back in that moment, but I should have. 'It's nothing. I just said it to get you to stop. God, you're like a dog with a bone,' I say. He watches me slowly as I take a deep breath and push my shoulders back. 'I've got better things to do than stand here in the blazing sun talking about pointless things from times gone by with you, Murad.' I whirl on my heels, intending to make my way back inside the villa. He grabs my hand, currents shooting from the point of contact, up my arm and through my body.

'If it's nothing . . .' Murad begins. 'Are you lying?'

I stiffen. 'I don't owe you any explanation for anything.' My voice croaks and I clear my throat.

'You were either lying then or you're lying now. Which is it?'

'Murad, please.' I try to affect annoyance in my voice.

'You were right,' he says gently and something about the softness in his voice makes my hair stand on end. 'I am like a dog with a bone. I won't rest until I find out the truth. Of course, you can save me the effort by telling me what I want to know sooner. You know where to find me if you do. But, rest assured, that one way or another, I will get to the bottom of this.' And with that, he walks away from me towards the cottage, leaving me feeling like he's sucked every last vestige of energy from my body.

I can't believe I gave myself away like that. For seven long years I've kept that secret from everyone I know. To be fair, there's been no one in all that time who I've felt able to share it with. No one who knew or cared enough to find out what secrets I held close to my heart.

98

The only other person who knew anything has been dead for three years and I know he never shared this particular secret with anyone. If he had, I would have heard about it and, more importantly, it would have exposed the part he had played in the whole debacle, and he wasn't going to do that. Instead, he took the secret to his grave with him and it's something I never forgave him for. Still haven't.

Murad will find out; it really is only a matter of time. How will he react? What will he say? Is it better if I just tell him everything? Get it out of the way so we can both move on?

In all these years, I've often thought about such a moment. Of me telling him the truth or of him finding out somehow and knowing that I did what I had to do, not what I wanted to do. Of course, it was all in my head, so it was as fanciful as anything, but in moments of deep loneliness and when I allowed myself the luxury, I did think about it. About him. About what he meant to me and how different things might have been if only . . . Like I said, fanciful.

'*Signorina*? Saf?' I turn and find Amadeo looking at me in concern. 'You OK?'

'Yes,' I say, weakly. 'I'm fine.'

I look around me in a daze and realise that I'm standing exactly where Amadeo and then Murad had left me. I don't even know how long I've been standing here like that, caught up in my own thoughts.

I smile at Amadeo, probably looking deranged and nod at him. 'Has everything been put away?'

Amadeo grins, his concern for me allayed as he launches into an explanation about where the bags of sand and cement are stored and the boxes of tiles we found at a really good price from a nearby wholesaler just yesterday, which I hope we might be able to use in the main bathroom. I know it's early to be buying things like tiles, but it really was a damn good price.

'Perfect. And the cleaning team?'

'They're ready to leave for today.'

We see the cleaning team off and, after thanking Amadeo for his help and hard work, I see him off too.

I look towards the cottage, but unease stops me from taking any steps in that direction. Instead, I go into the villa and make my way towards one of the rooms on the second floor which has glorious views of the lake and the sea beyond it. It kind of reminds me of Mombasa. I turn over a discarded wooden crate and slowly lower myself onto it.

The best part about living in Kenya was definitely the weather – it never got cold or wet enough to warrant winter coats. But there were definitely other things that I was more than happy to leave behind, like the power cuts. There was a laid-back vibe about the place, especially in the coastal town of Mombasa, where I reconnected with Daadi and Zafar. Until then, I had always grouped Daadi with Daada, believing that she had agreed with and supported all his decisions. It was only then I had found out that that wasn't the case, she hadn't, but she had been unable to do or say anything. It was after reconnecting with Zafar and Daadi that I managed to find the courage to end my toxic marriage with Ejaz and come back to London. It would be so easy to associate that place with him, but that would be unfair.

Much like this place. It's beautiful and serene, but I'm here with the one person who makes me feel agitated as opposed to calm, especially now.

I shake myself of my thoughts and look out at the view, taking in deep breaths in an effort to find a small semblance of calm amid all the chaos inside me.

Murad's face flashes before my eyes. Not from earlier, but the Murad of seven years ago. The pain I felt from breaking his heart has never really left me. Selfishly, I had thought that I would get over it in time and so would Murad. We'd both think back on our relationship fondly, but would both move on from it. But that never happened. I ended up swapping a diamond for a piece of coal and have come away with nothing but dirt on my hands in the form of emotional scars.

I had set out to hurt Murad because I knew that was the only way to save him from what my grandfather had threatened. If I hadn't broken his heart as thoroughly as I did, he would never have left me, and if I had told him the truth, he would have most certainly stood by me and I couldn't have that on my conscience. I'd hate to go back in time and go through any of that again, but I would likely make the same choice over and over if it meant protecting Murad from my grandfather's dirty machinations.

I sigh loud enough for the sound to echo softly through the empty room and I rest my head against the wall beside me, keeping my eyes on the horizon beyond the window. It's like a metaphoric reflection of my life, looking through a window and seeing the glorious possibilities there but not being able to reach them, though I've managed to break away from some of my shackles. Maybe it's just a matter of time before I can break away from the rest of them and maybe then I'll be able to truly feel free, something that feels further away than ever.

14

Murad

'I've searched everywhere. She's not here.' Amadeo pants as my heart sinks further. *Where is she?*

After our confrontation in the courtyard, and her enigmatic statement about all of it being for my sake, I holed myself away in my room, trying and failing to concentrate on some work. Nothing distracted me enough to stop Safiya's words from going round in my head on loop, but I forced myself to stay there. Otherwise, I would have only gone in search for the truth like a bull in a china shop. I needed the time to bring my thoughts and pulse to calmer territory so I wouldn't say or do anything rash.

All those noble thoughts, however, flew out of my mind when I realised Safiya was missing.

Amadeo had come and asked after her when a late delivery arrived, saying he'd looked everywhere but couldn't find her.

'What do you mean you can't find her? She wouldn't have gone anywhere without saying, that's not like her.'

I had tried calling her, but after a few unanswered rings, her phone had gone to voicemail.

I had gone downstairs, only to find a slightly frantic Bianca. 'I've checked, Signorina Saf is not here. I've not seen her for a couple of hours now.'

'She's not in the courtyard or at the villa?'

Amadeo shook his head. 'We locked the villa together after the cleaners left and I've looked everywhere else, I can't find her.'

I decided to go with Amadeo and look around the local area to see if she might have gone for a walk and got lost or something. She always had decent navigational skills, but it was a new area for her, so it wasn't outside the realms of possibility that she might be lost, though surely she'd have called or returned one of my calls.

Amadeo and I made our way towards the town and the area by the main lake. Being familiar with the area, Amadeo searched the smaller side streets, while I looked around the lake, neither of us having any luck in locating her.

'Should we call the police?' Amadeo asks now and my heart skips a beat. Waves of hot and cold wash over me as my panic levels peak. *Where are you, Fiya?*

I swallow the lump in my throat and try to keep a hold of my rationality. 'Let's go back to the cottage first. She might well be there.' I'm not sure if I'm saying it for his benefit or my own, but I hold onto the thought like a talisman as we make our way back to the cottage in silence.

When we pull into the courtyard, Bianca's standing just outside the cottage doorway, her hands clutched together and a hopeful expression on her face, which falls as soon as she sees me and Amadeo, who shakes his head in silence.

I take out my phone to try hers one more time before I have to do the inevitable and call the police. The phone rings and, as I wait, my eyes land on the door to the villa. The bolt across the double door is undone and the padlock is hanging off it but the door is closed.

My heart starts racing and my mouth goes dry as Safiya's voicemail kicks in again and I end the call. I walk towards the front door of the villa and slowly push it, only for it to swing open. I turn and look at Bianca and Amadeo, both of whom are looking between me the open door with wide eyes. I try Safiya's phone again as I make my way into the villa.

'Fiya?' I shout as I end the unanswered call for what feels like the hundredth time. I run through the downstairs, trying to find her in the dark until I nearly fall over crates lying in the middle of one of the rooms. I pause, pulling in a deep breath before turning on the light on my phone and then checking each room systematically before heading upstairs. 'Safiya?'

I reach the landing, my pulse now thundering in my ears. If I don't find her here, I don't know what I'm going to do. I see her face in my mind's eye, standing in the courtyard as I threw our history at her, her eyes sad and troubled. If anything happens to her . . . I don't allow that thought any air as I push open one door after the other.

'Safiya?' My throat feels hoarse.

Over the whooshing in my ears, I just about hear a faintly voiced, 'I'm here,' and my heartbeat stutters before it begins pounding like the hoofbeats of a herd of wild horses on the loose. It sounded like she's on the second floor and I don't even think twice before leaping up the stairs, taking them two at a time.

I see her come out of one of the rooms, brushing hair out of her face. 'What's going . . . Uff.' I don't even let her finish her sentence before I pull her against myself, breathing in her scent and relishing the weight of her in my arms. The pounding of my heart and whooshing in my ears still hasn't subsided when I pull back enough to run my hands down her arms before I cup her cheeks with both my hands and inspect her for any signs of hurt.

104

My breathing is ragged and the adrenaline pumping through me makes me feel like I can barely stand still until a hand rests against my chest and another tentatively lands on my cheek. 'Hey. Murad?' She says it softly and I feel all my energy leave my body as I pull her against myself and wrap my arms around her once more.

'Thank God! I thought I had lost you, Fiya. I've been going frantic looking for you.'

'Huh?' She pulls away slightly, but I'm loath to let her, keeping my hands on her hips. I glance down at her. Her nose is wrinkled and she's looking up at me in confusion.

Amadeo bursts into the room then and I reluctantly pull away from her, my fear from earlier finding its voice. 'What the hell have you been doing in here? And why didn't you answer your phone when I called you?'

Before she can say anything, Amadeo speaks. 'I'll go and tell *Zia* Bianca we've found Saf. Are you OK, Saf?'

She nods and Amadeo leaves while I now glare at Safiya.

She gives me a look and then moves past me, making her way downstairs and out of the villa. When I come through the front door, she reaches behind me and, fishing a key out of the pocket of her jeans, she bolts the door and then locks it. She's about to pull away so I curl my fingers around her wrist, holding her in place.

'You didn't answer my question. What were you doing in there and why didn't you tell anyone where you were? I began assuming the worst.'

'I just wanted some space after . . . I was resting against the wall and I fell asleep. It wasn't deliberate.'

I pull my hand away from her wrist, but I can feel the warmth of her touch. I shake my head, running my fingers through my hair before I turn and walk to the cottage, pausing outside the door and waiting for her. She precedes me into the cottage, where a panicked Bianca comes and hugs her close.

'I got so scared when they couldn't find you. Are you all right?'

Safiya nods and smiles tentatively. 'I'm fine, Bianca. I was in the villa and I fell asleep.'

Bianca shakes her head. 'You're working too hard and not resting enough. Have a hot shower while I lay out dinner for you and Signor Murad.'

Safiya faces me. 'You've not eaten?'

'He's been looking for you. He went around the local area with Amadeo to see if he could find you.'

I can see she's surprised, but I'm feeling too tightly wound to say or do anything sensible right now, so I move past her and go upstairs to my room. A tremor goes through my body and I lower myself onto the chair as I curl my fingers in on themselves, resting them on the desk and staring at the wall in front of me.

The guilt and panic that surged through me this evening is unlike anything I've ever felt before. It brought a crushing weight on my chest, making it hard to breathe, but I pushed through it all to try to find her and I would have kept on going for however long it took. It was only through a sheer stroke of luck that I spotted the unlocked villa door. The sense of relief that had washed through me when I'd seen her had nearly brought me to my knees.

I get up and make my way onto the balcony, taking deep breaths with my eyes closed and trying to tune into the sounds around me in a bid to calm down. I'm not sure how long I stand there for but when I hear a tentative knock on the bedroom door, I'm relieved that I'm no longer vibrating with tension. I step into the room and slide the patio door closed behind me as the door starts swinging open and Safiya pokes her head around it. Her hair is wet and her cheeks look clear, the scent of her shampoo wafting towards me as I close some of the distance between us. 'Hey.'

I clear my throat. 'Hi.' I sound like I've swallowed a frog. I wave my arm towards the chair but she shakes her head and so I take it instead, feeling the need to sit down.

She comes and leans against the desk, barely an arm's length away from me. 'I'm sorry. I didn't mean to worry everyone. I just . . . I needed some space.'

Guilt knifes through me afresh at her words. The only reason she needed space was because I'd behaved like a brute. 'I thought . . .' I shake my head, unable to articulate myself properly.

'That I was lost. Yeah, Bianca said as much.'

'No. Yes. But I thought you had wandered off because of me. Because of everything I said and the way I spoke to you before. It's not you who should be apologising. It's me. I'm sorry.' I lean back in my chair and glance up at her, my arm brushing her hand as I move it back and we both look down. Warmth climbs up my arm from where it touched her hand and when I look towards her, I feel the edginess within me slowly begin to subside. I observe her closely, more than I have until now and I can see the passage of time on her face. It doesn't take away from how attractive she is, if anything she looks more so.

'What made you look for me?' she asks softly.

'Amadeo said he couldn't find you and neither could Bianca. You weren't answering your phone. Amadeo said that you guys had locked up the villa after the cleaners had left so we didn't think you were in there. To be fair, there was no light on in the villa. It was only by chance that I saw the unlocked front door and went inside to check, though you still weren't answering your phone.'

'I don't know how I fell asleep like that,' she says prosaically as she scrunches her nose.

The answer's so innocuous, I can't help but laugh. It bubbles up out of me and I can't stop it as it gathers momentum. Safiya looks at me and smiles and it doesn't take long for her to join in too, her eyes sparkling and her cheeks rosy. I let out a deep sigh as she dries her tears of laughter with the pads of her fingers before moving away from the desk.

'Let's go down and have some dinner.' Her smile is open and I feel a sense of lightness slowly settle in my chest.

'Yeah. Come on.'

I follow her downstairs, where Bianca's laid out a lasagne for us. Given the late hour, I insist she and Amadeo join us and we spend the next hour eating and chatting, my fraught nerves gradually settling down as Bianca regales us with stories about her life in Perla Rosa before telling us about her children and grandchildren.

'I have a question, Bianca,' Safiya says as she pushes her empty plate away.

'*Sì.*' Bianca brings a tray of cannoli to the table after instructing Amadeo to bring coffee before she takes her seat again.

'Perla Rosa means pink pearl, doesn't it? How did the town come by that name?' I watch as Safiya bites into a cannolo, the filling clinging to her lips along with flakes of pastry, and I swallow to ease the dryness in my mouth. What on earth is wrong with me?

I turn and resolutely face Bianca, whose smile seems to have dimmed slightly.

'It's not a very happy story. There was a pirate who found a precious pink pearl on one of his many adventures. When he came to this town, he gave the pink pearl to the princess as a token of his affection and expressed a desire to marry her. The king refused the match because he said the pirate had nothing to offer, so the pirate told the princess that he would come back when he had amassed enough wealth to satisfy the king, telling her to hold onto the pearl when she tried to return it, as a symbol of his promise.'

'Did he not come back?' I find myself asking.

Bianca shakes her head. 'He did, but soon after he came back, the princess died. The king gave up his throne, but the pirate stayed here for the rest of his life because he felt closer to the princess. Thereafter, the town became known as Perla Rosa and the lake is called Lago Rosa. It's to celebrate the love of the pirate and his princess.'

'Oh no.' Safiya sounds genuinely upset.

'But there's a happy legacy of their story. Legend has it that if true love comes to Perla Rosa, then it will always find its way, no matter what. The people of Perla Rosa believe it's a blessing from the pirate and his princess.' Bianca looks pleased with herself as she drains her coffee and begins collecting the dishes on the table, while I make a conscious effort not to look in Safiya's direction.

Stars are sparkling in the night sky, the silence broken every now and then by the hooting of an owl or the ambient noises of other creatures not visible under the cloak of darkness. I find myself physically tired but, mentally, I'm wide awake.

I hear the patio door of Safiya's room slide open and, a moment later, she steps out. Not wanting to scare her, I alert her to my presence by clearing my throat. She turns to face me, the light from her room casting a soft glow over her.

'Can't sleep?'

She shakes her head. 'I want to, but I can't seem to settle down. Bianca's story about the pirate and the princess keeps going round in my head.' She comes and stands not too far from me, looking over the lake – Lago Rosa, not that we can see much in the dark.

'I'm not sure if it was true or a folk tale. You know? Like Heer Ranjha and Romeo and Juliet. Maybe this is just another version of that: star-crossed lovers and a tragic love story.'

'Is that what's kept you up as well?' she asks.

'Not really, no. I was thinking about us.'

She doesn't respond and I'm not keen to build suspense.

'I'm not going to pretend that this afternoon didn't happen, Safiya, or that I didn't hear your admission. If you choose not to say anything, that's up to you. Of course, I'd prefer you to, but I've decided I'm not going to push you. I have no right to do that and I'm sorry for trying to do so earlier. Whenever you're ready, I'll be happy to listen to whatever you've got to say, and if not, then . . .' I shrug. 'But, in the meantime, I'd like to put our differences to the side – or behind us even – and maybe, if you're up for it, get to know each other again. As friends. You tried once before and I rebuffed your efforts, but would you be willing to try again? Start afresh?'

Safiya looks at me for a long while, her expression not giving anything away in the dim light. It probably seems like a huge turnaround to her, and the truth is, it is. If someone had told me this very morning that I'd be offering Safiya Saeed friendship, I'd have thought they'd lost their marbles. But that's exactly what I'm doing. I don't know if it's the effect of what she said to me when we were standing in the courtyard this afternoon or what I went through thereafter when I thought she was lost. Maybe it's

110

a bit of both. When I found her in that villa, it had taken a Herculean level of effort on my part to let go.

It's moments like that which make one question what they're doing. Of course, I still want answers from her about what happened seven years ago. But in the grand scheme of things, aside from assuaging my curiosity, what would be the point? It's not like it would change anything. But, for however long we're working together, do I want to carry all that heartache with me? All that emotional baggage and all those unresolved feelings? What purpose does it serve, except to burn a hole in my gut whenever I think about any of it? None.

So, I figured it's better to try to find an amiable way forward – much like she suggested in the first place, but I was too pig-headed to pay any heed.

She smiles as she covers my forearm with her hand, her touch warm and comforting. I try not to feel anything beyond that, but I can't help myself from edging closer, watching as her smile reaches her eyes, making them rival the stars with their brightness. 'You're a good man, Murad Aziz, and I want nothing more than to put the past behind us and move forward as friends. But . . .' She swallows as she lifts her hand from my arm and tucks errant strands of hair behind her ear, my pulse skittering as her smile dims. 'That's it. We can be friends, the best of friends, but—'

I pick her hand up and squeeze it between both of mine. 'I get it. Just friends.' What we had is gone, it's in the past and can't be recaptured or revived. This is probably the best either of us can hope for. So why does it cause a dull ache in my chest?

Up until this morning, I thought, and strongly believed, that I wanted nothing to do with Safiya. I wouldn't have said I hated her, but I was indifferent to her – or at least

I wanted to be. There wasn't the slightest desire in me to befriend her or, heaven forbid, try to rekindle what we had. But hearing her allude to it and saying it out loud makes me feel a profound sense of loss and sadness. Why? Is it grief? Was I too angry and wounded to grieve seven years ago? Maybe. But at least we have an opportunity to move forward in a healthier way and I'm going to focus on trying to be happy and content with that.

15

Safiya

'I'm picturing the chandelier we took down from one of the reception rooms here, with re-laid flooring and paper on the walls. The ceiling will need work, but I think we should get a specialist in for it because I'd like to preserve the intricate plasterwork on it. You don't get work like that anymore'

'Mmhmm.' Murad's eyes are on his phone as I go through the revised designs for the villa with him on my laptop at the dining room table in the cottage.

'And these are the plans for the kitchen. Maybe we can install a bathtub in there.'

'Hmm.'

I raise my eyebrow at that. It's been a few days since we decided to put the past behind us and move on and it's been an interesting time. Of course, there's still a sense of awkwardness between us, but there's an effort on both sides to try to move beyond it. It's taken time, but I'm beginning to feel lighter and freer in a way I haven't since coming back from Kenya.

'And I was thinking of putting a swimming pool in the front reception room. Maybe have some mermaids in there. And a big taxidermied grizzly bear at the front door to welcome people.' Murad looks up at that, his expression contrite as I scowl at him. 'You weren't listening.'

'I'm sorry.' He puts his phone face down on the table and gives me his full attention. 'I am now. You said something about a bathtub.'

I groan and point at the design for the kitchen. 'I was showing you the revised plan for the kitchen. I'm thinking of using this room.' I show him the design and wait for his reaction.

His eyebrows furrow and he tilts his head to one side. 'You're going to have to explain this one to me, Fiya.'

My breath hitches at the sound of my nickname. He was the only one who ever called me that. *Fiya*. It felt like something only the two of us shared, a secret only we knew. It made me feel precious, cherished, and *his*. It's been years since I've heard it. I wonder if he has realised what he has said. Maybe he hasn't.

He clicks his fingers in front of my face. 'Hello! How will this room work as a kitchen? The walls are almost entirely made of glass. It might let a great amount of light in, but you're not leaving yourself any space to put up wall units or even base units in there.'

I clear my throat, snapping myself out of my thoughts. 'Look here,' I point at the plan and explain the concept behind my design and the alternative storage solutions.

He nods, then his pursed lips turn upwards into a large grin. 'It's bold,' He comments and my stomach twists. 'But that's you, isn't it? Bold and daring to the core.'

A huff escapes my mouth, his words surprising me. 'Not so much, anymore.'

He narrows his brows. 'Why not?'

'Oh you know,' I say casually. 'Tiny little thing called life, with a generous sprinkling of circumstances.' I close the laptop lid, standing up with a forced smile, not wanting to delve into this particular conversation with Murad.

Certainly not now. Our truce is in its infancy and I don't want to overcomplicate things. 'Anyway, we have work to get on with, so shall we?'

He doesn't say anything, but there is a flicker of concern in his dark eyes. It reminds me of his concern when he thought I was lost. Of how concerned and caring he was. He doesn't push. Maybe he thinks the same thing – that we shouldn't say or do anything to complicate our working relationship.

'Well?' I say.

He doesn't take his eyes off me for a long while and when he eventually does, I breathe a sigh of relief. He gives me a boyish grin and gets up. 'Let's go.'

'You, Murad Aziz, have the worst judgement when it comes to plumbers and electricians. I could see from a mile off that this guy was doing a bad job, but you insisted on giving him the benefit of the doubt, and now look where we are.'

He's lying on his back, his upper body stuffed under the bathroom basin which hasn't stopped leaking since the dubious plumber Amadeo found and Murad made fast friends with came and 'fixed' it this afternoon.

We're in the second bathroom of the cottage, which has been out of use since we've been here. It worked for all of half an hour after the plumber and then Bianca and Amadeo left. Since then, it's been dripping incessantly and, within the hour, it's filled a small bucket.

'If you could stop griping for one second and pass me the pliers, I'd really appreciate it.' His voice is strained as he wrestles with the hardware under the basin.

'*Griping*?! How dare you?! I'm not griping, I'm merely stating the obvious.'

'Well, don't. Not these ones, the other ones.' He hands the tool back to me.

I roll my eyes as I fish around in the toolbox for the second pair of pliers he wants, pulling them out and passing them to him. He grunts as he continues to wrestle with the parts while I surreptitiously watch the play of muscles in his arms.

He's wearing a plain cotton T-shirt, which has his arms exposed all the way to his shoulders, his biceps and triceps bunching and flexing. He wipes beads of sweat off his forehead and an ache grows in the pit of my stomach.

'Fiya?'

He was always athletic but never this muscular, from what I remember. He went to the gym reluctantly, preferring to go for walks, reading or doing a jigsaw puzzle. I wonder when he decided to focus on fitness like this, because that kind of muscle definition only comes through discipline and determination to push yourself beyond your comfort zone.

'Earth to Safiya,' he says, loudly, causing me to jerk my knee against the toolbox.

'What?'

'I think I've got it. I'm going to move out, and then we'll turn the supply back on.' He shimmies out from under the basin, his T-shirt riding up his torso as he does, showing me definition similar to that on his arms adorning his abdomen. *Well.* I look away, trying to remind myself that admiring arms is one thing, but ogling the man's abs is quite another and very much inappropriate, given that we are supposed to be *friends*. I shouldn't be doing either, strictly speaking.

I put some of the tools lying on the floor back in the toolbox and get up from my cross-legged position on the floor.

Murad makes his way towards the stopcock. 'Put the bucket back under there, please.' I do as he asks and he turns the water supply back on.

We both stand in silence and when we don't hear or see anything untoward, Murad makes his way towards the basin and crouches down to inspect the pipework underneath.

'Looks good. See, it was a simple enough fix.' He pats the side of the basin and a few drops of water fall into the bucket. We both watch it, Murad frozen in his crouched position while I stand just behind him, bent over. The few droplets become a steady drip and suddenly a spray of water shoots out from where Murad had been working, hitting him straight in the face and chest.

He lunges forward and presses his hand in front of the spray, but water being water, it finds a way out, steadily filling the bucket underneath and also covering the floor. An errant spray hits me and soaks the front of my T-shirt, the cold water making me gasp.

'Turn the stopcock. Switch the supply off. Quickly.'

I move towards the stopcock at Murad's prompting and grasp the handle. I pretend to try to turn the handle. I put my second hand on it and make a show of trying again, as though I'm giving it my all but the stopcock isn't moving.

'It won't turn.' I look in Murad's direction and find him completely soaked now, glaring at me as water drips off his face.

'What do you mean it won't turn? I just used it and it was fine.'

I pretend to try again, but keep my hands in place as water continues to spray at him.

'It won't move, Murad.' I put two hands on the handle.

'Oh, for God's sake.' Murad pulls his hands away from the leaking pipe and comes towards me, putting his hand on top of mine and pushing the handle firmly.

The water stops after a few seconds and there's silence in the bathroom.

I curl my lips in on themselves and refuse to look at him, though I can feel his eyes burning a hole on the side of my face. I sneak a peek and can see his expression is thunderous, before I look down at our hands. His is firmly on top of mine, the warmth of it making my hands tingle in a delicious way.

I hear a soft growl beside me and a giggle escapes me before I can stop it. I look the other way, trying to get a handle on my laughter, but the more I try to stop it, the harder it is until I stop trying. I look in Murad's direction and he's scowling at me, water dripping from his hair into his eyes. I can't help but laugh even more, tears of mirth rolling down my cheeks.

'You think it's funny, do you?' He takes his hand off mine and reaches for the handheld shower in the bathtub and aims it at me, turning the tap. A pathetic amount of water dribbles from the shower head and that makes me laugh even more.

'You are such a numpty. We just turned the water off!'

Murad looks at the shower head in horror before lowering it into the bathtub and making his way towards the bucket that's filled with water under the basin.

'Don't even think about it, Murad! If you do that, I swear I'll kill you.'

He grabs a small jug off the windowsill, tipping its contents of washing-up gloves and sponges into the basin before half filling it with water and then tossing it at me, making me gasp as cold water saturates my hair and T-shirt even more.

He laughs at me and I glare at him before making a lunge for the bucket and tugging it towards me. Water

118

sloshes over the side, some of it catching him and some of it catching me until it empties of water over us as we play tug of war with the bucket. Both of us end up collapsing on the floor with laughter in a wet heap.

The bathroom is a colossal mess and there's water everywhere, but I can't find it in myself to be serious about it. 'Bianca's going to be furious if she sees this.'

'We'll clean it up before that,' Murad says as we both lean against the side of the bathtub. 'Actually, you should do it, since it was you who pulled the prank.'

'It was too perfect a moment not to take advantage of.' I grin, feeling inordinately proud of myself and he looks at me in surprise, shaking his head, though I can see him biting the inside of his cheek.

'Devious. I suppose we should get cleaning.' He leans forward, surveying the carnage.

'Hmm. Murad?'

He looks at me over his shoulder. 'Yeah?'

'Thank you.' His eyebrows lower in confusion. 'For making me laugh.'

He smiles at that, his eyes pinned on me, making me feel like he's seeing a lot more than I realise. 'I think we both made each other laugh and we both needed that more than either of us appreciated. But you're welcome. Fiya.'

I look at him, intently, and a small smile teases the corners of his lips as he watches me. Something tells me that him calling me *Fiya* isn't as unintentional as I thought it was.

Perhaps we are getting somewhere.

16

To: Murad Aziz
From: Safiya Saeed
Subject: Progress

Hey Murad,
Hope you're enjoying your time back home while I slave
away at the villa. How do you sleep at night, knowing
I'm toiling away here while you're lapping up wet and
cold weather there? Anyway, I just wanted to let you
know that the roof is finished, as is the structural work.
You'll be pleased to know that I found some quality
plumbers and electricians and they're working as I'm
writing this. No busted pipes or unearthed wires.
Imagine that?!
Speak soon.
Saf

To: Safiya Saeed
From: Murad Aziz
Subject: Re: Progress

I am — Sumi and I baked cupcakes earlier and then we
played hide-and-seek for the hundredth time. I'm sleeping
pretty well actually, thanks for asking, and the weather's
been surprisingly mild here given the time of year.
Thanks for the update. Only time will tell what the

workmanship of these electricians and plumbers is like.

M

P.S. – I met Baz before coming to Birmingham. He didn't send his regards.

To: Murad Aziz
From: Safiya Saeed
Subject: Re: Progress

At least one of us is having fun! I've attached samples for paper and paints that I've shortlisted and hope to send to Antonella for sign-off. Make sure you actually check them this time. There might or might not be some pink in there ☺
By the way, when are you planning on coming back?
Saf
P.S. – When you see Baz next, tell him I send my best wishes.

To: Safiya Saeed
From: Murad Aziz
Subject: Re: Progress

I've attached my thoughts on the samples. Have you finalised any furniture? Make sure whatever you get is easy to move out in case we make a quick sale. Not sure yet, why? I didn't think I was needed for anything yet, unless that's changed?

M

To: Murad Aziz
From: Safiya Saeed
Subject: Re: Progress

No reason in particular – just wondering. Nothing's changed. I forgot that Antonella wanted to sell this place

121

– it's such a shame because it's gorgeous. I'd never sell such a place. The views are incredible and as we're working on it, its character is really beginning to come out. In fact, you'll be shocked when you come and see it. I went and saw parts of Perla Rosa with Bianca the other day when the builders left early. It's stunning. Have you seen much of it? The lake doesn't look big from far, but it's actually huge.
Saf

17

Murad

I look at the latest progress email that's come in from Safiya. She's taken to sending me an update almost every day, and as time has gone on, they've become more detailed – and not necessarily details about the work. She's started dropping in details about her day, what she does – by herself or with Bianca or Amadeo.

There's a huge difference between the Safiya from that first day in the conference room and the Safiya of now. Her confidence is coming back, along with her sass and playful nature. I'm happy seeing more of her old self come out, but the problem with that is that it was this old self of hers that I had fallen in love with. While I'm pleased for her, it doesn't bode well for me.

The whole point of me hightailing it out of Perla Rosa as I did was because I was beginning to have trouble with the lines we had drawn. It was nothing major, just the accumulation of the micro moments that were becoming harder to ignore. Like the light touches and brushes of contact. She would rest her hand on my forearm, making me tense on reflex before forcing myself to relax. Or she would start bickering and bantering with me playfully and I'd be thrown back in time to when we used to do that before. The rules we had established gradually slipped out of my mind until they were simply forgotten.

Then there was that day of the leaking pipe in the bathroom. Her playful jokes, messing around and then laughing the way she did. All of it had me feel things I have no business feeling – at least not for Safiya, not any more.

We had cleaned up the mess we had made and the ease with which we had worked together had set off alarm bells in my head. Within a couple of days, after seeing that work was well under control in Perla Rosa and I had no immediate responsibilities there, I decided to make my way back to London. I needed distance and time to get my head in the right place again; the close proximity to her was messing with my equilibrium.

I came back and checked in with all my ongoing projects, set up a few meetings and after a week in London, I headed to Birmingham to spend some time with the family. I'll need to get back to Perla Rosa soon, I've already been away for a week and I don't feel it fair to leave Safiya taking care of everything by herself, even though she's more than capable. And if a part of me is missing her and wants to be back where she is, then I ignore it – or at least, I try to.

'Here, you look like you could use this.' Zubair puts a mug of tea in front of me and takes the seat opposite at the dining table I'm using to catch up with my emails, a pack of biscuits tucked under his arm. I close my laptop and reach for the tea while he opens the biscuits.

'Thanks, mate. Where have you been?' I pull out a biscuit for myself – a crumbly, buttery treasure with sultanas.

'Husband and dad duties today. Meerab had a bridal make-up client, so I dropped her there. I then dropped Sumi with your parents at the soft play centre and then I took Irfan for a walk in the park. I've just put him down for his nap and I'm absolutely knackered. Talking of which . . .' He pulls out the small baby monitor device from his back pocket and places it on the table.

'I'm knackered just hearing all that.' I take a sip of the brew.

'I wouldn't change it for the world, though. As precious as my wife and daughter can be sometimes.' He grins boyishly.

'You're a good guy, Zubair. I'm happy for you and Meerab.'

'Me too.'

I shake my head at him.

'So,' he looks at his watch, 'I've got anything between thirty seconds to thirty minutes before someone needs my attention. Fill me in. What's been happening and what are you doing here instead of basking in the warmth of Perla Rosa?'

'I don't need to be in Italy for the entire duration of the project. I don't think Safiya does either, but she wants to stick around.'

Zubair leans forward, 'How are things with Safiya? Complicated or *complicated*?'

I can't help but chuckle at his question. 'That's one way of putting it.' Zubair knows everything about my history with Safiya. We became good friends soon after he started dating Meerab and when she mentioned my heartbreak in front of him once, I soon ended up telling him the whole story. Zubair didn't make any judgement or even curse Safiya to seventh heaven, unlike Meerab. 'We called a truce on any hard feelings and have forged a friendship.'

'Really? And how's that going?' His expression is one of keen interest as he grabs another biscuit.

'Tremendously awkward to begin with. Neither of us really knew how to navigate such terrain. The last time we had been friends like that was when we were children. But we warmed up over time and things got more comfortable.

125

Things are going well now, I'd say, much better than I anticipated when we first got the project.'

'Hmm.' Zubair eyes me over the rim of his mug. 'And what aren't you telling me?'

I swallow hard as I lift my own mug. 'What makes you think there's more?'

'Ha. Your niece carries some of your expressions. And you're looking remarkably alike right now. She also looks exactly like this when she's not giving me the full story.' He circles his finger around my face, but not close enough for me to swat his hand away like I want to.

'Get lost.'

He chuckles. 'I'm serious. I feel like there's more you're not telling me, but if you're not ready to, then that's fine. Tell me, how are you finding being friends with her? Are you OK with it?'

'I'm the one that suggested it. I mean, she had made overtures before, but I wasn't interested and then I realised the futility of what I was doing. The truth is, I'm best friends with her cousin, who we both happen to now work with. I'm bound to see her at some point or other, so what's the point in not maintaining a civil relationship with her?'

'Because you loved her once upon a time.'

My heart plummets at Zubair's softly voiced statement. There's no intonation or jokes or sarcasm from him, just a simple statement of fact.

It's also the reason I felt the need to get some space when I did, because I was afraid that those old feelings might not be as dead as I thought, and what if they come barrelling back in my life? What am I going to do? There's no hope for any of that between us now.

Is there?

No, there can't be. We're too far apart now to bridge

126

the gap between us and it's for the best. I just needed time and space to remind myself of that pertinent fact and once I've shored up my defences, I'll be ready to see her again.

At least, that's what I keep telling myself.

'Oh my God! You're back! You should have told me you were coming back today.' Safiya marches towards me, but as she gets close, she stops and then awkwardly sticks her hands into her pockets, clearly unsure about what to do with herself. To be fair, I feel the same way, unsure about whether to hug her, give her a high five or just verbally say hello.

I'm saved from doing anything when Bianca comes through the cottage door. 'Signor Murad. Welcome back. So good to see you again.'

'It's good to be back, Bianca.' I turn and face Safiya, unable to stop myself from smiling at her. 'Glad to see everything is still standing.'

Her smile is wide and bright, all those earlier hints of hesitancy from weeks ago gone, replaced with a sparkle reminiscent of the Safiya of old. 'Wait till you see the inside. It's nowhere near finished, but it looks so different with the layout change. Your mind will be . . . poof.' She mimes a mind-blowing action.

'I look forward to seeing it.'

'I'll let you get settled and everything. See you at dinner.'

'Yeah.'

She hunches her shoulders as she smiles and wrinkles her nose before walking off in the direction of the villa, her ponytail swinging with her gait. It's so much like how she used to be, I stand dumbstruck for a moment, wondering if I've stepped back in time.

Going back home was supposed to give me a better sense of perspective, but I seem to have come back to

Perla Rosa with a heightened awareness of Safiya and the way she is, which fills me with renewed concern.

I try to shake off the thought, making my way inside the cottage and heading upstairs, only to be surprised again as I stand in the doorway to the room I was using before I left. None of my things are where I left them. In their place are all of Safiya's things. I glance in the direction of the room she was using and see my things neatly arranged in there.

'I did that.' Her voices comes from behind me and I turn and stare at her in surprise. 'I remembered as I headed towards the villa that the room swap will probably confuse you, so I came to . . .' She waves her hand around, encompassing the two rooms. 'I know you're not fond of lace.' She grins cheekily. 'I was just being a nuisance on purpose that day by taking the other room.'

'I knew exactly what you were doing. You didn't have to swap the rooms back, though. I was fine with it once I got used to it.'

I wheel my suitcase into the room decorated in soft greens and blues and she follows me inside, pausing in the doorway. Her expression has morphed to uncertainty as she chews her bottom lip.

'I felt bad. I want . . . I don't want to be the cause of any kind of—'

'Fiya. It's fine. I'm happy either way.' I groan inwardly at the use of that name. I'm supposed to stop calling her that, but it's been slipping out since we called our truce. How am I supposed to maintain a healthy emotional distance from her if I slip into old habits as easily as breathing?

She sighs dramatically. 'Good. So,' she walks further into the room and leans against the desk heavily. 'How was your trip back home?'

She peppers me with questions as I unpack and then we make our way to the villa, to see the progress since I've been away.

She was right, the villa, while looking the same but cleaner from the outside, looks vastly different on the inside. Of course, it's still starkly bare, but the removal of some walls and the erection of glass partitions in their place has transformed the inside. The front foyer has opened up and looks even bigger. The staircase has been moved and rather than being on the side, it now has centre stage and looks magnificent branching off left and right at the top.

We're heading up the stairs, Safiya walking ahead of me, when I see her wobble slightly. 'Woah!' I immediately put my hands around her waist to steady her. The instant I feel the heat coming off her, I know something's not right. I take the two steps between us as she lifts a hand to her head. 'What happened? Are you OK?'

'Mmhmm. I just felt a bit unsteady, that's all. I'm fine.' She lowers her hand and smiles at me and I look at her intently. Her cheeks are flushed and beads of sweat dot her hairline.

I lift a hand and place the back of it against her forehead and cheek. 'Fiya, you're really hot.'

She grins at me and I groan at my choice of words. 'Glad you think so.'

'I mean you have an elevated temperature. You have a fever. Come on, we're going back to the cottage.'

'But I want to show you the rest.'

'It can all wait. The villa's not going anywhere and neither am I.'

'Promise?' she asks softly as I turn her on the steps carefully to go back down. I pause at her question. Her head is lolling forward a bit, and she's leaning against me, as though in an instant she's given up the fight against her body and is giving into how she's feeling. She's got a temperature, so she obviously isn't fully alert to what she's saying or how it's coming across, so I don't say anything.

I guide her down the rest of the steps and we slowly make our way back to the cottage, outside which Bianca is trying to shoo a cat away with a broom. She spots us approaching and her face is immediately filled with concern.

'She's got a fever, Bianca. I'm just going to get her settled upstairs,' I explain.

'I'm fine,' Safiya protests but is ignored.

'She's been working herself to the bone, Murad. I've been telling her to slow down, but she's like a bee.' Bianca hurries into the cottage ahead of us, making her way upstairs and turning down Safiya's bed.

'She's exaggerating,' Safiya's whispers to me but sags a bit more heavily against me.

Were there signs that she was unwell? Had I not paid close enough attention? Her cheeks had looked bright, but I had thought . . . I mentally shake those thoughts off. There's no point in second-guessing myself right now. The thing to focus on at this point in time is Safiya and making sure she's looked after.

I guide her into her room, where Bianca's now pulling out some clothes from the chest of drawers. 'I'll let you get comfortable and check in shortly, OK?'

Safiya nods and then squeezes her eyes shut and I look at Bianca in concern.

'I'll get her settled in. Why don't you go and get changed? You must be tired after the journey.'

I nod at Bianca as Safiya lowers herself onto the end of the bed, her colour high as she gives a little shiver. I'm loath to leave her, but I know she's in good hands, so I back out of the room, letting Bianca do what she promised and having a quick shower myself.

By the time I get back to Safiya, she's huddled under the duvet complaining about it being freezing, even though her face is flushed thanks to her fever. I head downstairs, where Bianca is stirring something on the cooker, the aroma of herbs and spices infusing the air. 'Bianca, do you have a big bowl I can borrow?'

'Is she feeling sick?'

'No, no. I'll fill it with water and use it to cool Safiya down a bit. My mum swears by it.'

'*Sì*.' She pulls out a bowl and grabs a couple of small towels. 'I'm making a wholesome chicken soup for her. This should make her feel better. Honestly, that girl has been working non-stop since you left. She took a break for one weekend when I forced her to, but even then, she didn't rest much.' Bianca shakes her head as though she's failed.

'Don't worry about it, Bianca. She's a law unto herself. I'm back now, so I'll make sure she takes it easy.'

'Hmm. I'll bring food up for both of you. You need to eat too.'

I leave Bianca bustling around in the kitchen and when I go into Safiya's room carrying the bowl of water, she seems to have fallen asleep. I gently lower the bowl onto the table and pull a chair up to her bedside, staring at her as guilt roils in my gut. A single thought keeps going round in my head. I never should have left her.

18

Safiya

My body feels like it's aflame and every single muscle seems to be in pain. I can barely lift my head off the pillow. A cool weight rests against my forehead and a moment later I feel the same cool sensation on one cheek and then the other and I groan at the slight relief.

'I know it's uncomfortably cold, but it's to cool you down.' The weight from my forehead is lifted and I shuffle in protest, but even the slightest bit of movement is difficult and I can barely move. 'I'm just refreshing the towel. Give me a second.' The cool weight is back on my forehead and I sigh in relief. 'There.' Murad's voice is soft and deep, his hand a welcome weight on my forehead on top of the cold wet towel. 'Do you think you can get up to have some soup?'

I try to shake my head, but it's a bad idea because it makes me moan in pain.

'All right, all right. No soup. Got it.' He chuckles softly and my lips go up involuntarily as I feel myself lulled back to sleep, comforted by the knowledge that he's there.

I turn over onto my back and feel a sense of stiffness in my muscles, but thankfully there's no pain. I blink my eyes open slowly and look around the bedroom. There's the slightest movement of the curtain in front of the patio door, which I can see is open a few centimetres. There's faint light in the room, suggesting it's either dawn or dusk. I'm not sure which because I have no idea how long I've been out of it.

A soft sigh comes from my side and I turn and find Murad sitting in a chair, his feet resting on the end of the bed as his head lolls to the side. He's fast asleep with a thin blanket covering him, his socks peeking out where the blanket's too short for him.

I look around for my phone to check the time. It's gone half past six in the morning. I try to get up as quietly as I can and use the bathroom, brushing my teeth and retying my hair so it looks less like I've stuck my finger in a socket.

When I look marginally more presentable, I come out of the bathroom, only to find Murad standing outside it, looking sleep-rumpled and seriously sexy, with his mussed hair and five o'clock shadow.

'Hey, how are you feeling?' Concern washes over his face.

'Much better, thanks. My head doesn't feel like it's going to explode and I think my stomach rumbled.'

He looks visibly relieved as he cracks a smile. 'I'm glad to hear it. Let's get you back into bed.'

I know he doesn't mean anything by that, but for some reason, my brain is short-circuiting this morning.

'I suppose it's inevitable that your tummy would rumble when you've not eaten for nearly two days. You had nothing yesterday, except a few spoons of soup and nothing the day before according to Bianca, except a quick break-fast before I arrived.' He guides me back to the bed and I settle under the duvet, relishing the warmth under it.

Murad opens the curtains covering the patio door and turns to face me. 'What would you like for breakfast?'

133

I look at him, overcome with emotion that, after everything that's happened between us, this man has spent the last day and a half taking care of me, giving no thought to his own comfort or tiredness.

'What is it? You OK?' A sense of worry immediately colours his expression.

I smile at him as I hold my hands out towards him. He closes the distance between us instantly, holding my hand, looking at me with a furrow between his eyebrows.

'You're the best,' I say softly and, gradually, his expression clears. I feel him begin to pull his hands away from mine, but I hold onto one of them. 'I really appreciate your help and you taking care of me the way you did. You didn't have to do any of that, but you did it anyway. You're a star.'

His smile is shy and his cheeks have colour in them as he avoids making eye contact with me. 'Yeah. Well, I think I'll shower and then put something together for breakfast. Shall I get you some juice in the meantime?'

I nod and loosen my grip on his hand. He slowly pulls it away before leaving the room and despite everything, a sense of deep contentment fills me in this moment. I'm feeling better, it's a bright sunny day outside and Murad is here and he looked after me.

An hour later, Murad comes upstairs bearing a tray with breakfast on it. I only manage to nibble on a cornetto and take a few sips of tea, while he demolishes his eggs, mushrooms, toast and my second cornetto, after which he heads downstairs and I make my way to the bathroom, hoping to feel more human after washing my hair and having a long hot shower.

When I come downstairs, Bianca's at the cooker.

'How are you feeling, *cara*?' She cups my cheek and gives

me a once-over, much like my grandmother would, and I feel a wave of longing for home wash over me.

'Much better. Thank you so much for taking care of me, Bianca.'

She waves her hand in the air. 'Oh, it was nothing. Murad did most of the nursing. He was very worried about you.'

The thought makes my heart skip a beat, but I do no more than smile at Bianca and then head outside, needing some fresh air, though I'm feeling pretty tired. I settle down on one of the wrought-iron chairs in the courtyard, noise from the villa and the work going on in there filtering through to me, and I let the rays of the sun warm me.

Even though I can't see him, just knowing that Murad is there makes me feel different, as though the energy around me is charged. The funny thing is, I was fine with him going back home. Of course, I missed him too, but that was only because we had started getting on really well before he left. It had felt like we had truly put the past behind us and were putting as much distance as possible between us now and the ugliness that happened seven years ago, which I'm still aware I've not told him about properly.

While Murad was gone, I kept myself busy with finalising all the details of the design for the villa and working with the construction team leader on getting the work well underway, dealing with challenges as they cropped up. I kept Murad in the loop via email, but I enjoyed the time by myself too. It was the first time, since coming back from Nairobi, that I was truly by myself.

When I first got back after my divorce, my family were constantly around me, fussing over me and wanting to make everything better and while I understood their reaction and need to help, it became almost suffocating after a while. I barely got the chance to just be by myself and think. Connecting with Vaz had been a godsend. We had been best friends since we were practically babies because our mothers and my Auntie Farida are friends. But when I went to Nairobi and got married, we lost contact – no thanks to Ejaz's toxicity, ruining my life in yet another area. Thankfully, once I came back, Vaz and I picked up where we left off and she gave me the chance to move in with her rather than having to stay at home.

But it's not until now, being out here, that I've had enough silence around me to hear my own thoughts. It gave me a chance to pause and see where I was, where I wanted to be and what I wanted to do and the answers weren't quite what I had thought they would be a few months ago.

I thought I didn't want to work in design anymore, but working on the period conversion flat and this villa has made me realise that this is exactly what I want to do. In fact, I want to up skill, see what I've missed and fill in the gaps in my knowledge. I want to pick up my bucket list and start adding new items on there and checking them off.

'Penny for your thoughts?'

I smile as Murad lowers himself onto the matching wrought iron chair with a sigh. 'You'll be pleased to know that work progressed just as well while you weren't here. Signs of a good plan, I believe.'

'I'm glad. So, what were you thinking so hard about?' he asks, his attention on me.

'Just that I'm enjoying my time here. It's given me a chance to connect with myself – something I've not done in a very long time – and, in a convoluted way, I've got you to thank for that.'

'Me? How did you figure that out? Antonella hired you because of you, not me.'

'Yes, but if you hadn't let me work on the period conversion – which you would have been well within your right to do – I wouldn't have got this chance. So thank you.'

He looks at me intently, not saying anything for a minute, his expression inscrutable. He stares off into the distance and then, seeming to come to a decision of some kind, he looks at me once more. 'I didn't want to. Have you work on the flat, that is. But I felt like I had no choice. It was either that, or tell Zaf the truth. I felt stuck between a rock and a hard place.'

His words cause a twinge behind my solar plexus. I appreciate his honesty and, to be fair, he's not wrong. I would have likely felt the same way. But that doesn't mean it doesn't hurt.

'But I'm glad things worked out the way they did. You did a magnificent job on that flat and it brought us better results than we were hoping for. And I know you're going to smash this project as well. I went through the villa yesterday with the construction leader while you were sleeping. Your vision is incredible.'

My chest swells with pride at his words. I can't even remember the last time someone spoke to me with such praise or confidence in my ability. The thought brings tears to my eyes and I can't stop them from coming.

'Hey. Fiya, what's wrong? What did I say?' He's out of his chair and crouched in front of me, his warm hands covering mine on my knees. 'I'm so sorry. I didn't mean to—'

I shake my head, sniffling. 'It's nothing you said. Well, it is.' His face drops and I rush to explain. 'You complimented me and my work. You lifted me up, despite everything that's happened and that . . . it means more to me than I can even say. No one's done that in a long time, Murad. All I got from Ejaz was criticism. All he ever did was knock my confidence instead of building it up, making me second-guess all my decisions until I felt like I was incapable of deciding anything worthwhile. Ow.'

He squeezes my hand so tight I yelp. He loosens his grip instantly, massaging my hand between his. 'Sorry. I didn't mean to.'

I smile at him as he slowly pulls his hands back. 'I'm glad you like how the villa's turning out. Fingers crossed the end result will be good.' I try to get back to what we had been talking about before I went off piste. 'What's going on in there anyway? I think I should go in and have a look.'

I stand up and Murad does too, the space between us less than an arm's length. I look up at him as he looks back at me, his eyes moving from my hairline down to my lips, making every part of my face tingle as though he's physically touched it.

A loud crash from the villa has both of us springing apart and looking towards the villa in horror.

19

Murad

'He said the cat ran at them as they were trying to fix the glass and it caused a big commotion.' Amadeo translates as an irate workman gesticulates towards the cat sitting impassively on an upper shelf.

I massage my temples. I'm not sure whether I'm pleased or vexed about this situation. Vexed for obvious reasons – a huge single pane of glass has been broken and it was made to order, which means going through the laborious process again. Pleased because the commotion put an end to a conversation which was making me feel emotions which I had thought long dead. I had felt a wave of rage come over me at Safiya's description of her ex-husband and I'm not really a quick-to-anger kind of guy.

I look at the angry workman and then at the cat, who Safiya is now making cooing noises at.

That mix of emotions washes over me once again: the anger at how Safiya was treated by her ex-husband, an instinct to hold her in my arms, a desire to tell her how brilliant she is and whatever it takes to see that sparkle in her eyes again. A need to kiss her – which I firmly stamp out of my mind and refuse to give any thought. All the feelings I had sensed before and had made me head for home in the hope that they would disappear – wishful thinking on my part, obviously.

What didn't help was the fact that as soon as I came back, she fell ill. Bianca's convinced she had worked herself too hard, and I can well believe that. She's on a mission of some sort, which only she knows about, but I've noticed that she has multiple things on her mind and to-do list, which she's always doing or thinking about.

Thank God I came back when I did. Seeing her unwell made my heart clench and I found myself unable to move away from her bedside, during the two nights she was ill, sitting in a chair next to the bed in case she needed me. Though it could be argued that it was me who needed to be near her, none of which bodes well for me. I try and shake off my thoughts and focus on the present situation.

'Where has it come from?' I ask Amadeo as I point at the completely unrepentant and purring feline, who licks its paw, having no clue at all – or care – at how it has put a huge dent in the renovation.

'It's a local nuisance. Nobody wants him – at least we think it's a him.' Amadeo shakes his head in disbelief.

'Well, can we arrange for the cat to be shifted so that work can resume and no more damage occurs? Maybe call a cat rescue centre or something?'

Amadeo nods. '*Sì*, I can do that.' He pulls his phone out and moves away as I make my way towards Safiya, who is still cooing at the cat.

'Careful, Fiya,' I warn. 'It might be feral.'

Safiya shrugs, with a soft smile. 'The poor thing seems to hate people. Won't come down from that shelf no matter what. I think we should leave him alone. He'll come down when he's ready. Won't you, cutie?'

I resist the urge to smile, then watch the workmen go about cleaning up the broken glass.

'I think we should go back to the cottage,' I nudge her with my shoulder. 'It's not like we can do anything. And you're still not fully recovered. You should rest.'

Safiya frowns. 'Oh, I'm so bored of being in bed and I don't feel like going back to the cottage. What do you say we play tourist for a bit? Get some lunch.'

'I don't think that's a good idea. You need to build up your energy.' While I'm genuinely concerned about her need to recover fully, I'm not sure doing what she's suggesting is a good idea even if she is feeling well.

'My energy's fine. I'm not suggesting we go hiking or mountain climbing. Let's go for a short walk around the lake. Have lunch. We can borrow Bianca's car rather than walk if it makes you feel better.' A familiar smile makes its way across her face, causing a crease around her eyes, and I'm thrown back in time again.

Lately I've been finding it harder to say no to her, willing to do whatever to make her smile. Purely for selfish reasons. For the warm feeling that settles in me when Safiya is happy. But this smile? It makes a sucker out of me each and every time.

'I don't think so, Fiya. You've only just got out of be—'

'Fine,' Safiya relents. 'But we have to go exploring tomorrow. Promise?' Her eyes crinkle in anticipation and before I can stop myself, I find myself responding.

'Promise.'

'Oh. My. God.' A gasp punctuates every word as Safiya glances at the sight in front of her.

I grin, briefly glancing at her t-shirt. *Though she be but little, she is fierce.* Truer words couldn't be said for her.

'Are we going on this?'

'Yeah.' I make my way to the scooter, taking one of the helmets and putting it on her head. My fingers brush

141

against her cheek, sparks buzzing at my fingertips, and I clear my throat.

Just an electric shock, I remind myself, *nothing more.*

I put on my helmet and make my way to get on the scooter.

'You can ride pillion,' Safiya says, as if it were obvious, but her voice wavers. She sounds a little breathless. I try not to read into it, instead reminding myself of our forgotten rules.

'What? No.' She might be stubborn, but two can play at this game. 'No way. *You* will ride pillion because I'm insured on this and you're not.'

'Hang on a second. How did you manage this?'

I grin at her as I get on the scooter. Annoyingly, her gorgeous green eyes are hidden by the sunglasses. 'I have contacts.'

'Oh,' she says, using the handlebar at the back to hold on to, which I'm thankful for. I obviously hadn't factored this part in when I arranged for the scooter. The only thing on my mind at the time was that she would love it and I wanted to give her that.

We arrive at Lago Rosa, Perla Rosa's famous lake, all too quickly and I secure the scooter. Safiya goes towards the edge of the wall below which the lake spreads out for hundreds of metres, surrounded by a wide gravel pathway. The water looks calm, glittering under the rays of sunshine and making the vista seem magical.

The elevated level we're on has independent shops selling Perla Rosa merchandise and trinkets, cafés and a small church, but if you follow the downhill path, it eventually joins the gravel pathway that traces the perimeter of the lake before giving way to short cliffs.

The shops and cafés are bustling with people – tourists and locals alike – and you can just about hear the lapping of the water over the laughter and shrieking of the children who are playing on the small green not too far from the lake.

Safiya is stood by the edge of the wall, her hands resting on it. There is awe in her eyes as she looks down at the lake and surrounding scenery, breaking it momentarily to look at me. 'It's so vast. It just takes your breath away,' she says, quietly. 'Do you ever feel that way? When you see something so beautiful, it's like you have to hold your breath just to enjoy it. To hold onto that one moment in time.'

'Yes.' I glance at her and hold my stare perhaps a second too long. Her cheeks redden and I look over at the lake. 'It is pretty big. But you can swim in some parts of it. I mean, if you want.'

She snorts. 'God, no. Things like this are better seen from a distance. I'd never swim in it. Who knows how deep it is and what might be lurking under that glittering surface. There could be a Lago Rosa Monster – a long-lost relative of the Loch Ness Monster.' She gives a theatrical shudder and I roll my eyes at her dramatics before turning and watching a few adventurous people take out small boats in a section of the lake cordoned off for that purpose. There's a sense of peace here and I can feel my shoulders relaxing as I stand and watch the water. A sense of peace which I've not felt in a very long time, maybe even as long as seven years while I kept myself busy chasing down one goal after another in my professional life. I glance Safiya's way. Perhaps that sense of peace has alluded me since Safiya and I broke up and I'm just fooling myself in trying to attribute it to other things.

We start walking along the coastal path, Safiya looking around with bright, wide eyes and a serene smile on her face. She looks content and that makes me feel content. We walk past a small hut where boats are available for hire and next to which are changing rooms for the swimmers.

Safiya picks up her pace as we go past, making me laugh. She turns back and grins at me as she walks backwards for a few steps. Some things never change.

Whenever we went out with each other, it was always Safiya who would do the monkeying around. She'd be very enthusiastic about going somewhere, but as soon as she got tired and hungry, she'd make sure I knew about it and she was very clear about her likes and dislikes. She was very much an all-or-nothing kind of girl.

It surprises me that I'm able to think back without rage burning a hole in my gut. That I can think about how things used to be with a smile. I don't want to feel that kind of intense anger anymore. It never did me any good – and, to be honest, every day, every second, that anger is fading.

Whatever the truth she holds close to her heart might be, I don't want to hate her anymore. I *can't*. I'm not a fool, I'm well aware that we can't go back to how things were before. We can't have what we had then, but maybe we can try something else: being friends. We're just two people who knew each other once – loved each other, hurt each other – but have moved past it. That's progress. It's certainly more than I imagined we might ever have that day in the conference room.

We make our way to the edge of the crystal-clear shimmering lake. I let out a sigh and take in the perfect harmony of nature: the ridges of lush cliff-like mountains, the white swirls of clouds and trees peeking out in the distance. I stop by the edge of the lake, watching as sunlight plays on its surface, while Safiya moves a bit further ahead to read an information board.

When she joins me moments later, her eyes are brimming with tears, a sombre expression on her face which instantly tugs at my heart. 'What is it?' I face her fully, my hand reaching for her shoulder. 'Are you all right?'

20

Safiya

Legend has it that the name of Perla Rosa came from the love story between a pirate and a princess who had met at this very lake. They fell in love and he gave her the pink pearl as a token of affection . . .

I glance at the board, feeling a heaviness behind my breast-bone that I can't shake. I can't ignore the similarities between the things that came between the pirate and princess and the obstacles Murad and I faced. Even if it is a folk tale, the issues are sadly just as real now as they might have been when this tale was written and that thought fills me with sadness.

Murad's hand tightens on my shoulder. 'Fiya?' He looks at me in concern, a furrow notched between his eyebrows, and a wave of affection for him goes through me.

I smile tremulously, shaking my head. 'It's nothing. The pirate story got me again.' I sniffle and shake my head once more, trying to shake this sombre pall off. I turn and spot a cute little gelateria just off the path facing the lake and my mind goes straight to my list in my little book of dreams.

A portly gentleman is standing outside it, wearing an apron over his clothes and a broad smile, which widens further when he sees me. I leave a bemused-looking Murad by the lake and make my way towards the kiosk. The vendor tells me about all the flavours he's got and after I've chosen two and paid for them, I turn to make my way back towards the edge of the lake, only to find Murad standing right behind me, a smile on his face.

'How did you know which flavour I'd want?' he asks, an eyebrow arched.

'I took a punt. But I've got a feeling you'll like this one.'

I hand one of the cones to him as we sit on one of the small tables set outside the gelateria. Mine's a swirling mix of chocolate and vanilla, but the one I've handed him is creamy in colour. He takes a cautious bite and I watch as his wary eyes brighten before he takes another mouthful, bigger this time. I can see he's trying to figure the flavour out because it's not obvious what it is.

'It's called *fior di latte.*' I smile at him, supremely pleased with my selection on his behalf. 'It's a plain milk and cream flavoured gelato. Perfect for your slightly senior tastebuds, but not quite vanilla.'

He grins back at me, taking my sass in his stride just like he used to. 'You were right, I do like it. And vanilla's a perfectly respectable flavour, I'll have you know.' I give him an arch look, glad that the sombre mood after reading that story is beginning to lift. 'Which flavour have you got?'

'Stracciatella. Vanilla with shards of chocolate in it. And I've never had a problem with vanilla. Sometimes it's the only flavour that hits the spot.' I take a mouthful of mine and the flavour is absolutely perfect, the blend of vanilla and chocolate in perfect harmony.

We sit at the little table, people watching and chatting about inconsequential things as we eat our gelato, before we make our way back to the scooter. Murad hands me one of the helmets and then puts his own on. 'Where to next? Home or a bit more exploring?'

★

The sun set some time ago and the sky is dark except for the moonlight. I lean forward against Murad, and think about how surreal being here feels. Sometimes it's as though I'm dreaming and, any minute now, I'll wake up and find Murad gone. At other times, it feels like the past seven years have just fallen away and we're back where we had been before everything had gone to hell in a handbasket. Sometimes I sense an undercurrent between us, like when I catch him looking at me intently, or when I can't stop watching him. Or when he brushes past me and all my nerve endings become hypersensitive. Waiting, hoping, *longing* for another accidental touch.

The scooter screeches to a stop, startling me. I had been so lost in my thoughts that I didn't even realise where we were. There's a woman standing a few metres in front of us. She's thin, with dark circles around her eyes and her greasy hair is in limp curls hanging around her shoulders. Her arms are outstretched on both sides, standing in the middle of the road, slowly staggering towards us, but she stops well out of reach.

Murad rests his foot on the road and I let go of the handlebar I had been holding behind me and grip his T-shirt at his waist, something about the scene making me feel uncomfortable and my hackles rise. The isolated street is too quiet.

'I don't like this, Murad. Let's go,' I say.

'I can't. She's in the middle of the road,' he says, concerned. We both keep our eyes on the woman in front of us.

Her beady eyes sweep the street and then land on Murad. 'Help me, please,' she says in English. My senses go on high alert. 'I need money for food. My baby needs milk.' I look around but don't see anything or anyone.

Murad takes one hand off the scooter's handlebar and reaches towards his back pocket, as though he's going for his wallet, and I grip his wrist. The woman's eyes dart from left to right and I see a shadow out of the corner of my eye. A second later, a man with a mean-looking knife is looming towards us.

'Murad!' I let go of his wrist and grab his shoulder as I point towards the man with my other hand. Murad tries to move the scooter off, but the woman is standing right in front of it now, blocking us as she nervously looks up and down the street.

'Give us the money and valuables and no one gets hurt.' The thug looks at me, his knife glinting in the dim light from the street lights. 'Jewellery, phones, money. All of it.'

He edges towards us and I feel Murad's arm come between me and the man, pulling me back and angling himself in front of me as best as he can while seated on the scooter. 'All right. All right. Stay back. You'll get everything. Just don't come close.' Murad's voice is clear, each word enunciated with precision but laced with anger.

He keeps his arm as a barrier in front of me and a wave of tenderness goes through me. The last thing I want is for this bozo to rob us blind – or, worse, for Murad to get hurt trying to take care of me. I look at the pair standing in front of us, pleased to be preying on unsuspecting people and robbing them of possessions they've worked damn hard to get. Well, not on my watch. Anger erupts in me at the injustice of the moment.

I swing my leg over the back of the scooter and hop off, distracting the man and taking his attention off Murad, who's paused with his hand on his wallet.

'Fiya!' Murad's warning tone through clenched teeth comes my way. He gets off the scooter and the woman edges back, looking nervous as the four of us face off, the running scooter providing background noise.

'Ah, ah, ah,' Bozo says, waving the knife in an arc. 'No messing around. Hand over the goods and you can go.'

'Come and get them,' I say loud and clear as I tilt my head and sidestep away from Murad to give myself a bit more room, not taking my eyes off the man with the knife.

'What the hell, Fiya? He's got a bloody knife,' Murad grits out, closing the distance between me and himself until we can touch hands.

'And he won't touch either of us with it. I won't let him. Trust me.' What Bozo doesn't know is that he's picked on the wrong person today. With the cocktail of emotions swirling inside me and the spike of adrenaline in my bloodstream, if anyone's going to leave here hurt, it'll be him and his sidekick. There's no way I'm letting him lay a finger, let alone a knife, on Murad or me.

'Little lady has a big attitude, huh?' Bozo smiles, showing off stained and crooked teeth. A quick glance at his companion reveals that she's backing away, half a step at a time. He takes a step towards me and shows me the edge of his knife as I get a strong whiff of alcohol off him.

'Stop right there. I'll give you what you want, just don't come any closer. This isn't a joke, Safiya,' Murad says, sternly.

I turn to face Murad, keeping a side eye on Bozo the whole time. 'We're not giving him anything.'

Murad looks at me, his expression angry and worried. 'He's got a knife!' he says again, as though I missed that fact the first time. 'And none of these possessions are worth more to me than you or your safety.'

149

That gets me right in the feels, but I firm myself against it, picking up on his former statement and more determined now to see this through my way. 'I saw the knife when he first pulled the bloody thing out, believe it or not. I'm not blind.' And Murad's safety is just as important to me.

'Hey!' Bozo shouts to get our attention.

'One second, sunshine,' I say dismissively, while keeping my attention mostly on him and some on Murad. The woman is looking between the three of us, her retreat paused for the meantime as she folds her arms at her waist and watches us warily.

'Are you kidding me? This really isn't the time for you to be contrary, Safiya.'

'I know what I'm doing, Murad. I'm not going to let you stand in front of me to possibly get hurt or give up even a penny for this joker.'

'Oi! I'm not a joker. See this?' Bozo calls out to me and shows me the knife again, having taken another step towards me.

'Safiya!' Murad says murderously, while I gauge the distance between me and Bozo. He takes half a step towards me and it's all I need. I move in, ducking beneath the knife he swings my way and coming up in front of his face. I jab hard with my left hand and follow straight through with a right hook, hearing a satisfying crunch as I connect with his nose, pain ricocheting all the way up both my arms with the contact.

Bozo shrieks, while his companion screams, and taking advantage of his distraction, I knock the knife from his limp hand, kicking it away and, in the next second, I lift my knee to connect with his crown jewels. He howls in pain as he keels over and I'm about to go in for another right hook when my arm is pulled back firmly.

'Enough!' Murad's voice booms around me with the force of a gunshot. 'Let's go.' He pulls me towards the scooter and in a handful of seconds, we're riding away.

The journey is conducted in absolute silence, but I can feel the heat and anger coming off Murad like a tangible force. We pull up outside the cottage and I can see from his expression when he takes his helmet off that he's livid. Well, so am I. Hopefully that thug and his accomplice will think twice before pulling another stunt like that.

Murad opens the front door to the cottage and steps back to let me go in first. He closes the door behind us and then locks it before going to the kitchen and opening the freezer. He pulls out ice cubes, dumps several into the middle of a tea towel and then stalks towards me. 'Hands.' His tone is unlike anything I've ever heard from him before, practically vibrating.

I extend my arms and, in complete contrast to his harsh expression, he gently places the makeshift ice pack against the knuckles of both hands, arching an eyebrow at me as I hiss through my teeth, pain asserting itself as the adrenaline begins to drop. I smile at him tentatively, but he doesn't look amused in the least.

'He asked for it, Murad. I would have given him a lot more of that – and his sidekick too – had you not pulled me back.'

'Shut up, Safiya.'

I huff moodily but go quiet, while he stands there broodily, his jaw clenched tight, as he gently moves the ice across both my hands, lifting it for a second before inspecting the epic bruising already coming up. I won't say as much to him, but it hurts like hell.

'Sit down.'

I do as he asks and he sits opposite me, not letting go of my hands as he holds the ice against them.

'I didn't want him to hurt you or rob you.' He doesn't say anything, but his jaw is doing overtime. 'I was suspicious straight away when she spoke to us in English. How did she know what language we spoke or where we were from?'

He ignores me and concentrates on what he's doing and, after a few minutes, he pulls the tea towel away and gets up to dump the ice. He then pulls out his phone, tapping the screen rapidly before pressing it to his ear.

After ten minutes of being ignored by him, I leave him to his phone calls as I go upstairs to shower and get changed, hoping that by the time I come down, he's calmed down enough to actually have a conversation with me. I get that he was worried about me, but people like that thug aren't trained fighters and I know how to defend myself. I learnt how to when I knew I could only rely on myself. My one small effort to claw back some sense of self when I felt I was losing sight of who I am.

I wince as water hits my knuckles, making quick work of showering and getting into some comfy jogging bottoms, my spiked adrenaline from earlier having completely crashed now. When I go back downstairs, it's to find Murad talking to Antonella's brother, Gianfranco, and a uniformed policeman. The policeman asks for my account of events, with Gianfranco translating for us both. After a few minutes, the policeman leaves the cottage.

Gianfranco comes towards me. 'You were very brave today, Safiya. The police will take care of everything now. I was just telling Murad that I should have warned you two about some of these opportunists who hang around and see that people have come from outside Perla Rosa and then they target them. I'm sorry.'

I smile at him reassuringly. 'You have nothing to apologise for. Hopefully we taught him a good lesson and he'll think twice before trying to rob someone else.' He grins at me, but Murad continues to stand there stone-faced, still not having calmed down enough to crack a small smile.

There's a series of knocks on the door and when Murad opens it, the same policeman is standing there. He speaks in Italian with Gianfranco on the doorstep for a few minutes and then with a single '*Arrivederci*' for everyone, he leaves once more and Murad closes the door.

Gianfranco fills us in. 'Well, the officer had some good news for us. The offender and his accomplice have both just been arrested not too far from where they tried to steal from you and it turns out that before you, they had already threatened someone else and actually stolen from them and those people had reported the crime too. The miscreants will be off the streets and not bothering anyone anymore.'

'That's a relief. Did you hear that, Murad? All's well that ends well, eh?!' I smile in a bid to appease him.

Murad gives me a blank stare and I gulp down any other smart comment I might be tempted to pass. He's supremely pissed off and had it not been for Gianfranco's presence, I'm sure he would have torn a strip off me by now. In fact, he still might.

Gianfranco doesn't hang around for long and as soon as Murad's closed and locked the door behind him, he double-checks everything in the cottage and then makes his way upstairs, not uttering a single word to me. I hear the bathroom door slam shut and then the sound of the shower goes on in the silence of the cottage.

I lower myself onto the sofa, a sense of misery coming over me in complete contrast to the day we'd had before being ambushed by muggers. The day had started off so beautifully and I feel like we had finally found an easy rhythm and a level of comfort with each other without layers of awkwardness, only for it to end disappointingly. Murad is upstairs, fuming and I'm sitting here, nursing bruised and stinging knuckles.

21

Murad

Rage courses through my bloodstream and neither the blast of hot water nor the cold have done anything to temper it. I keep seeing the glint of the blade as it waved over Safiya's head, missing it by no more than a couple of inches, and my life flashing before my eyes.

The whole scene couldn't have lasted more than a minute or two, but it felt like a lot longer than that as I watched Safiya duck under the swinging knife and punch the bastard square in the face and then again on the cheekbone, and while I might have instinctively winced when she kneed him in the nuts, it was no less than he deserved. The little bloodthirsty tornado wanted more, I could tell, but it was time to cut and run. I didn't want there to be any chance of Safiya getting hurt because the guy retaliated or his partner jumped into the foray – although it was unlikely given how she had backed away – or for another accomplice of theirs to step out of the shadows.

Even now I can feel tension thrumming through almost every muscle of my body, it just won't leave. I turn the taps off and, wrapping a towel around my waist, I make my way out of the bathroom. I pull on a pair of shorts and as I'm scrubbing the towel over my hair, I hear a soft tap on my bedroom door and then Safiya comes in holding two mugs in her hands, her expression sheepish but with a side of defiance.

Her eyes widen as they land on my bare chest and my subconscious delights in the slight pink that tinges her cheeks as she utters a soft 'Oh,' before turning her back to me. 'I can come back when you're . . . done.' She waves a free hand in the air. Had I been in a slightly better mood, I might have smiled right now, but I'm not. I'm still supremely angry.

I grab the T-shirt I had left on the bed and put it on, throwing my towel in its place. 'I'm done.'

She turns around carefully, as though disbelieving of my statement, and when she's satisfied that I'm fully dressed, she straightens and turns properly, extending one of the mugs she's holding towards me. I see her sore knuckles and my emotions spike even more.

'I come bearing a sugary hot drink.'

I stare at it, then at her before shaking my head and walking past her towards the door. I make my way downstairs and I can hear her following behind me.

'Oh, come on, Murad. I knew what I was doing. Stop being like this, please?'

Needing something to do, I fill a glass with water and stand with my back to her in front of the sink as I slowly drink it, hoping the cool liquid will cool my temper enough that I can have a conversation with her. Unlikely, but here's hoping.

I drain the glass and then, putting it beside the sink, I turn to face her, folding my arms across my chest. 'Answer me with either a yes or a no. Do you realise how dangerous that situation was?' I can't help but grit my teeth towards the end of my question.

She's put the mugs down on the coffee table and is standing beside the sofa, her sweatshirt sleeves pulled over her hands as she regards me. 'I knew what—'

'A yes or a no, Safiya,' I say in a raised voice and she rears back slightly but answers me with a single word.

'Yes.'

I shake my head, a part of me still unable to process the emotions that raced through me in that moment as I voice my concerns. 'You had no idea how skilled or unskilled that man was with a knife. Or the fact that the woman could have been armed. Or they might have had more accomplices hiding nearby who could have jumped out at us. Did you even consider such possibilities?'

'Yes. But I had greater confidence in *my* skills. I knew I'd be able to disarm him. I could smell the alcohol off him and I could have broken that woman in half in a matter of minutes. Besides, you were with me.'

Her belligerence has the effect of oil on the fire of my rage and it makes me see red. I close the distance between us in a few strides and hold her by the shoulders, pulling her towards myself, whether to make a point or to reassure myself that she is unharmed, I can't say for sure.

'You obstinate woman! What if he'd managed to use that knife? What if you'd been hurt?' The thought fills me with terror anew, my breathing going ragged.

'Murad?' She says it so softly, like the touch of a petal, completely in contrast to my harshness.

'What would I have done? Do you have any idea what I went through when I saw you take a step towards that man and he swung his knife at you? I felt fear in a way I never have before.' I squeeze my eyes shut as those images make a reappearance in my mind and bile rises up my throat. I can feel Safiya trembling under my hands as beads of sweat roll down my spine, my pulse thundering in my ears like the beat of the loudest drum in the world. I try to take a deep breath, but something is constricting me, so I can only take shallow breaths.

I feel the warmth of her palm as she places it on my chest, as light as a butterfly, and she says my name again, just as softly as before. 'Murad. I'm fine. I'm here, right in front of you. Look at me. Please?'

My hold on her shoulders slackens and she moves her second hand to the other side of my chest, gently moving her hands up to my shoulders and then back down as my arms fall to my sides.

'I'm absolutely fine. Standing here right in front of you. Unharmed,' she croons at me and I gradually feel the noise in my ears recede. I realise that it was me who was trembling, not her, because tremors are still going through my arms as I clench my fists tight, opening my eyes and looking down at her.

I see her gorgeous, dear face and when she gives me a crooked smile, I finally manage to fill my lungs all the way with some much-needed oxygen.

'Don't ever do that to me again,' I plead, my voice sounding as though sand is coating my throat and it breaks on the last word.

She wrinkles her nose, her hands still soothing me. 'Really? I mean you really should have seen the other guy—'

I don't let her finish her sentence, wrapping her tight in my arms on a squeak and crushing her against me. Her head is tucked under my chin and I rest my face against the top of it as I breathe her in, the scent of her shampoo, her shower gel, *her*. It infuses the air I breathe. I feel as though I've been broken and then put together again, my chest aching with the force of my emotions.

I hold her close, so close, and she lets me. Her body relaxes in my arms and then I feel her arms wriggle out from between us and snake around my waist, holding me just as tightly as I'm holding her. I don't know how

158

long we stand there for, but we both seem content to be doing just that. She snuggles into me as though I'm the comfiest duvet she's ever used and even hums in appreciation, and for the first time in seven long years I feel a sense of contentment. A sense of peace that has eluded me for that long.

Warmth builds up inside me. If I could, I would spend the rest of my days like this, a thought that should scare the hell out of me, but right now, my adrenaline levels are controlling my thoughts and feelings and they couldn't give a damn. There's still so much to unpick between us, but in this moment none of it matters. All that matters is that Safiya is safe and unharmed and content in my arms.

A succession of chimes pulls us out of our bubble and we both ease away from each other. Safiya looks up at me, tucking loose strands of hair behind her ear shyly as I stick my hands into the pockets of my shorts. Her cheeks are highlighted with colour and she's nibbling on her lower lip before she mumbles, 'I should see who that is.'

She goes across to the sofa and picks up her phone, while I make my way to the coffee table and pick up the forgotten mug of hot chocolate, taking a sip of the now lukewarm beverage.

I suddenly feel the need to sit down, so I lower myself onto the sofa, feeling a lot older than my thirty-four years. Safiya's standing, tapping away at her screen. I feel a shiver go through my body and pull the blanket off the back of the sofa and lay it over myself, really embodying the whole senior vibe as I sip my hot cocoa.

Safiya picks her mug up and wrinkles her nose, but then shrugs and sits on the opposite side of the sofa, tucking her feet under one end of the blanket. We're silent for a few minutes and I try to relax the muscles in my body, but there's still a great deal of tension in them and I can't seem to warm up.

'Is it me or is it cold?' I ask as I close my eyes and rest my head against the back of the sofa.

'It is a bit cool in here. Hang on.' Safiya gets up and goes upstairs and, moments later, I hear her come back down. I crack one eye open and see her standing there with one of my jumpers and her duvet. 'You're in shock, Murad. Put this on' – she lifts the hand holding my jumper – 'and then we'll snuggle under this.'

The idea of snuggling under the duvet with her infuses some warmth through my bloodstream, but there's an ocean of unresolved issues between us before we can get to that. *If* we can get to that. A part of me realises that it's a bad idea, but I can't bring myself to not indulge right now. I grab the jumper and put it on.

It might be an idea to go up to bed, but I don't quite feel ready to try to sleep yet. Maybe Safiya's right and I am in shock. I've never experienced anything like this before. Those images are still way too fresh in my mind. Safiya pulls the blanket off me and a shiver goes through me again, a bit more forceful this time. She lays the duvet over me and I get a wave of *her* wash over me before she puts the blanket on top of the duvet and then comes and sits next to me. She taps on her phone some more and then the room is filled with the soothing sound of steady rainfall.

Safiya snuggles against my side, linking her arm with mine, and then she rests her head against my shoulder. 'You need to warm up,' is all she says as we sit there in silence for a few minutes, the only sounds in the cottage coming from our breathing and the sound of rainfall from her phone.

Gradually, I feel warmth imbue my body. Safiya's like a mini radiator attached to my side, but the warmth she's emanating makes me feel comfortable. Safe. My heart rate regulates enough that I can't feel the thundering of my pulse any longer and thankfully the trembling has subsided too. I feel closer to my usual self.

For her part, Safiya seems content to stay exactly where she is, she's barely moved a muscle and I'd have thought she was fast asleep if she hadn't spoken. 'I went for boxing classes while I was living in Nairobi.'

I raise my eyebrows in surprise at both her comment and the fact that without me prompting her, she's offering me a small insight into her life after *us*.

'I guessed you might have had some training, I've never seen a hook like that in real life. You never expressed an interest in boxing or any kind of combat sport before?'

'Yeah. It wasn't out of interest as such,' she says softly.

A different kind of fear snakes through my body and I stiffen. 'Why did you feel the need to have boxing classes?'

She pulls in a deep breath and pulls her head away from my shoulder, allowing me to turn and face her. Her face is in profile, but I can see the set of her jaw and the seriousness of her expression. 'I wanted to . . . I needed to do something different and completely outside my comfort zone. I didn't know what at the time, but I felt like I was beginning to lose myself and I happened to see a poster for nearby classes. I gave one a go and then . . .' She shrugs.

'Have you ever needed to use your training before today?' I ask, praying that the assumption I'm making about her married life isn't true. I breathe a sigh of relief when she shakes her head.

It'll be a miracle if I can get through the next twenty-four hours without having a heart attack. My concern for this woman – despite spending the past seven years telling myself that I don't care a whit about her – is being tested left, right and centre today, making me think that I really need to have a sit-down and evaluate how I feel about her. Have my feelings over the past seven years been a big fat lie? Or were they honest, but commingled with other feelings?

'Nothing happened. Ejaz was . . . not a good man, but he never hit me,' she says as she pries my fist open with her delicate fingers. I don't even know when I had done that, but the tension in my arms tells me that I need to relax, though I have a feeling that hearing her speaking about her ex-husband and what he was like isn't going to help. 'I'll talk, Murad, but you have to promise me that you're not going to keep reacting like this. We're both here, in this moment, safe and sound. Just remember that, OK?'

I eye her sceptically, wondering what she's going to tell me and if I'll be able to temper my reaction. I nod once, hoping I can, and she smiles before linking her fingers through mine where they rest on top of the duvet and blanket covering us and I swallow hard as I try to relax my muscles once more. Her touch is having an extraordinary effect on me. It feels like dormant parts of my body are waking up to a unique call only Safiya can make.

'Ejaz is a narcissist. If things aren't about him, then they're not important. Over time, he chipped away at my confidence, manipulated situations to make me feel like mistakes were mine and my judgements and decisions – the few I made – were always wrong, until I honestly started believing that. I didn't work while we were married and whenever I raised the topic with him, he'd convince me it was a bad idea. He got into my head and I began losing sight of myself, of who I was and what I could do. It was a moment out of the ordinary in which I decided to do boxing classes. Had it been an advert for learning flamenco, I might have gone for that too – it just happened to be boxing and something I managed to persist with.'

'I hate the fact that you had to make a decision like that in the first place.' I had no idea about the kind of man Ejaz was. I had always assumed the guy was the next best thing since sliced bread because Safiya had dumped me and married him. On the off chance I spared him any thought in those early days, I assumed he was perfect in every way. Mostly, I avoided any mention of Safiya and anything to do with her. Hearing what he was like with her fills me with anger, needless to say, but it also fills me with an acute sense of sadness.

'Hey, it's a good thing to know. It'll never put you at a disadvantage to know how to defend yourself. Came in handy today, didn't it?'

'Don't remind me. And can I just say, for the record, that with less skill than you demonstrated, I could have thrown a few punches myself but I was keen to extricate us from there more than I wanted to rearrange that lowlife's face.'

She grins at me, and as I usually do with her, I shake my head. Strangely, I can't help but smile at her, but at the same time, there are so many questions in my mind about her marriage and her choice to stay with a guy so obviously dreadful.

'If he was that toxic, why did you stick it out with him for six years?' I can't help but ask.

Her expression closes up, but I don't regret asking. It's about time we addressed the herd of elephants in the room. 'Does it matter? I'm not with him anymore. I'm trying to get my life on track, so . . .' She shrugs her shoulders, as she stops the sound of rainfall on her phone, but I'm not convinced. Silence falls over the cottage.

'It does matter. To me. Talk to me, Fiya. What happened?' Safiya's the one to tense up now, her shoulders hiking up to her ears. I'm not sure if, given what I've heard thus far, I'm ready to hear what she has to say but then I don't know if I'll ever be. What I do know, is that for us to move forward, however we choose, I need certain blanks filled and something tells me that Safiya needs to get out everything that's pent-up inside her to truly heal.

22

Safiya

My heart plummets all the way to my toes and I feel like diving under the duvet Murad tossed off at some point and hiding for the rest of the night. But knowing Murad like I do, he'll probably be sitting there waiting when I peek out from under it tomorrow morning.

Today has been an absolute rollercoaster and it's beginning to catch up with me. But I wouldn't change today for the world and if the confrontation with the thugs has to stay for the rest of it to remain unchanged, then so be it, because going around parts of Perla Rosa and exploring it with Murad made me feel alive in a way I haven't in years. Sharing moments with him, the gelatos, having conversations about nothing, having conversations about something, silences. All of it.

The altercation with the muggers ruined the harmonious mood between us. Though, if I'm honest, I can't be entirely unhappy about it because while I hate that it happened, it led to a very beautiful moment between me and Murad. He'd taken me in his arms and the sense of peace and belonging – of being *home* – had filled my entire being as he held me close. I'd be willing to face down a hundred muggers to have Murad hold me like that again.

And then we had to ruin it by talking about Ejaz Baig of all people. But maybe it's time to stop delaying the inevitable and just tell Murad the truth about everything. I have no idea how he'll react and given the shock he went into after this evening's drama, I'm unsure about what to expect, but I can't let that stop me. He deserves to know the truth.

I turn my face towards him. 'If we're going there, then I want to get some tea first.' Ten o'clock in the evening isn't the best time for me to caffeinate myself and I'm totally stalling, but he lets me.

I make my way to the kitchen and make two cups of tea, trying to breathe through the slight sense of panic I'm feeling at the prospect of telling Murad everything. I grab a box of biscotti and then go back to where Murad is sitting, tucking my legs under the duvet on one side of the sofa as I face him. He sits looking at me, his arm resting along the back of the sofa while his other hand holds his tea.

I huff out a nervous laugh, probably sounding a bit hysterical while he looks back at me calmly. 'I don't even know where to begin.'

He gives me the gentlest smile, a bit crooked, and takes a sip of his drink before speaking. 'How about I ask you a question and you answer it? Maybe you can carry on from there or I can follow it up with another question. How does that sound?'

I nod my head at his suggestion and nibble on a biscotti. 'Why did you stick it out with Ejaz?'

There's no easing into it with that question. He's gone straight for ripping the plaster right off and this is it. My chance to tell Murad the truth and then wait and see how the chips fall. I lift my shoulder and let it drop. 'Because I felt guilty. I had broken your heart, hurt you in the worst way possible. I didn't deserve to be happy and being with Ejaz for six years made me very unhappy, so I thought it was well deserved.'

Murad's jaw, which had relaxed earlier, has tension marring it once more, his expression grave. He shakes his head, his expression incredulous. 'You can't be serious?! God, Fiya,' he mutters under his breath. He takes a mouthful of tea and looks at me intently as I carry on nibbling on my biscotti. 'Why did you break my heart?' he asks softly after a lengthy pause.

'You're going straight for the jugular with your choice of questions.' I laugh, but he doesn't. His expression, if possible, is even more serious than it was earlier.

'The fact that you felt you deserved to be punished for doing it makes me think that there's more of a reason behind your choice than simply that you didn't want to be with me anymore. Otherwise, you would have thought nothing wrong with your choice and not believed you deserved to serve a sentence with Ejaz.'

'So perceptive.' I take a deep breath and go for it. 'My grandfather found out about us. You remember what he was like, don't you? So-called patriarch, leader of the family. A my-way-or-the-highway kind of power-hungry guy.' I curl my fingers into a fist, my fingernails biting into the palm of my hand before I force myself to relax them.

Murad lowers his eyebrows. 'I do remember, but maybe not the same way you do. He always seemed like a nice guy to me, if a bit stern. He was certainly stuck in his ways and they didn't always translate to the present, but overall, he was—'

'Someone who single-handedly destroyed what I held very dear to me.' Murad's perception of him doesn't come as a surprise. My grandfather had cultivated his image outside the family to be exactly that, while he easily went about manipulating people and situations around him to suit his agenda. 'He suspected there was more to our friendship

167

than we let on and one day he asked me about it, coming across as though he wanted a granddaddy/granddaughter moment of sharing a secret. Deep down, I had always wanted his approval and when he showed me attention and took an interest in my relationship with you, I fell for it hook, line and sinker, the fool I am. He wasn't interested in the way I thought he was.' I shake my head as I remember my gross naivety, shadows of that old sense of helplessness nipping at my heels.

'I never got the feeling that he loved me as such, but I didn't realise he disapproved so strongly. I suppose he tolerated me for his favourite grandson's sake,' Murad says with no small amount of surprise in his tone. Being Zafar's best friend gave him more freedom to hang around us than we ever realised.

'Who needs his approval anyway?!' Anger is creeping into my tone and I make an effort to calm down before I carry on. What I'm telling him has already happened and getting angry right now won't serve any purpose; I need to remember that.

'So, what did he say?' Try as much as he will to sound mildly interested, I can tell Murad's emotions run a lot deeper. There's colour on his cheekbones and his hand, which is resting along the back of the sofa, is fisted again, a sure sign of the tension coursing through his body.

'He told me about his contacts and the things he could do. How he could put a word in the right ear and make or break a person. He even showed me how he had done that with someone who had tried to take him on professionally, though I can't remember the details. Once he'd flexed his muscles, so to speak, he told me that if I didn't end things with you, he'd destroy you. He didn't want us together.' I can't keep the bitter note out of my voice, as a cocktail of frustration, resentment and disgust courses through me.

Murad's face clears of all expression and I know I've shocked him. It's nothing compared to the shock I had felt when my grandfather had actually said those words to me. 'He said that to you?' he asks in disbelief.

'Yup.' I tip my mug against my lips, swallowing the bitter dregs of tea.

'So, you broke up with me. Why didn't you say anything?' The hurt in Murad's voice scores a fresh gash on my heart, but I knew this would happen. I knew if I eventually told him the truth, it would hurt me that much more than it did when I actually had to live through every single moment of this nightmare, because I would see every emotion I had felt then etched on his face.

I shake my head. 'No. That's not when I broke up with you. I told my grandfather that I wouldn't break up with you. I didn't need his approval or his blessing; if he didn't approve, then so be it. I would forge my own life with you. He didn't say anything at first and I didn't say anything to anyone because . . . I suppose I wanted to pretend it hadn't happened. I don't know. To be honest, I don't know who would have sided with us against him. But then you went for an interview soon after graduating and you didn't get the job, remember?'

His eyebrows lower in confusion. 'I interviewed for many jobs I didn't get, Fiya. One man can't have that kind of influence. It's different if he had been the king or something, but—'

'It was him, he told me himself. He then started telling me facts about you and your family which he could only have found out through digging for them. He told me that he could let the right people know that you weren't to be

169

touched professionally and word would eventually spread. It would destroy your career and your life before it had even begun. I knew how much succeeding meant to you. The struggles your parents had gone through for yours and Meerab's sake. I knew how much you wanted to make a success of yourself, for their sake as much as your own.'

I feel the same sense of helplessness and suffocation I did seven years ago when my grandfather had explained this grotesque scheme of his. I get up and make my way towards the window overlooking the front courtyard and open it a bit to let some fresh but warm air in.

'Jesus Christ,' Murad huffs, sitting on the edge of the sofa with his arms resting on his legs, his head hanging. 'I had no clue.' He gets up abruptly and paces the length of the room, his restlessness mirroring mine.

But there's still more he needs to know.

'I asked him why he was doing this and he told me that you weren't good enough to marry the granddaughter of Zafar Saeed I. He had a very high opinion of himself, you see. Do you want to hear the funny part?'

'None of this is funny, Fiya.'

I ignore what he's said, finding a cruel irony in the situation my grandfather had created. 'He never approved of me and Qais because he didn't approve of our mother. My father married a woman of his own choosing and my grandfather never forgave him for that and punished me and Qais for that transgression by always treating us like outsiders. You'd think that would give me the freedom to do whatever the hell I wanted with my life, but no, sir. That wasn't the case. He said he should have known that any child of my parents would show such a rebellious streak and he needed to break that trend before it caused his family and his reputation any more damage.

'He negotiated a match between me and Ejaz, with his father, and told me that if I went ahead with it, he'd leave you alone. If I married you against his will, he would destroy you and your family.' I take a deep breath and turn to face Murad, who's now leaning against the wall, his expression bleak, but his eyes burning with fury. 'I loved you too much to watch him destroy you. I would never have been able to live with myself knowing I was the cause of any hardship you or your family faced. I also thought if I did what he said, there might be something close to redemption in there for my parents or Qais.' I feel my limbs deplete of every last iota of energy and stagger towards the sofa, slumping down on top of the duvet as I stare ahead blankly.

I'm familiar with the rage Murad is feeling, I've been living with it for seven years. I had thought it might subside over the course of time, but I don't think it ever has. It just hits me in peaks and troughs. I can go weeks, in fact, months, and not think about it, but then, out of nowhere, it'll hit me and I'll feel intense anger consume me at the unfairness of it all. At my grandfather's manipulation and handling of everything, his abuse of power and control.

'Was there?' he asks and I look at Murad blankly. 'Redemption for your parents and Qais?'

'Ha! There was never going to be anything of the sort. I was just a naïve fool for thinking there might be.' I lean back on the sofa and close my eyes, a dull pain pulsing through my temples. 'And, after all that, the man he thought was good enough to marry his granddaughter turned out to be as toxic as he was.'

23

Murad

If what I felt earlier was rage, then what I'm feeling now can only be described as incandescent fury. An anger so all consuming, it's only by sheer force of will that I'm not smashing the cottage up around me. The urge to destroy anything and everything in my path right now is so strong, it's making my skin feel tight and my blood like lava.

Safiya's sitting there, the epitome of both fatigue and defeat, and I feel like roaring in anger and frustration. In helplessness. In sadness and desolation. The tumult of emotions running inside me is so immense that there's no way I can get control of it or even begin to articulate any of it.

'My grandfather thought that a man like Ejaz Baig was a suitable match for me rather than a man of my own choosing who happened to have a humbler background.' Safiya sits up and looks my way, her expression sombre. 'And all for what? His own pride? Ego? To punish my father for exercising his right to choose?'

'I could say something inane, like I wish you had told me, but we both know it's a pointless thing to say.' I can't imagine being in the predicament Safiya was in and having to make such a choice. To be used as a pawn like that by her own grandfather . . . I can't even begin to comprehend it.

'Hindsight is a cruel thing, Murad. It makes everyone second-guess their decisions and choices and it always makes the option one didn't choose look more favourable. Seven years is a long time to sit and reflect on one's choices and, trust me, I've done plenty of that. I've gone through all the various scenarios in my head. If I had chosen *this*, then *that* might have happened. If I had chosen *that*, then such and such might have happened. You get the picture.' She waves her hand in the air and then lets it flop down in her lap.

She's right. There are plenty of things I've done in life which now, in hindsight, I'd do differently. If only it were that simple.

I heave a tired sigh and join her on the sofa, pushing the duvet back. I don't think either of us is inclined to sleep, even though it's ridiculously late. God knows whether I'll actually get any sleep tonight, my mind is like a hive of activity, hardly conducive to a good night's sleep.

'So, what made you leave Ejaz when you did?' I wonder out loud.

She turns to face me, her head still resting against the back of the sofa. 'I reconnected with Zafar and Daadi when they came to Mombasa last year.'

'Oh.' I remember Zafar going for a wedding on Reshma's side of the family out there. He mentioned reconnecting with Safiya, but I deliberately kept myself out of the loop because at the time, I hadn't wanted to know anything about her. What difference would it have made knowing though? Of course I feel nothing but sympathy for Safiya having endured what she did and I feel worse still because she largely did it for my sake. But it's like she said, hindsight is a cruel thing.

'Mmhmm. I hadn't spoken to anyone after leaving, but when Zafar and Reshma came to Mombasa with Daadi, and I happened to be at the same wedding, Zafar and

I had a good catch-up. We kept in touch when they went home. Connecting with my family again gave me a renewed perspective and made me stop and take stock. It made me see where I was and where I was going and none of it filled me with hope. I realised I had punished myself enough and decided to call it a day with Ejaz. Of course, it wasn't as easy as that, but I was determined to get away from him, even if I was coming back to nothing.' A sense of sadness imbues her voice and I feel a prickling sensation in the corners of my eyes.

We're silent for a few minutes as I toy with the edge of a cushion. 'Did you ever speak to anyone about us?'

She shakes her head.

'Not even Vaz?'

'No. I didn't want there to be any issues for anyone about keeping a secret or watching every word or action with the fear of being found out. I thought it best to keep it to myself. Did you?'

I nod. 'I spoke to Meerab and then her husband, Zubair, but they've never said a word to anyone else about it.' A corner of her mouth turns up, but she doesn't say anything. 'I'm glad you ended your self-imposed punishment, Safiya. Not that you ever needed to punish yourself.'

I've spent seven years believing that Safiya broke up with me because she thought I wasn't good enough for her. She did a damn good job of convincing me that she believed that and with her going ahead and marrying another man who, as far as I knew, she hardly knew because he lived in a different country but was everything I wasn't, I truly did believe I wasn't good enough for her.

And to now discover what I have . . . it'll certainly take some time to come to terms with it all. Especially the fact that the whole thing had been orchestrated by her grandfather, a man I had respected and admired till now. I hadn't even realised he was capable of such ruthlessness, and that too with his own flesh and blood. It beggared belief.

Safiya doesn't say anything in response and, after a few minutes, she gets up and tugs her duvet off the sofa. 'That was it. The big reveal.' She grins at me, but there's none of her cheekiness behind it.

'Don't downplay it, Fiya. No one should have to go through what you did,' I say. 'You know that, right?'

Her eyes are filled with sadness when she responds. 'Yeah. I'm going to head upstairs. Goodnight, Murad.' She turns to leave, but pauses for a few moments, before she turns back. She comes towards the sofa and I sit up a bit straighter, our eyes locked on each other. She keeps her duvet held close to herself as she slowly closes the distance between us and lowers herself until she's barely a handful of centimetres away from me, her scent filling my senses. She turns her head and slowly, softly presses her lips against my cheek, holding it there for a few seconds, hardly enough time for me to take in what she's doing before she pulls back. 'Sweet dreams.' And then she's gone.

After everything she's just shared with me, and given the day we've had, the end seems somewhat anticlimactic, but what more is there to say or do?

I stay downstairs, my mind and body buzzing with thoughts and feelings as I try to will it into stillness, hoping for the oblivion of sleep. I doze off here and there but not enough to feel well rested. At some point, I hear Safiya go into the bathroom upstairs and turn the shower on and I realise that it's morning, time to get up.

I ease off the sofa and groan as my back, neck and shoulders all make their presence felt as one in protest. 'You're getting old, Aziz.'

I make my way upstairs and once the bathroom is free, I use it, the hot water helping ease some of the tension in my upper body. The tension in my mind, sadly, is here to stay. Learning that Safiya didn't want to end things between us and she had only done so to protect me and ended up spending the next six years in a miserable and toxic marriage makes my heart bleed. The thought just won't leave me.

I go downstairs to find Safiya in conversation with Amadeo as she munches on a cornetto at the kitchen table. Unlike all the other mornings we've been here, I pause when I catch sight of her, marvelling at how much she's endured by herself all these years. And while the anger from last night hasn't quite subsided, not a single part of it is directed at her. Not anymore. For her, I now feel a desire to make things right. To ensure that she finds the sense of joy and happiness which her grandfather and then her now ex-husband took away from her and that she herself has kept away from for seven years.

I don't know whether we can ever go back to having what we had before her grandfather decided to blackmail her, using me as leverage. God, the thought of it has acid churning in my gut. I had no idea he was so calculating. And to think that he used to see me after that and was just as cordial as he'd always been, asking after my parents and wishing me well. Except, towards the end. There was a difference towards the end. I'd catch him every now and then, watching me closely, as though seeing something he hadn't before, or like he wanted to say something but decided not to at the last minute. Was it anything to do with Safiya? I'll never know, will I? And what difference would it make? It's too late to make amends.

'*Buongiorno*, signor,' Amadeo says cheerily.

176

Safiya looks my way and smiles and I respond with one of my own, making my way down towards her.

'*Buongiorno*, Amadeo. Good to see you.'

The sound of a horn comes from the front courtyard and Amadeo leaves to see to it.

'Morning.' I turn to face Safiya. She's in a faded pair of jeans and worker boots and a plain red T-shirt, bringing out her sun-kissed complexion and the green of her eyes. She appears no different to how she usually does, but I feel a difference in her. There's a lightness about her, a sense of freedom in the smile she sends my way.

'Morning. Did you sleep well?'

I shake my head and she gives me a sympathetic look.

'I know just the thing.' She turns and starts on the coffee and I make my way to the table, finding scrambled eggs on two plates with toast and some wilted spinach. 'I was hoping to prepare the breakfast of champions, but a combination of me oversleeping and Amadeo turning up early put paid to that, so we'll have to make do with half a breakfast of champions. Though I think we might have an avocado left which we can share. Bianca's gone to some farmer's market this morning.'

'We don't have to share it. Feel free to have the whole thing,' I say as I load a piece of toast with some eggs and start making a dent in it. I'm hungrier than I real-ised. 'Avocados have got to be one of the most overrated foods in the world. They've hardly got any flavour, are temperamental with their ripeness and are almost always overpriced,' I say with great satisfaction.

'Wow. I had no idea you were such a hater.'

'I'm not a hater. I just find them overrated. Now give me a solid grapefruit and we're talking.' Just as I'd hoped, she bursts out laughing and I even get a swat on my arm.

'Get out of here, you.'

I grin as she joins me at the table with two coffees and we make quick work of our breakfast, ready to join the small army of workers gathering in the front courtyard to begin the day.

There's definitely something different in our vibe this morning. It seems like we're both on the same page in terms of not raising any of last night's conversation, though we're not pretending it didn't happen either. I'm sure we'll revisit it at some point, but I'm quite content to let it be for now and maintain the status quo on our friendship.

We both need to concentrate on the job we're here for.

The next several weeks pass in a blur of furious activity and spring is practically upon us. Work on the villa is coming along nicely, but with Easter approaching, we decided to take a short break to coincide with the holidays. Safiya made her way back to London and I made my way to Birmingham to spend the holidays with my folks.

'God, what have you been feeding him? He's doubled in size.' I look at my sister in faux horror and she gives me an amused look in return before handing me her son. He's like a miniature version of my sister.

'You did last see him when he was barely a few months old,' Meerab says as she sits back on the sofa, looking as tired as you'd expect a mother of two young children to look.

'Still. He's like dough, leave him for a few months and he doubles in size.' My baby nephew gives me a frown and after a little drum roll from his backside, he grins at me. 'Attaboy!'

'Uh, men!' Meerab gripes, but I know she dotes on all the men in her life. 'So, how's the Italian adventure coming along?'

'It's coming along pretty nicely, actually. When we go back, it should be the home straight and very much full-on, but it's nice to see it all come together. To be fair, my work doesn't end there. I need to arrange its sale.' The end of the project will also mark the end of being teammates with Safiya and that makes my heart sink, but I push that thought to the back of my mind, refusing to consider it just yet. The last several weeks have been easy and comfortable between us, completely unlike before when I could barely stand the sight of her and that's something I want to hold onto for just a bit longer.

I lift Irfan against my shoulder as he gnaws on his fist, my big hand pressed against his tiny back. He's still got that baby smell and I feel a wave of longing go through me. I've always wanted children, especially after the birth of my niece and nephew, but after the fallout with Safiya, I never thought it would happen for me. I tried to content myself with being a part of my sister's children's lives, but today, seeing little Irfan kicking his legs and cooing seems to have brought those thoughts to the forefront of my mind once more. How different might things have been if . . .

There I go again! That's been happening a lot lately, me thinking of *what ifs*. What if Safiya's grandfather hadn't interfered in our relationship? What if I hadn't taken what Safiya said at face value? What if . . . the possibilities are countless.

'What about working with Safiya?' Meerab asks oh-so-casually. Being the warrior older sister she is, she's hated Safiya since our break-up, and while I felt the same before, now I know better. And I think it's time to share that information with Meerab, though I have no idea how she'll react.

'Maybe you can put the kettle on and I can tell you about working with Safiya. But first, please change this stinker's nappy. That trumpet from his backside heralded something.'

179

24

To: Murad Aziz
From: Safiya Saeed
Subject: Progress update

Murad
How are you? Hope you're having the best time with everyone. I spent the first few days back shivering but since then I think I've consumed my body weight in Easter chocolate. Vaz said that anything from the Easter bunny is to be considered a gift and consumed without any guilt so I'm sticking to that positive attitude and will try to remember it when I finish the last of my Easter eggs later. How much chocolate have you had?
Saf

To: Murad Aziz
From: Safiya Saeed
Subject: Re: Progress update

Sorry. I pressed send without saying what I had actually intended to say . . . lol! Did you see the photographs of the finished flooring throughout the villa? Thoughts? I'm glad we went with the lighter finish on the wood in the reception rooms – it brightens them and to be fair it will darken over time anyway. I think the floor tiles in the kitchen look amazing – great choice Mr Aziz! I have to

*say, I am concerned about not being there whilst the
staircase is being reworked.*
Saf

To: Safiya Saeed
From: Murad Aziz
Subject: Re: Progress update

*I'm pleased for you. That kind of positive thinking is
what we need more of in the world. I regret to inform you
that I only had a single Crème Egg. Sadly, Sumi the
chocolate monster got to my Easter egg before I did. She
got chocolate everywhere – even on Irfan – and her mother
was not best pleased. I, however, thought she looked really
cute (photo attached). Maybe she has the same thoughts as
Vaz when it comes to chocolate from the Easter bunny!
I did and I agree. Didn't you say you wanted to get
some rugs? Did you hear back from the stone mason?
Relax, it'll be fine. Didn't you go through the plan about
ten thousand times with the entire construction team?*
M

To: Murad Aziz
From: Safiya Saeed
Subject: Re: Progress update

*That is such a cute picture! She's gorgeous. And those
cheeks . . .* 🐼
Very funny 😔 *there's no harm in making sure we're all
singing off the same hymn sheet! Yes – all set to go with the
stone mason. I might even be back in Perla Rosa by then.
Any plans for later? I'll be going to see my folks and
catch-up with them. I'm sure my mum has plans to stuff
me with as much food as is physically possible!*
Saf

Sumi's taking me to the cinema and then shopping apparently and then if she's feeling generous, she might feed me. Of course, when I say she's taking me, I mean I'm taking her in my car and I'll be paying for everything but I get no say in what we do or how we do it. She calls all the shots. And Irfan is strictly not invited – girls only she said. I don't think she gets it but I'm not going to be the one explaining that to her. Zubair can. Tell your parents I said hi.

M

25

Safiya

'I'm so pleased you came home for a break, sweetheart. I want to hear all about your project in Perla Rosa,' Mum says as we settle on the sofa.

I'm in London for a few more days before I return to Italy and it's been great to be back. I had a catch-up with Vaz a few days ago and today, I decided to drop in and see my parents.

'It's going really well actually. Of course, there've been some hiccups, as there are with any major project, but in the grand scheme of things, it's good. How have things been here?'

'I'm so pleased to hear that. Things have been fine, just the usual. Your father's been busy in the garden and I've not seen Qais in a few weeks now. How's Murad? I've not seen him in so long. How is it working with him?'

The mention of Murad makes my pulse race. Try as I might, I can't seem to stop myself from reacting to the mention or presence of the man. He just has to walk into the room and I'm hyper aware of him and I don't even know when that started happening. It certainly wasn't the case when we initially started working together. But now things are different. We're working together almost seamlessly and since being back in London, we've been catching up via email or messages. I never thought I would, but

I'm actually missing him. 'He's fine. He's in Birmingham, visiting his family.'

'They've moved to Birmingham?'

'Yeah, his sister got married and moved there. She's got two children now.'

'And how about Murad?'

My racing pulse stutters at that. 'What about him?'

'Is he with anyone?' Mum watches me carefully but I have no idea why. She doesn't know anything about my history with Murad.

'He's not married. And I don't think he's with anyone. He's certainly not mentioned it.' It's something I've not braved asking him about, though whatever the answer, it shouldn't affect me.

'Saf? When did you get in?' Dad walks into the room and I get up and squeeze him around the middle as he holds me close against him.

'When you were gardening.'

'I was in the shower. Your mother refuses to let me in here unless I take a detour to the bathroom after gardening. I heard Murad's name, is he here? I've not seen that kid in a long time. Zafar's wedding was the last time, I think.'

I stare at my dad in confusion. 'Why would Murad be here? We're just working together, Dad. He's gone to see his family in Birmingham. Mum asked about him.'

Dad looks at Mum meaningfully and it puts my spidey sense on alert.

'What's going on?' I ask, looking between them.

'Time for tea.' Mum gets up, but I raise my hand to stop her.

'Ah ah, no. What was that look between you two? I might not have been here awhile, but I know that exchange had loads of subtext.'

'You always were a tenacious child. Come and sit down and we'll talk,' Dad invites.

I sit on the sofa near Mum, while Dad sits in an armchair.

'It's no secret, Saf, that I failed you as a father.'

I let my shoulders slump at that. 'Dad, please don't—'

'You wanted to know, so let me speak please.' He gently reproaches me, a smile on his face. 'I should have stood up to my father. Stopped him from controlling my children the way he did, but I . . . I sought his approval.' He looks at Mum and she leans forward and squeezes his knee. 'You already know that your grandfather didn't approve of me marrying your mother. And he never let us forget that fact, letting it impact his relationship with you and Qais as well. And after Zafar's birth, he made it a point to treat you and Qais differently.' He sighs, looking heartbroken.

'Daddy, why are you going over history which brings no one anything except a deep sense of sadness?'

'I just wish that I had put a stop to him arranging your match when you didn't want it. I thought he was finally showing an interest in you and your future. I thought it was his way of moving forward and that it would change things, and when you agreed, I didn't talk to you to make sure that that was what you truly wanted. I should have.'

My heart twists at the sorrow and guilt that's clear as day on my father's face and in his voice. I get up and make my way towards his armchair, sitting on the armrest and resting my head on top of his as I hug his shoulders. 'I want to put all that behind us, Daddy. I want us all to move on and look how far we've come. You and Mum have made a home for yourselves here. Qais has done so well for himself and I'm trying too. I've come a long way too.' I'm surprised to find that I mean what I've said. After my time in Kenya, I thought the only direction I had moved in was backwards but in recent months, that's changed.

'I know you have, my angel, and I'm so proud of you. But before your grandfather passed away, he told me something about you and Murad.'

My heart stops at that as I slowly pull away from Dad and look between him and Mum, who nods at me with a sad smile on her face.

'What did he say?' I ask with no small amount of trepidation.

'That you both liked each other, but before anything could come of it, he arranged your match with Ejaz and you went ahead with it.' I roll my bottom lip between my teeth as Dad squeezes my knee. 'I'm not for a minute suggesting that you pick up where you left off. I appreciate that you've come out of an unwanted relationship after six years and it'll take time for you to heal and decide what you'd like to do going forward. I think you're doing a brilliant thing by focusing on building yourself up slowly and concentrating on your professional life.' He huffs a soft laugh. 'Another thing I should have protected on your behalf but didn't.'

I get up from the armrest and kneel down in front of my dad, my heart twisting at the sight of unshed tears in his eyes. 'Daddy.' My voice is barely above a whisper. 'None of what happened is any one person's fault. Well, except maybe one person and he's not here anymore. It's perfectly natural to want approval from your dad. I did the same, I went ahead with what Daada said because, somewhere along the line, I was seeking his approval too. I wanted approval for myself, for Qais and for you both.'

'It wasn't your job to do that, sweetheart. But it was absolutely our job to take care of you and we didn't do a good enough job,' Mum says from her place on the sofa.

'If that was the case, and if I believed that, then I wouldn't be here and nor would Qais. The fact that, after all that, we can still be together, as a family, is testament that you didn't fail. We were all just let down by someone who should have done better.'

They both look at me in sadness but with understanding.

'I asked about Murad because of what my father had said and we just want you to know that, whatever you decide, you have our unwavering support,' Dad says with a smile. 'But by no means does that mean we want one thing or another. We just want you to be happy with whatever and whoever you choose – or don't. OK?'

I swallow the lump in my throat and nod at my parents, their unwavering support making me feel light in a way I haven't in a long time and so contrary to how my grand-father made all of us feel.

Dad leans forward and grasps my face in his hands, kissing me on my forehead affectionately.

'I don't know whether to be outraged that you didn't tell me or outraged that you went through what you did. But, suffice to say, I'm outraged.' Vaneeza leans back against the sofa, her hand landing on Biscuit's head as she doses in her lap.

I wince as she looks at me with wounded eyes. 'It's a thing of the past, Vaz,' I say as I replace my cup in its saucer. I always thought rehashing the past was a point-less exercise and that was why I never shared any of what happened with Vaz. But talking to my parents has made me realise that there's a sense of freedom in finally talking about things openly with the right people. I also think that finally sharing the truth with Murad has also enabled me to make peace with my own guilt.

'No thanks to your grandfather.' Vaz says heatedly. 'Jesus!'

We sit in silence for a few minutes and my mind drifts to Murad, wondering what he's up to. Has he shared this stuff with Meerab or has he kept it to himself? I had got so used to seeing him every day. With him not here, it's like there is something missing.

After that night, which feels like it happened just recently but, at the same time, ages ago, we've had a really easy rapport. We've been working in perfect harmony with each other. Murad's been helping with the villa fully, giving me his opinion whenever I've asked for it and encouraging me throughout. He even told me that, though he didn't say as much at the time, he loved what I had done with the period conversion.

It wasn't the first time my work had been complimented, but it made me feel particularly warm and fuzzy to hear that from him. He had pride and admiration in his voice as he spoke and he kept assuring me that the villa would look amazing when it was finished. His belief makes me believe in myself in a way I haven't in a long time.

We've also started bantering more with each other. The other day, when I went to the supermarket, I saw an exceptionally large grapefruit and knew I had to send him a picture of it. I held it next to my head and sent him the selfie and, not long after, he sent me a picture of his niece eating an avocado, her face covered in green mush as she grinned at the camera, her nose scrunched as she did, while Murad was next to her making a gagging face as she held a spoonful of smashed avocado towards him. His message had been one word – Heathen. I can't help but smile at the thought.

'Oh my God,' I hear Vaneeza say ominously.

I snap out of my thoughts and look at her pointedly. 'What?'

She doesn't say anything but picks up her cup and tries to hide behind it.

'What is it?'

'You've got that look about you, Saf. You were smiling while lost in thought and I think it might be because of your rekindled' – she waves her hands around in lieu of using a noun – 'with Murad.'

'Well.' I sit back. Do I? Surely not. 'Nothing has been *rekindled* between me and Murad. We cleared the air and are being perfectly civil with each other. Friends even. That's it. Nothing more,' I say with more force than the mini speech requires.

'Me thinks the lady doth protest too much,' Vaneeza remarks with her nose in the air and Biscuit barks softly. 'See?' She widens her eyes and points to her dog, as though Biscuit's some sort of authority on the matter.

'Me thinks you're full of shit,' I grumble and we both laugh, Biscuit yipping along with us.

But Vaz's insinuations make me feel restless. I'm just about getting used to the idea of Murad being in my life again and enjoying connecting with him as a friend. It's only been a few months, for God's sake, and it's not like our feelings for each other are what they used to be. Those feelings were left behind seven years ago and I'm sure he's moved on since then. Obviously, I know he's not married, but that's about it. It's impossible to imagine a man like Murad not being snapped up and, from what I remember, he always wanted marriage and children.

While he's not told me about his relationships, he has told me about his parents and their shift to Birmingham, his sister and her family, and how they're all encouraging him to move closer to them. He's always been close to his family, but the thought of him moving to Birmingham permanently to be with them and me not being able to see him leaves a hollow feeling in my gut. Had it been before, I might have welcomed the idea because it would have meant not seeing that hostility from him, but now? Now, it's different. And I feel like that should bother me, but, for some reason, it doesn't.

26

Safiya

'OK, so the floors are done. The staircase has been reworked. The ceilings are done – looking fantastic, if I say so myself. The walls are prepped and ready to go. And . . .' I pause and glare at Murad. 'You're not listening to me.'

Murad looks up as he puts his phone down and he grins at me, something that's becoming a regular thing recently. Whenever I look his way, I catch him smiling, just like he used to. Grumpy Murad seems to have left the building for good. I don't know exactly what the turning point was, but I find myself slowly being lulled in, feeling calmer, more positive and optimistic than I have in a long time. I feel happier, even if I am faux-moaning at him. There's a certain sense of joy in that too.

'Of course I'm listening. I'm always listening when you speak,' he says cheekily.

'Cut the charm, Aziz. We have work to do.' I point my pen at him for emphasis even while warmth courses through me at the exchange and being the recipient of his charm.

'No, Fiya. Our work for today is done.' Joy swells within me at the sound of that name coming from him. He freely calls me that most of the time now. 'You're just emulating that workaholic cousin of yours right now, not knowing the difference between work and rest. Though, to be fair to Zaf, recently he's been really good about taking time off and delegating more.'

I sigh as I lower my notebook onto my lap. 'I just want to do a good job, Murad.'

'And you are. In fact, you're doing a better than good job, but you don't have to do it at the expense of all else. We can chill out in the evenings and on the weekends. You don't have to prove anything to anyone,' he says rather perceptively.

We're sitting in the courtyard outside the cottage as the sun sets on another glorious day in Perla Rosa. There's a pinkish hue to the sky and the air is still warm from the day's uninterrupted sunshine. Work has been carrying on steadily since we came back and I'm pretty pleased with the progress, though there's always a doubt in my mind that I'm forgetting something or something's going to fall through or at the end of it all, Antonella's going to hate it. Which is why I'm finding myself unable to switch off and enjoy the setting and the company, going through my to-do list with Murad for the umpteenth time instead. Or at least I'm trying to, but he's not co-operating.

'Hey.' I feel Murad's thumbs against my eyebrows as he smooths them across my forehead, his palms cupping my cheeks. 'If overthinking had championships, I'd expect you to get the gold medal every single time.'

'Very funny.'

He grins as he eases back from me and my cheeks feel the warmth seep out of them as he pulls his hands away. In a few short weeks, I've got used to Murad's presence and his occasional touch when he's done it without realising, because when he's paying attention, I find him keeping a polite distance between us as though one of my brothers are watching.

'What's on your mind, Fiya? Talk to me.' He eases back in his chair, his long legs stretched out in front of him as he keeps his eyes on me and picks up his glass.

'Choose a topic,' I say flippantly as I put my notebook and pen on the table next to me and pick up my forgotten drink, a cool mocktail Bianca made a large jug of, which I've been drinking like it's going out of fashion.

'Oh-kay. What's concerning you about this project?' Murad asks as he sips his own mocktail.

'Nothing specific. But I just want the whole thing to go smoothly.'

'And it is. It's running on time and progressing just how we want it to, with all the usual hiccups a project like this has. In fact, I'd go as far as saying that we've been lucky. If it helps ease your mind I can see if Baz fancies coming out here to help out with the electrics.'

I widen my eyes at that and he grins mischievously. 'No thank you. We're managing perfectly well without Baz, even if I can't understand a word this electrician was saying and he thought I was crazy. Thank God Amadeo turned up in time to translate for me, otherwise we'd have had wall sconces on the ceiling in that bedroom.'

Murad scoffs. 'It wasn't that bad.'

'Close enough. The electrician thought *I* wanted wall sconces on the ceiling, he thought I was bonkers. He was gesticulating so hard, I thought he might pull a muscle. After he left, I checked to see what "pazza" means. It means crazy.'

'You and electricians.' He shakes his head in amusement. 'To be fair, you do have a crazy glint in your eyes when you're working. It probably freaked the poor guy out.'

'Lots of jokes coming from your corner this evening.' I stretch my lips in a fake smile.

'And you're yet to smile properly.' He leans forward and presses a finger lightly against my cheek. 'I know when you're really smiling because you get the faintest of dimples just on this cheek. It only ever shows when you smile fully or laugh and that's when your eyes sparkle like emeralds. Something that doesn't happen as often as it used to,' he says softly and my heart skips a beat. Classic Murad, saying things that go straight to my heart without even trying.

I smile sadly and he eases away. 'Time has a way of leaving its mark on a person, Murad. You're hardly unscathed. You've changed too, though I can see glimpses of the old you more recently. You're more ready with your smiles and there's a certain lightness about you which wasn't there when I first saw you in that meeting room.' Something I welcome wholeheartedly. 'You're cracking terrible jokes once more.' I say in a bid to lighten the moment but he does no more than lift a corner of his lips.

'I think it's fair to say that we're both victims of circumstances, Fiya. What happened to us wasn't ideal, but it's in the past. It's up to us how we move on from it and how much we bring that into the present with us. I want to move on and I'm sure you do too.'

God, he makes it sound so easy and wonderful, and I suppose, in theory, it is that easy, but in reality? Not so much. And life is about reality, not theories.

I'm a fighter by nature, but there's only so much fight in me. There are some demons I just don't have the strength to slay – the biggest of them being guilt. Every single promise I made to the man sitting in front of me, I broke and while he might be able to forgive me for that, how can I forgive myself for hurting him the way I did? I had claimed to love him more than anything else and yet . . . I knowingly said things to him which I knew would cause

194

him pain. A person like that doesn't really deserve to move on and put it all behind them, do they?

Murad clicks his fingers and snaps me out of my thoughts. 'We've established that there's nothing about the project that should be causing you concern. So what else is on your mind? Is Zafar flapping again?'

That makes me laugh. 'When doesn't that man flap? But no, he's eased off over time. His wife's helped a lot with that. Otherwise he can be worse than my dad.'

'You've become good friends with Reshma?'

'Yeah. She's great. It's been nice to connect with her and to reconnect with Vaz again after coming back.'

'Did you not have many friends in Nairobi?'

I shake my head, a wry smile on my face.

'What? How?' he asks incredulously. 'You were there for six years, Fiya. And you've always been friendly and one of the first people to start talking to others in a room, so what happened over there?'

'I tried in the early days, when I thought there was a remote chance things might work out, but very soon I realised that wasn't going to happen. Most, if not all, of the people belonging to Ejaz's social circle weren't my kind of people. I had nothing in common with them and when things started going south with Ejaz, I knew I'd never be able to count on any one of them for true friendship or support. They wouldn't know how to even spell the words honest or genuine. So, I kept to myself. I made a few friends with my boxing class goers, but not on any deep or meaningful level. Things were pretty lonely out there.' And that was putting it mildly.

We're silent for a few minutes, the sounds of nature surrounding us. A soft breeze, insects buzzing here and there and, in contrast to that, the very distant sound of a car horn every now and then. Murad doesn't take his eyes off me and I can see sorrow swirling in their depths in the faint evening light.

'I also felt guilty,' I say it softly, but he hears me crystal-clear.

His eyebrows lower into a frown at that statement and his voice sounds more suspicious and less curious when he asks, 'About what?'

I debate saying anything more. What good can come of it? There's nothing to be gained by going over old ground, but . . . but I feel a sense of catharsis talking to Murad about it. He's the only person I've shared any amount of detail about the past seven years with. There's not one member of my family who knows the stuff I've shared with him – aside from the few brief conversations I've had with my parents, Qais or Vaz. So many things from the past seven years are crammed inside me and there's something poetic about Murad being the only person I share these details with. He was just as much a victim of what happened as I was, albeit unknowingly.

'Us.' That one word clears the frown from his face, upon which I now see annoyance.

'Not that again. Why?' he asks through clenched teeth.

'*Why*? Need you ask?'

He scoffs. 'You've already said you treated the six years of your marriage as something of a sentence. I had no idea you were such a martyr, Fiya. What happened to the dynamic and fierce woman I knew? The one who never backed down no matter how high the odds were stacked against her.'

'She got caught up in her grandfather's manipulation. And you're talking as though you kept going just as you were after everything. There's a world of difference

196

between the Murad of then and now. There's a hardness about you that I put there.'

He looks away, his eyes not meeting mine as he responds. 'That's not true. I had a lot of growing up to do. It's not all on you.'

'But at least some of it is. You can be honest with me, Murad. Just like I'm being honest with you. I hurt your feelings. I crushed your faith in me. I made you feel less than. I broke your heart. None of those things are forgivable.'

'Is that what you want then? For me not to forgive you? To punish you more than you've punished yourself? What will it take for you to accept that everything was out of our control? Your grandfather orchestrated things so you saw no way out and you did what you thought best at the time. We do that, Fiya.' There's an urgency in his voice as he leans forward towards me, his eyes focused on me once more. 'We make the best choice at the time, with only what we know at that point in time. No one knows what the future holds. No one knows how the chips are going to fall or what will be a success and what will be a failure. We just do our damned best and we hope for the same. You did what you thought best. I trusted you then and, believe it or not, I trust you now.'

There goes my heart, swooping again. I feel like I'm on a never-ending rollercoaster with Murad.

'You're supposed to be smarter than that, Murad,' I scoff, letting some irritability come through into my words. How can he say such things? 'Let me ask you this, then.' I decide to test the waters. 'Why haven't you found someone and built a future with her. You always wanted marriage and children, it was no secret, so why hasn't that happened? Why haven't you moved on? Why does it feel like there are certain parts of your life which are exactly where you left them seven years ago?'

He's quiet, avoiding eye contact with me as he looks into the distance. It's darker now and the outdoor solar lights are beginning to glow and gradually brighten. The light casts half of Murad's face in shadow, but I can see that he's in deep thought, any semblance of joviality completely gone from his expression.

'I've been concentrating on other aspects of my life.' He says in a very matter-of-fact manner.

The fact that he's not acknowledged any relationship gives me a sense of relief I shouldn't be feeling. It's ridiculous. I should be encouraging him to move on rather than be pleased that he might not have. It's not like *we* have any future. I hold that thought as I try to get back on track.

'There's no denying that you've focused on some aspects of your life in spectacular fashion. You've made a massive success of yourself in the last seven years. I know you've worked hard to get to where you are, but that doesn't preclude you from being in a relationship, does it? Many people manage both things and I know you're more than capable of doing that.'

He's quiet, doesn't respond to me.

I drain my glass and then pick up my notebook and pen before standing up. 'You don't have to share anything with me if you don't want to, Murad. These are spontaneous conversations which we're having in the moment, but they don't have to mean anything more than that if we don't want them to.'

I squeeze his shoulder and feel the muscles beneath my hand tense. I leave him sitting there and make my way upstairs, ready to call it a night and hoping that the turn of conversation this evening doesn't mean a sleepless one.

27

Murad

I shiver a bit as I eventually get up and my stiff backside protests the duration it's spent in a wrought-iron chair. It was warm throughout the day, but for some reason I'm feeling kind of cold right now, though it might have nothing to do with the temperature and more to do with how I'm feeling physically and emotionally. I could have got up when Safiya left, but I stayed where I was, her words circling through my mind on loop as I tried to find answers and explanations that would appeal to my understanding and justify why I was where I was, and why I had made the choices I had, consciously or subconsciously.

I make my way into the cottage and, after locking everything up, I go upstairs. My mind doesn't feel at ease or ready to rest as I lie there, staring at the ceiling in the faint light coming in through the patio door, so I let it wander.

Safiya had been right when she'd said that she had hurt my feelings. In fact, that's a bit of an understatement, but the point stands. She *had* crushed my faith in her. She did make me feel less than. And yes, she did break my heart. She said none of those things were forgivable, but I can't quite bring myself to agree.

Now that I know her reasons for doing what she did, I can't lay the blame for all those things on her doorstep. She gave me her reasons and I believe her. She hurt my feelings and broke my heart to protect me from her grandfather's machinations. If she had gone into it any more lightly than she did, I might never have believed her, and then what?

She needed me to hate her and I did, she made sure of it. She took my reality and turned it into insecurities and used them against me. But, deep down, in the depths of my heart, I don't think I ever hated her like I believed I did or might have wanted to, otherwise, why would I want to be around her even now, despite all her explanations? But I do. I find myself being drawn to her like a moth to a flame, slowly circling and closing in until it's too late.

I turn onto my side and try to get comfortable, hoping sleep will come and rescue me from these thoughts, but I feel wide awake.

Over the years, I had tried my best to forget about her and I had succeeded to some extent. I could go days, sometimes weeks, and not think about her. But then, out of nowhere, something would trigger a memory and it would hit me like a juggernaut. All the feelings would come flooding back and I could just about keep my head above the water as the memories washed over me like one gigantic wave after another, crashing on the shoreline and not stopping until they were good and ready and I was completely spent.

I would go through an array of emotions. Sadness and devastation. Anger and frustration. Loneliness and inadequacy. Confusion. That used to be the hardest sometimes, because aside from feeling confusion about the sudden turnaround and lack of lead-up to such a spectacular break-up, I used to feel confused about my mixed feelings towards her. Sometimes I could hate her with unadulterated loathing and yet there were times when the thought of her not being with me filled me with utter desolation. An abundance of grief would pour forth from me and I couldn't understand how I could feel like that for someone who thought I wasn't good enough for her and within months of breaking up with me had gone on to marry someone else.

I don't think I ever hated her enough to wish ill on her, though. That's not me. I might have said various things to save face, but none of that would ever come from the heart, because from there I can only ever feel love for Safiya. My heart doesn't know any other feelings aside from love when it comes to my Fiya.

I sit up, the sheets falling to my lap as I cover my face with my hands before pushing them through my hair and clasping them at the back of my neck. My heart is pounding hard in my chest and I can feel the drumbeat of my pulse in every part of my body. I'm feeling clammy but cold. I close my eyes and take a few deep breaths to try to calm my heart's gallop and when I do, I see Safiya's face from seven years ago.

She's smiling at me, that playful smile of hers which gives that dimple a chance to appear. She lifts her hands and touches her finger tips and thumbs to make a heart before kissing her palm and blowing her kiss towards me.

And then I see Safiya from the day we broke up, her eyes dull and puffy, their appearance a clear indication that she hadn't been sleeping. Her lips are pinched and then, after a moment of looking at me as though it's the last time she'll see me and wants to take it all in, she raises her chin and one eyebrow imperiously, her look one of contempt.

But as I look more closely, I can see the emptiness in her eyes. An isolation and a grief which I never saw before because I couldn't see past my own hurt.

And then there's the Safiya of now, the sight of whom still makes my heart leap. This version shows the toll the past seven years have had on her and it makes me want to pluck the moon from the sky and lay it at her feet if it would make her smile like she used to. She's suffered enough, and for what? She deserves to be happy, for her life to be filled with joy and love and for the sparkle to come back to her eyes and I want to be the one to do that. I want to banish all the pain and vanquish all her demons.

Because I love her.

I open my eyes as that truth suffuses my body, my heart and my soul.

I love Safiya. I never stopped loving her. All I did was try to bury that feeling as deep as I could, but the strength of it was such that all it took was a few months and some exchanged confidences for it to break through all my defences and take back its place, as though it had never left.

And why not? Why shouldn't we have back what was so cruelly snatched away from us? That wasn't our choice. Our choice had been taken from us, not respected as being worthy because of one man and his ego and prejudices.

But those aren't our circumstances anymore. We're not the same as we were seven years ago, and neither is the situation. What happened, happened, we can't change that. But we should be able to move on, and as well as putting what happened behind us, we should be able to build a future of our own choosing, and if that includes each other, then why not?

None of what happened seven years ago is real, it was all manufactured for a purpose and it isn't relevant anymore, so why should either of us lug the load of it here and now?

An energy I've not felt in a long time courses through me and I find it difficult to keep still. I throw the covers off and, after grabbing a jumper, I make my way towards the patio door, sliding it open softly so I don't disturb Safiya, and step outside. The sky is dark, the stars clearly visible and twinkling like diamonds encrusted on the darkest blue velvet. I lean against the railing and feel a strong sense of calm fill my body as my jumble of thoughts finally resolve themselves into clear and decisive ones. Ones which I can action and which, hopefully, will bring me and Safiya that feeling of peace that has eluded us both for seven long years.

'Can't sleep?'

I turn at the sound of her voice. She's standing in the doorway to her room, the bedside lamps casting a soft glow of light behind her and through the flimsy curtain covering the patio door. She steps out and, cupping her elbows in her hands, she comes and stands next to me.

She sighs softly. 'The sky looks gorgeous, doesn't it. Look at all those stars. You know, doing this is on my bucket list. Stargazing. This has got to be the most stars I've seen though – enough that I think I can tick that item off my list.'

'What else is on your list?' My voice comes out gravelly, like I've not used it in days.

She smiles at the question, her eyes lighting up in a way that puts the stars to shame, at least in my humble opinion. 'A few things, and we've already ticked one item off – to have a gelato at a gelateria in Italy. I think I've only got one item left from my old list and that is to see a Formula One Grand Prix at Silverstone. I need to think of new things to add. So far, I've ticked off . . .'

She goes through her list, her face animated as she tells me about each thing and I savour this moment of closeness to her. The fact that she is standing next to me, when a few months ago I would never have believed such a thing possible, would have never even admitted to wanting such a thing. The subtle fragrance of her perfume fills my sense of smell and when she goes silent, I turn and look at her. She's looking at the sky, a serene smile on her face, her arms still folded across her body as she holds the sides of a light cardigan together. She's the most beautiful person I've ever seen and seeing her right now, in this moment and after my own moment of realisation, makes me feel stronger and more resolute. Yes, this is my person and who I want to be with.

'Can I ask you something?'

She glances my way and gives me a single nod.

'If what happened seven years ago hadn't happened, where do you think we'd be?'

Though she's not moving, I get the feeling that she stills at my question, before her expression fills with anguish and she turns to look into the dark distance. Her expressive eyes talk more than she does, telling me how she feels, and it makes me want to close the short distance between us and gather her in my arms, soothe away the pain and grief she's been carrying with her all this time.

'What's the point of such a question, Murad? What purpose does it serve for either of us?' Her voice now sounds deflated but I don't let it deter me.

'Humour me. Please.'

She takes a deep breath and sighs, her hands now on the rail in front of us. 'I'd like to think that we'd both succeeded in careers of our choice. You doing what you're doing now, I suppose, though whether that would have been with my family, I'm not so sure. I'd like to believe that I would have worked as a designer for some company before maybe starting up my own business.'

She's prevaricating from answering what I actually asked her and she knows it because she won't make eye contact with me and then, when she eventually does, she huffs in annoyance.

'What's the point of this, Murad? You're asking me to tell you something knowing that it's impossible for it to ever come true. Since when do you derive pleasure from pain?'

I reach across and put my hand over hers. 'Why does it have to be impossible, Fiya?'

She looks back at me in confusion.

'I don't think it has to be impossible. I tell you what, I'll answer that question and then you can.'

She scoffs a laugh and turns to face out again. 'This is the height of silliness, Murad. At stupid o'clock in the middle of the night, we're standing here talking fantastical nonsense.'

I ignore what she says but keep my eyes on her side profile. 'If things had been different seven years ago, we would have still been together.' She's silent, but her lips tighten. 'We would definitely have been married. I would have romantically proposed and you would have said yes before I'd even finished my speech. We'd have had a place of our own which we would have had heaps of fun decorating together, it would have been the best project either of us would have worked on – our favourite. We might have bickered about some colour choices or pieces of furniture, but I'm sure you would have talked me round to your ideas by the end – except pink of course. We would have travelled because I know how much you always wanted to travel, but we would have also had some time at home with just each other because that's more my thing.'

She's watching me intently now and I can see the changing emotions on her face, a yearning and longing creeping into her eyes as I describe what could have been an ideal life for us. She swallows hard, but I don't let that stop me.

'I'm sure we would have had children, though I can't say how many we might have had by now. We would have wanted at least one of each.'

205

'Stop it, Murad. There is no point in you doing this apart from causing both of us more pain than we need. Haven't we suffered enough?' She moves, as though she's about to leave, but I put my hand on her arm, stopping her.

'What if we can have what we dreamt of having, Fiya? What if we treat the last seven years as a delay that was beyond our control and did now what we had wanted to do then?'

Her eyes widen as I speak, her hand lifting to cover her mouth. 'What?' She whispers the word in disbelief.

'Yeah. We can fulfil the dreams we had. What's to stop us? Who will object now? There's no reason why we can't be together anymore, Fiya. You asked me earlier why I hadn't found anyone? The reason is pretty obvious. It's only ever been you, Fiya. And there never will be anyone but you for me, my love.' I feel like I'm laying myself bare but it also feels supremely right.

She looks at me in horror and pulls her arm away from under my hand. 'There can never be anything between us again. You need to get that thought out of your mind before it can take root. Any chance we had is long gone and the best we can now hope for is to be friends. Really good friends.' She gives me a smile which fills her face with sadness, her eyes filling with tears. Then, with the subtlest shake of her head, she goes inside, leaving me staring after her.

28

Safiya

'This is the not-so-secret ingredient.' I show Bianca the little tub of cream and then pour a generous amount into the simmering chicken curry we're making.

When I got back from London, we made a deal. She would teach me an Italian recipe and I would show her a South Asian recipe, after which followed a lengthy discussion about how much a basic recipe, be it Italian or South Asian, could vary depending on which region's recipe you followed. There were many variations and no one was right or wrong so we agreed to show each other our family recipe.

Her cheeks are glowing and her eyes widen as she stirs the cream in and watches the colour and consistency of the sauce change. 'Ah.'

'Mmhmm. You could use yoghurt, but where's the fun in that? Now we just need to add some fresh coriander and a sprinkling of garam masala. You can have this with rice or naan. I actually love having it the next day with toast.' I give her a chef's kiss and she smiles back at me broadly.

'I've already prepared the dough for the naan. I checked the recipe online for that and it's very easy. *Grazie mille*, Saf. My grandchildren will love this when I make it for them.' She hugs me tightly and a wave of longing goes through me as I think of Mum. I've been thinking about her a lot today. I'm not sure if it's because I'm using a recipe she taught me or something else. Maybe I'm just homesick.

Leaving Bianca to finish off what she's doing, I head to the sitting room and settle down on the sofa and decide to give Mum a call. Over time, things have been getting better between me and my parents and more so after my visit home and our lengthy conversation. She answers the phone with a smile in her voice. 'Hello, sweetheart.'

'Hey, Mum. Guess what? I made your creamy chicken curry recipe today.'

We chat for a while before she asks, 'And how's Murad?'

The mention of him fills my limbs with tension. Of course, she has no idea that, not twelve hours ago, he dropped a bomb on me which rocked the ground beneath my feet.

'He's fine. I think he's gone out for a run.'

'Oh, OK. So, when do you think you'll wrap things up there?'

'Soon, I hope.' More so now than I did last night.

The strange thing is, I actually missed this place when I went back to London and was really happy to come back to it. Now? Now I can't wait to return home, because after last night, each minute I spend under the same roof as Murad has his words going round in my head on loop.

I can barely process that conversation and the things he said. In fact, instead of dealing with it, I'm doing a really good impression of a tortoise, hiding inside my shell whenever he's around. It was part of the reason I initiated an impromptu cooking session with Bianca when the builders left a bit earlier than usual. Murad saw us together in the kitchen and then went off somewhere, thank God. I know I can't avoid him forever but I've done a pretty stellar job so far.

'The pictures you sent me of the progress in the villa were great.' Mum's voice pulls me back to the moment. 'I love the kitchen especially. When you're back, you can work on our house.'

Dad joins us on loudspeaker for a bit before I get off the phone. As I do, Murad comes down the stairs, fresh out of the shower in a pair of chinos and a pastel pink T-shirt. His jaw looks like he's just shaved and his hair looks like it's been trimmed. I swallow hard and force my gaze away from him and try to act like I would have before his craziness last night. Because that's all it was – sheer craziness. As if any of that was possible.

'I thought you went for a run?'

He gives me a half-smile, like I'm missing something obvious. 'I went for a haircut. Didn't fancy needing to borrow your hairband. I tried that once with Sumi and she got the hump.'

I can't help but laugh at his silliness. 'Very funny.'

'I can be sometimes. I took her headband and put it on my head and she didn't speak to me for a whole five minutes.' He comes towards the sofa and sits on the opposite end of it, leaning back with his arm across the back of the sofa and one leg bent on his other knee. His hand is no more than a dozen centimetres away from me, a sleek watch strapped on his wrist. His forearm looks well defined from here, dusted with fine hairs, and I can see the delineation of muscle above the elbow too, where the sleeve of his T-shirt hugs his bicep.

He clears his throat and I look up at him and he grins at me knowingly, having caught me. I roll my eyes and look away, hoping that my cheeks don't give me away. Once I'm sure I can keep my eyes on his, I turn to face him once more.

209

So far, thankfully, he hasn't raised the topic of us being together. He completely blindsided me when he spoke about us like that. It was the last thing I had ever expected from him and I felt like the ground had tilted beneath me.

For a split second, I had been ready to agree. He was voicing and offering me the one thing I had always desired most. I wanted to say yes to what he was suggesting. To throw caution to the wind and embrace the possibility he was dangling in front of me, to spend the rest of our lives together, much like we had wanted to before my grandfather had made me choose between being with Murad and Murad's future and wellbeing and, as a result, the future of his family as well.

And then reality crashed down on me like a tonne of bricks. I couldn't do that, not in a million years. How could Murad even ask me? I had taken something precious and beautiful and smashed it to smithereens, and irrespective of the circumstances, I had caused him an immense amount of pain and sadness. I had hurt him in the most callous way and gone on to marry another man and, after all that, Murad thought it would be a good idea for us to simply pick up where we had left off? How delusional was he?

Even if he wanted to ignore all those things, how could he expect me to? The irony of the whole thing is so tragic, I felt like bawling my eyes out. I broke up with him, telling him he wasn't good enough for me, when the reality is that he's always been perfect and it's me who's not good enough for him and I never will be. How can I spend my life with a man who deserves the best in everything, when I know I'm not worthy in the least. I don't deserve a man like Murad Aziz and I never will. And the worst part of it is that I destroyed the chance of that happening.

'Ah, you're here, Murad. Good.' Bianca comes towards us, her bag already on her shoulder. 'I don't have to give you any instructions for dinner today because it's all your work anyway. I've made the naan and kept them in the warming oven.' She looks at me as she speaks.

'Did you take out some of the curry and naan for yourself?' I ask her as I get up.

'I took more than enough. Enjoy your evening both of you.' She gives us a big smile and leaves and then it's just me and Murad – the moment I've been dreading.

I make my way to the kitchen, it's better than sitting there with Murad, where awkwardness seems to be creeping up one degree at a time since *you know what*. I take out plates, only to turn and find Murad right there. He takes them from me and makes his way to the table, that grin still in place as though he knows a secret I don't. I don't know how he can be so calm and content when my nerves feel practically fried thanks to him. I refrain from growling and grab the cutlery and napkins and follow after him. Once we've got everything we need at the table, we sit down to eat, our meal punctuated by a mixture of awkward silences, stilted conversation and Murad acting like he's on top of the world without a care in the world.

'That was sensational. You're a great cook, Fiya. I remember how you hated cooking before. Is there anything you can't do?'

As much as I don't want it to, his praise goes straight to my soft centre and warms me up. Moments of praise have been few and far between in my life over the past seven years. Being back with my family has had me on the receiving end of compliments, but it's taken some getting used to, and coming from Murad, it hits differently.

'I would have more, but if I do, I won't be able to move off this chair. You'll have to roll me around the room.'

'I'm glad you liked it.' I bypass the reference to *before*.

We start clearing away and there's now more a companiable silence between us. My nervousness is slowly beginning to abate and if we can get through this evening, then I'm sure we'll be back on an even keel from here onwards. We can forget about last night and carry on on the same trajectory as friends. Sadly, my hope is short lived.

I put away the last of the dishes as Murad puts the kettle on for some tea.

'Have you given any thought to what I said?' He sets out cups and takes out the milk.

'About what?' It's a redundant question, I know exactly what he's referring to and his look my way confirms that he knows that I know. I should have known there was no getting away with it when it comes to Murad. 'Don't start, Murad. That conversation is over.'

'I don't think it's fair for you to say it's over without even giving it any thought. How can I allay your concerns if you won't share them with me? At least talk it through with me. Because, from where I'm standing, I can't see any reason for it not to happen.' He pours the boiled water into two cups. 'Look, I know I came out of nowhere last night and surprised you with what I said, but that doesn't make any of it wrong or untrue. I still stand by everything I said.'

'It can't happen,' I say through gritted teeth.

He folds his arms across his chest and stares at me, his expression firm and his gaze direct. 'Give me one good reason why.'

29

Murad

Her cheeks redden as her eyes blaze at me across the kitchen. She looks incredible to me all the time, but Safiya in full angry mode is a sight to behold. Her shoulders go back and her chin goes up. If she doesn't curl her fingers into her palms to form fists at her sides, she'll rest her hands on her hips, and often, it's a good indicator of how angry she is. If she's absolutely vexed, it'll be the fists, and if it's less so, it'll be the hands on her hips, which is what I get now.

'What part of no are you struggling with? The N or the O?' she seethes.

'Neither, love.' Despite her anger, I keep calm, knowing that reacting in any other way won't help. 'I just want to know *why* you're saying no. Surely you can explain that.'

'I don't need to justify myself to you. And don't call me that.'

That makes me want to smile, but I don't want to antagonise her any further. 'You're right, you don't need to justify yourself. But don't I at least get a chance to have a conversation with you as to why you think it can't happen. You didn't object when we were together the first time around, so I want to know what's changed. Maybe then I can try to understand your point of view. I'm not saying this to be cruel or harsh – that's not me, and you know it – but I didn't get a say the last time. You made the decision for us and I went with it.'

'You didn't have a choice not to go with it, I made sure you went with it. That was the only option for you to take.'

'Exactly. It can be different this time, Fiya. We can talk about different points of view like adults and together' – I wave a finger between us – 'we can decide what we want our future to look like, rather than let one person do all the decision-making.'

Her chin dips and her shoulders hunch forward a fraction, that warrior-like stance less pronounced. I finish making the two cups of tea and take them to the table and then I hold a chair out for her. She takes her time, but I've got all the patience in the world.

Once she's sat down, I take the chair adjacent to hers and I waste no time in carrying on our conversation. I don't want silences and assumptions to do the talking for us. I don't want there to be any misunderstandings. Whatever we choose to do must be just that, our choice, and for that we need to talk, even if these conversations are hard and take us all night.

'Fiya—'

'Look, Murad,' she cuts in, her voice more defeated than angry now. 'I heard what you had to say and while it sounds great in theory, it's impossible for us to do in reality. We can't be together like that. Too much has happened and—'

'Woah. Let me pause you there. Don't give me generalisations, Fiya. When you say too much has happened, I need you to be specific. What exactly has happened?'

'Don't be obtuse,' she growls at me.

'I'm not. Saying "too much has happened" is not good enough. There are plenty of people who have a lot less than what we had and still give their relationships a second chance, so why can't we? We didn't even have a say in what happened seven years ago. Your grandfather did all the saying and deciding.' I say it with as much emphasis as I can to try to get through to her.

She takes a shuddering breath and I force myself to take a calming breath too. I need to keep my cool and not let my own temper get the better of me by bringing up her grandfather, it'll do neither of us any good.

We both take a sip of our tea, the only other noise in the room coming from a small ornate clock, with the odd, errant noise filtering in from outside. Other than that, we're surrounded by silence. A silence fraught with tension and unspoken words rather than the companionable silence we sometimes share.

'Murad,' she says with forced patience. 'Seven years is a long time. I've changed since then, as have you. I'm a divorcee. My ex-husband was a toxic man and my reputation hasn't come out of that situation unscathed. Have you thought about how that might affect you and your family? I'm working for my family with few prospects of my own and little experience to fall back on. In fact, I got the opportunity I did because of Zaf. Barring this one.' She adds the last bit tetchily when I give her a pointed look. 'You, on the other hand,' she smiles, but I can't bring myself to, 'you've made so much progress in that time. You're bright and successful and you've got a big heart with a lot of love to give. I know how much your parents wanted that success for you and I bet they're super proud of you. I know I am. You can't want to saddle yourself with an unworthy failure like me. You deserve so much more, so much better, and that's not me, Murad. *That's not me.* I lied when I told you that you're not marriage material, because

215

the truth is that *I'm* not marriage material and I've got a failed one to prove it. You're better off without me.' She sounds like she actually believes what she's saying.

'That's it for you then? One failed marriage will define you for the rest of time? So, what does the future you envisage for yourself look like?' My jaw aches because of the hardness with which it's clenched. I can't believe she's writing herself and any future for herself off like that, and all because of a grandfather and ex-husband who failed her. 'And when have I ever cared about what people have to say? People will talk. They always do. You matter to me. Not them.'

Silence descends once more as she fidgets with her empty teacup and I stare into mine, trying to process everything she's just said to me. After all that, there's only one question I can think to ask her.

'Can I ask you something?'

'Yeah, but no promises I'll answer.'

I huff out a laugh at that. She can't help but dish out the sass, but I shake my head. 'No. This question needs an answer and once I have that answer, I'll drop the subject and leave you alone if that's what you want. But I need an honest answer to the question and I want you to give me that answer without thinking about the past or the future. I just want the absolute, unvarnished truth from you and, ideally, it'll be in one word without any supplementary explanation or justification. Agreed?'

She hesitates, looking at me as though she already knows what I'm about to ask her. She swallows hard and I do the same, my palms suddenly feeling clammy. Everything pins on this one thing and if this fails, then I'll have nothing more to fall back on. This will be it.

I take a deep breath and ask her, 'Do you love me?'

216

I can feel my heart thundering in my chest and the silence around us feels like it's a physical being sucking the air out of the room. I wipe my hands on my jeans, but I keep my eyes on Safiya. Her eyes widen and her lips part, but other than that she's as still as a statue.

We sit in silence for a few minutes. I don't follow up with anything, wanting the question to stand on its own and hoping that she knows what it means. She's not looking at me. She's looking down at the surface of the table, where her hands are holding onto the empty teacup for dear life.

I want her to have the space and freedom to answer me honestly, so I push my chair away from the table and pick up my cup. 'I'll leave that question with you. When you know what your answer is, let me know and then we'll take it from there. Goodnight, Safiya.'

I don't wait for her to respond. I tuck my chair under the table and, after depositing my cup in the sink, I head upstairs, grabbing my tablet and making my way to the balcony.

It's a cool and clear night, so I throw a blanket over my legs before getting onto a fool's mission of trying to find something to watch on any one of the numerous streaming services I'm subscribed to, hoping that something will distract me enough right now to stop me from harassing Safiya for an answer. I only get five minutes into my search when my phone starts ringing.

'Hello.'

'Hi, Mumu.' Sumaira's angelic voice comes through the phone. She's supposed to call me Mamu Murad – the address for a maternal uncle – but somehow it became Mumu and it's stuck ever since.

'How's my favourite angel? Have you been good?'

'Uh yeah. I'm always good.'

'Puh-lease.' I hear my sister scoff in the background and suppress a grin.

'What did you do today?'

That's my niece's cue to launch into a lengthy monologue and I listen intently, enjoying her chatter and letting it soothe my rougher edges this evening.

I've left the ball in Safiya's court, but that doesn't mean it's not left me feeling on edge. I honestly don't know which way this is going to fall, and while one possibility will lead to euphoria, the other will be even harder to bear than our break-up the first time around because this time the decision will be entirely our own; no one else's opinion or choice has any bearing on it. We're calling the shots and I actually have no idea what Safiya's going to decide.

I hear Sumaira yawn and after bidding me goodnight, she passes the phone to her mother.

'Hey, Meerab.'

'What's up?' No preliminaries.

'Why would something be up?' I try to sound nonchalant.

She clears her throat and I can picture her folding her legs under her on the sofa and getting comfortable to make her point. 'Don't bullshit me, little brother. Us older sisters are born with an in-built radar which every now and then can get straight to the heart of the matter, provided we've had enough sleep, which, given the fact that I've got a baby with teeth on the way, means I'm not at full function.' I love how she caveats her bullshit. 'I know what can annoy you, what can make you laugh and what can bother you or how when you're bothered or stressed, you sound like you've got a sore throat. So don't waste our time and cut to the chase.'

'Now I know where Sumi gets the capacity to talk from.'

'She'll make a great leader one day. My baby girl knows her onions already.'

218

We both laugh and then there's a pause as I hear her gulp, presumably having her first peaceful cup of tea of the day while my brother-in-law takes over pre-bedtime parenting.

'Stop stalling. Is it Safiya?' she asks softly.

'Meer-rabb,' I groan.

'Ah. Bullseye. I'm switching to video.'

'No, don't—'

It's too late. Within seconds, her face appears on my screen. Her hair is in a bun on top of her head and she looks completely wiped out, not that I'd say as much. She'd launch into me with a sudden spurt of energy. A wave of affection goes through me at the sight of my sister. Aside from my friendship with Zafar, which has its own place, my sister is my best ally. If I say we're going to war, she'll pick up her sword and shield, no questions asked and she'd probably be the one to bring me a head on a platter. She's also my biggest cheerleader, my voice of reason, my sister/friend/part-time mother/my champion all rolled into one.

'Hmm.' She scrutinises me through the phone.

'Don't use the tactics you do with your kid on me please.'

'Don't behave like her then. Now, talk.' She does indeed have a cup of tea with her. In fact, it's a mug the size of her head. 'Do I need to pull on my big sister gloves and come there?'

'I'm not sure exactly how that would play out, but,' I shake my head, preparing myself for her to fly off the handle when she hears my next words. 'I kind of asked Saf if she wants to give our relationship another go and she said no.'

To Meerab's credit, only her eyes widen. She doesn't say anything or have any other expression. She takes another mouthful of tea and then nods for me to carry on and I do. It feels good opening up to her with my thoughts and feelings. I tell her everything that's happened, filling in all the details I didn't give her last time we spoke, about me reconnecting with Safiya, and by the time I finish, her eyes are filled with sadness.

'Poor you. And poor Saf. I feel a bit bad for hating her now.' That response is a turn-up for the books.

'Only a bit?'

'Yeah. She still did a number on you, whatever her reasons and as your sister I have to hate her a bit for that. It's in the rulebook.'

'You're such a child sometimes.' I can't help but smile, something I'm sure she intended.

'Ha. Says the man who came into the world two years after me. Wouldn't that make you a baby?'

'Can we keep to the subject at hand here, please?' Though I'd never outright tell her, I need my sister's advice and support right now.

'Yes, we can. So now you're just going to wait?'

I shrug my shoulders. 'There's nothing more I can do, is there? It's got to come from her, I've told her my thoughts and feelings.'

'Have you? You told her you still love her?'

Had I? I know I've acknowledged as much, but did I actually say the words to her? 'Well, no, not exactly, but . . .'

'Oh, Murad.' She palms her forehead and I scrub my hand over my face. 'How can you ask her to take such a giant leap of faith blindly without giving her something to try to reach for?'

'I didn't realise I hadn't actually said the words, Meerab.'

'I think you did, just not consciously. Maybe it was self-preservation. Not wanting to put yourself out there fully until you knew she'd also be there with you. Holding some of yourself back. You should tell her how you feel.'

'I don't want her to think I'm pressurising her into choosing me by saying that now. It won't sound honest, it'll sound calculating.'

'She deserves to know how you feel about her.'

'And I'll tell her, but not until she's told me how she feels.'

Meerab huffs and I can tell she's not entirely pleased with my answer, but she accepts it anyway. 'Keep me posted, OK?'

'Yeah. Thanks, Meerab. Love you.'

'Love you too.'

I end the call and drop the idea of watching anything, deciding to get ready for bed instead.

When I step out of the bathroom, I find Safiya standing pacing in the hallway.

'Hey. You OK?' I ask.

Safiya nods, her eyes not quite meeting mine as she twists her fingers. She opens and closes her mouth a few times as if she has something to say but doesn't quite know what. She raises her chin. 'My answer is no,' she says. 'I don't love you anymore, Murad. We can't be together. I'm sorry.'

She turns on her heel, heading back into her room, while I stand frozen right where she left me. Just like seven years ago. Except this time, my rule about not falling in love with her again is going through my head, mocking me, leaving me wondering how much of an idiot I am.

30

Safiya

The sound of the drill repeatedly going on and off is driving me absolutely insane. That and the guilt simmering in my stomach. My head is pounding, my heart aching and this infernal noise isn't helping. I wish I was at home with Vaz, watching *Bridget Jones* with a tubful of ice-cream and the remains of a Chinese takeaway strewn around me. The tried-and-tested heartbreak cure.

Because that's what this is: heartbreak. Though, in my case, I've done it to myself. So perhaps I deserve it. Deserve all of this.

Do you think anyone else would want you? Ejaz's voice reverberates in my head, echoing and making every insecurity of mine take on a monster-like form and stand before me baring its teeth.

I move towards the kitchen, where I hope the noise is less and those monsters can't find me, but I have no such luck. The builder working in here is using his bloody electric tile cutter. I just about hold back from screaming and leave the kitchen through the door that leads to the courtyard, only to be confronted by the cat who thinks of the villa as his – or her – domain and has made its displeasure crystal clear by hissing at everyone.

'If you don't clear off, I'll give your hissing a run for its money, I swear to God. Today is not the day to test me.'

It gives me a filthy look and then saunters off, leaving me feeling even worse than I am for aiming my wrath at the innocent creature.

I heave a heavy sigh, remembering Murad's hopeful eyes and how I had to break his heart all over again. Every day of my life I'll have to get by knowing I could have been with Murad, but chose not to. And, like he said, this time it was entirely my decision to make.

I know I could have slept on it, but what was the point? There was absolutely no sense in me dragging it out and keeping him hanging. I knew what my answer would be. What it had to be. I'm not the same Safiya he used to know. Not the Safiya he had imagined a life with.

Do you think anyone else would want you or your hollow sense of self-worth?

My breath hitches and I pace my breathing. If I close my eyes, it's like I'm back in Kenya. I used to pretend that Ejaz's words didn't hurt, didn't prick at the skin and eat away at my confidence. Because that would mean he won – he'd got what he wanted. I could pretend to him, and maybe even to the rest of the world, but I knew the truth.

And it only made the things I heard on the grapevine after my divorce worse. I knew they weren't true, but the fact that people held those opinions about me and my family bothered me. That they thought they had the slightest inkling of what had happened between Ejaz and me.

When a marriage ends, people always want to know why. And, in many cases, where the facts are unknown, somehow the finger always points towards the woman – as was the case with me. Ejaz seemed perfect to everyone. Charming, handsome, wealthy. An all-rounder. But with me? They saw a woman who had turned her back on her family after marriage. And how could that woman be a good wife? People remarked I hadn't given Ejaz any children, completely ignoring the possibility that Ejaz might have had something to do with it. Of course, where there was no relationship, there could hardly be any children, but people weren't to know that, they likely wouldn't even care. I even heard some people talk about me as though my life were over, as though I were damaged goods that should be consigned to the local dump site.

I know I should ignore it. People will always talk. But it still stings. And knowing all this, how can I subject Murad to that? How will it affect his family? I can't do that to him. What happened seven years ago was bad enough, I can't stand the thought of causing further damage to him with all my flaws and baggage of insecurities.

I sit on a chair against the wall by the wrought-iron table with a tired sigh, glancing at the never-ending fields in the distance. At the beauty of this place. Murad's words echo through my head. My *lie* echoes through my head. *That's it for you then? One failed marriage will define you for the rest of time? So, what does the future you envisage for yourself look like?*

Until recently, I was taking my life one day at a time. I suppose it was just survival. Just thinking about the next step, not my whole life. My forgotten dreams. I hadn't given my life as a whole any thought. I hadn't envisaged any future. I had once, but then it became clear that my plans were meaningless – my future was planned for me without me knowing. So now, the prospect of thinking ahead feels a little futile, because you never know what fate has in store for you.

Do you love me? Murad's words go through my mind again.

What was I supposed to say? Yes, of course I still love you. In fact, I probably love you more now than I did before. I know what it's like to lose someone that precious and I don't want to go through that ever again.

But what would be the point in sharing that with him? All my considerations still stand. And because of that, the future I envisaged last night, looked bleak. It looked bare of colour and joy. It looked bare of moments of laughter and moments of peace. It was bare of love, because it was bare of Murad, it was that simple and that complicated.

I'm so lost in my thoughts, I don't hear or see him until he pulls the chair opposite back with a loud scrape against the ground and sits, after placing two tall glasses filled with sparkling elderflower and mint leaves and lots of ice on the table. 'Courtesy of Bianca.'

I skipped out on breakfast and haven't seen Murad since last night and the sight of him now makes my heart clench and I will myself not to break down into tears. I glance in Murad's direction as he takes in the scenery around us. He looks forlorn.

'Thanks.' I grab the glass and take a small sip, except it goes down the wrong way and has me choking and gasping as bubbles tickle my throat and nose. Murad is out of his seat in a heartbeat. His big, warm palm resting on my back and moving in soothing circles as he encourages me to look up, tilting my chin when I don't respond. My eyes fill with tears and I'm not sure if it's because of the choking or if they're actual tears. He crouches down beside my chair, his hand on my back not stopping.

'Hey. You all right?' he asks gently, a kind smile on his face.

I feel my throat close up as he looks at me in concern, his eyes shining with what I know is pure love for me. I shake my head, tears filling my eyes to the brim and spilling over onto my cheeks.

225

He looks at me intently for a minute before he gets up and walks back towards the cottage and the sight of his retreating form fills me with pain, but it's what I asked for. I can't reject him and his offer and then expect him to hang around and comfort me. Tears blur my vision and I close my eyes as tears continue running down my cheeks.

A hand lands on my shoulder and I look up and find Murad standing before me, his hand held out in front of me. I look at his hand through the haze of my tears and then up at him.

'Let's take a break. I've spoken to the team supervisor and they'll be fine without us for a while. Come on.' He takes my hand and helps me up and then we're walking down a little path which I know leads towards a small harbour called Porto Rosa – very much named in line with everything else in this town.

We walk for ten minutes, Murad keeping my hand firmly in his as we make our way there. I know I should pull my hand away. In fact, I should have refused to go with him but I have no fight left in me. I feel like a piece of driftwood floating on the surface of the sea, moving wherever the waves take it. When we get there, he guides me towards a small bench facing the water under the shade of a tree. No more than a handful of colourful boats of varying sizes are secured to the harbour, bobbing up and down with the movement of the water, the sun glinting off the surface. On any other day, I'd lap up the peaceful vibe, but today it's all lost on me.

Murad pulls his hand away from mine and I nearly whimper in protest but hold back, clutching it with my other hand in my lap instead as we look out at the water, the afternoon sun doing nothing to warm up my ice-cold limbs. My jaw is cramping with the effort it takes to hold back from crying like I feel the need to.

I can hear Murad breathing deeply and evenly and, pretty soon, my breaths match his as we sit there. I feel my emotions begin to come down from their high in small degrees and my pulse isn't pounding in my cheeks anymore.

I don't know how long we sit there in silence for, but it's got to be at least twenty minutes before Murad finally turns and looks at me, his face clear of any expression.

'Better?'

I nod and try to smile, but my cheeks ache.

'I'm glad.' He turns to face the harbour again.

I want to say something to him, but my mind is drawing a complete blank right now. What can I say to him after telling him I don't love him? There is no follow-up to such a statement. And why is he being so nice to me? He should have left me to choke in the courtyard after what I said to him last night. In fact, he didn't even need to come and give me a drink in the first place. Why did he come and find me? He should ignore me like he did when I first came back.

'I realised that I'd been unfair to you yesterday.' His voice startles me, and when I process his words, I'm confused, though not for long. 'I asked all those questions of you but gave you nothing of my own thoughts or feelings. Of course, you've already given me your answer and I respect that. I told you that would mark the end of me bringing it up again and I stand by my words. I just feel that if I asked you to explain why you said what you did, I should too. I should have before you answered me and I would have, but then I didn't want you to think I was explaining myself in an effort to pressurise you into accepting what I'd said. Does that make sense?' He turns to look at me, his expression earnest, and all I can do is nod and then he's looking out at the water once more, while I look at him.

'When I asked you to give our relationship another chance, I think I made it sound like an option we could choose, when what I should have done was say to you that it was what I wanted. I wanted us to start a relationship with each other after finding out what had actually happened seven years ago because I'd realised that none of it was your fault, you were manipulated. I wanted us to give our relationship another chance because I remember how much it filled our lives with happiness. And when I thought about my future, I couldn't imagine it without you. And I suppose . . . well, I don't suppose, I know. I know that's the reason I've never entered into another relationship since then, not with full commitment. I've always held a part of myself back. I'm always looking for my Fiya in every other woman, when in reality there is only one Fiya.'

I swallow the lump in my throat at his words, my inhale more of a shudder. I can feel my heart breaking anew, piece by piece, and each piece causes fresh pain to engulf my body, while he smiles sadly at me before breaking eye contact once again to look ahead, but not before I see the sheen of moisture in his eyes.

'Please don't think I'm saying all this to get you to change your mind, Safiya. That's not what I'm doing. I completely respect your decision. You were right, we have changed in the past seven years and I'm sure you've gone through a lot more than you've said. From what you've described of him, Ejaz Baig wasn't an easy man to live with and you had to spend six years with him. And in contrast, as you said, I have come on leaps and bounds, but, believe it or not, you fuelled that. I was trying to prove a point, the Ferrari being a prime example, which you sussed out straight away. I remember us talking about it, so it felt like the natural choice to make when I was ready to get a supercar. I wanted to prove that I could flourish with a background like mine. I'm not sure if you're aware, but I invested in your family business, something that might well make your grandfather turn in his grave, now that I think about it, though at the time I thought I was sticking it to you.'

That makes me reluctantly smile.

'Despite all of that, I don't for a second think you're a failure or unworthy in any capacity. Please don't think that about yourself. You're one of the strongest people I know, a true fighter. You're selfless, giving and have a beautiful soul, Safiya, and there's no part of you that I don't love beyond any expression or that I'm not proud of. Anyone would be lucky for you to be a part of their life, not better off without you.'

My tears are freely falling now and I make no effort to stop them.

Murad swipes a hand across his face and looks the other way as we sit silently for a few moments before he speaks again.

'I hope you heal over time and open yourself up to love again. For what it's worth, I feel privileged that though our time together was short, I got to be with you, to love you and be loved in return, and those times are going to sustain me for the rest of my life. They'll be memories I can fondly and proudly look back on now rather than avoid thinking about.' He turns to face me and aside from the single silvery streak down his cheek, there's no other sign of tears, just that gentle smile of his gracing his gorgeous, dear face.

My tears, on the other hand, come thick and fast, blurring my vision until I can't see anything through them. I feel his arm come around my shoulders and then I'm resting my head against his shoulder as I let my despair pour out of me. Murad holds me close against himself, his hands linked around me as his head rests against the top of mine. I can hear the steady beat of his heart against my cheek as my tears soak his T-shirt. I can't see if he's crying, but I feel like he is and I tighten my arms around him.

You've got a false sense of superiority, Safiya. No actual substance, just a bucketload of pride. Do you think anyone else would want you?

Those words, which had been on replay ever since I left Ejaz, cross my mind again. But for once – for the first time – I brush them off. *Shut up Ejaz,* I think, and when I've got nothing more left in me, I pull in a shuddering breath and I feel Murad's hold around me loosen. I slowly pull away from him and when I'm far enough, I look up at his smiling face. The man who loves me, who has *always* loved and believed in me. My heart glows with love as he cups my cheeks, his thumb wiping away the last of my tears but the steel cage around my heart won't let any of my love for him escape or show.

'Let's go back home,' Murad says.

I nod.

31

Murad

I'd be lying if I said I hadn't hoped for a different outcome. In an ideal world, Safiya would feel the same as I do. She would want *us* as much as I do. And I want her to want that, to choose us. But, most of all, I want her to be happy – even if it is without me. And isn't that what love is? Letting go even if it crushes you because it's what makes the person you love happy and it's what they want. The sentiment feels hollow right now, but I'm hoping over time I'll truly believe it.

It has been a few days since our moment by the harbour. Safiya and I have both thrown ourselves back into work. In a way, it is kind of nice. Letting go of the resentment, making our peace with the past and present. And we work well together, we always have. And that's not me being biased, others have said as much.

'You and Safiya have worked wonders here.' Gianfranco eyes the villa carefully, a glint of approval in his eyes. 'Antonella's going to be very pleased with this. How much longer do you think it'll take? It seems like you'll be done within a week or so.'

'Ten days at the most, I reckon. Just some finishing touches left to do.' We're standing in the courtyard where the builders are now packing up for the day and Amadeo is leaning against his car with his phone glued to his ear until his aunt hollers for him to make his way to the kitchen. Gianfranco leaves once all the workmen have left for the day and I make my way into the cottage. There's no sign of Safiya, I only find Bianca as she straightens after putting something in the oven and closes the door.

'Bianca, is there any chance I can get a coffee, please? I can feel a headache coming on.'

Her expression is one of immediate concern and she bustles towards me. 'Oh, *caro*.' She places her hand against my cheek and, after clucking some, she goes back to the kitchen and I can hear her rummaging in a drawer as I go and sit on the sofa. She brings over a glass of water, a blister pack of tablets, a coffee and a plate with a small serving of pasta on it. 'I saw what you had for lunch and it wasn't enough. Have some of this before you have the painkillers or your coffee.' She pats my cheek and then backs away.

If eating pasta or painkillers would do the trick, then I'd gladly have them, but they won't. Nothing will do away with the pain or the emptiness I'm feeling. The pain and emptiness that I've been feeling since that night when Safiya told me she didn't love me and which will probably stay with me forever now, because Safiya and I are done. We're actually done. I took a chance and lost. We'll still be friends, but nothing more.

I told her I'd respect her decision and I do, but that doesn't mean I can't mourn the loss of the future I had hoped for. Last time there was an element of shock, whereas this time I've had a lead-up to it. Since I asked her the question, there was always the possibility that she might say no, but there had also been the hope that she might say yes. Last time there had been hate and anger mingled in with the despair. There had been a bitterness and it had all merged to fuel me for the next seven years. But this time around, there is none of that. There's just a strong sense of loss and grief. Of devastation and isolation. A sense of being adrift and not knowing how I'm supposed to move forward and navigate a future in which Safiya doesn't feature and I fear that this feeling, this void inside me, isn't going to go away any time soon, if ever.

'Antonella. It's lovely to see you.' I step forward and hug her. She kisses me on both cheeks before holding my hands in hers, tilting her head to one side.

'How are you, Murad?' she asks, her eyes knowing. Sometimes I feel she can read my mind.

'All the better for seeing you. Tell me, are you excited to see your finished villa?'

'I am.' There is a big smile on her face. 'Gianfranco has been torturing me with cryptic messages and blurry images. Little brothers are the worst.'

I let out a laugh, thinking of how many times Meerab has said that to me. 'Well, I won't keep you in suspense for very much longer. I'm just waiting for Safiya to come and then she'll take you on a tour of her latest masterpiece.'

And it is indeed a masterpiece. In the last week, Safiya has doubled down on finishing this project, working to iron out every last detail and finishing a few days earlier than the agreed deadline. Every aspect of the villa looks flawless, and if after this she still thinks of herself as only worthy of projects because of her family connection rather than her own talent, then someone needs to shake some sense into that woman. As though conjured by my thoughts, she comes through the cottage door and pain slices through my chest at the sight of her as it has done every time since that day by the harbour. It doesn't get any easier by the day and trying not to show how much it affects me has been one of the toughest things I've had to do in a long time.

Safiya closes the distance between us. She looks incredible in a mint green linen suit with a white blouse and high heels. Her hair is in loose waves around her shoulders, looking lighter thanks to her time in the sun, while her complexion appears golden, making her eyes look brighter, though I can see the sadness that's been lurking there since our visit to the Porto Rosa harbour. She tries to mask it with a blinding smile as she hugs Antonella and greets her exuberantly.

'I've been so excited for this.' Antonella looks at Safiya and then me as she speaks. 'I can't tell you how much I've waited to see what magic you two have done.'

'Well, I hope it lives up to your expectations,' Safiya answers, her tone heavily laced with nervousness. She licks her lips and glances timidly at me and I smile at her, hoping it offers her the reassurance she needs.

Gianfranco comes towards us from his car. 'Sorry, I was just taking a call. Right, are we ready?' He waves towards the villa, giving his sister a pointed look.

'Yes.' Antonella moves forward with her brother and Safiya and I fall into step behind them.

We go through the front door and into the main foyer, but Safiya pauses just inside the front door.

'You OK?' I stop just beside her, reminded of how she was the first time at the period conversion.

She turns wide eyes to me and I see her lips press together before she parts them to speak, wiping her hands on her trousers. 'She's going to hate it. I'm going to embarrass you and Zaf.'

I take half a step towards her and, on instinct, I touch her to comfort her, holding her face in my hands. 'No, she's not. She's going to love it just as much as you and I do. She's going to see that you've put your heart and soul into this place.' I lean forward and brush my lips across her forehead and I feel her press forward, as though she's savouring the touch, her hands fisting the fabric of my shirt at my waist. When I pull away, I smile at her. 'You could never embarrass me and I reckon Zaf will say the same. I have utmost confidence in you and your ability. Now go in there and show off your hard work.'

I move back, but she grabs my hand, shaking her head. 'You'll stay with me? We'll show her *our* hard work? Together?'

A shaft of pain goes through me at her earnest expression and words, but there's no way I can say anything other than, 'Yes.'

Safiya beams as we move towards Antonella and Gianfranco. 'I wanted this space to feel open, wide,' she explains, as the siblings glance at the huge, newly cleaned and polished chandelier, which we moved to take pride of place in the hallway. It's been lowered slightly to pull people's attention to it when they come in and the staircase has been moved as well. The effect looks classic and magnificent. 'This chandelier . . . well, it was far too beautiful to get rid of.'

Antonella gapes, wonder in her eyes. 'Oh, my goodness. That's our great-grandmother's chandelier. I was convinced it would be gone.'

'Your great-grandmother certainly had good taste,' Safiya says and Antonella puts her hand on top of hers.

'It looks superb, doesn't it?' Gianfranco says proudly. 'I told Saf to do away with it, but she said she had a good idea for it, and look. It's as though it always belonged here.'

We make our way through the villa. I take a back seat, watching both Antonella and Gianfranco marvelling at the way Safiya has brought the villa into the present while retaining some of its original features, much like she did with the period conversion.

'It's a bit unorthodox, I know,' Safiya says. We are standing in the main reception room which Safiya had the idea of moving upstairs. 'I just kept thinking that, with views like this, you'd want to always see it. Not just when you're going to bed and it's dark out, but you know . . . when you're living life.' I marvel at Safiya's vision for this place and how she's gone beyond just the design of the place and considered how it would be lived in.

Antonella nods. '*Sí*. I never thought of it like that. What an eye you have.'

We walk through the bedrooms downstairs as Safiya answers Antonella's questions. While I was aware how hard Safiya had worked on the renovation, I had no idea how above and beyond she had gone. There is a beautiful vase which she has sourced from Rome after hearing from Bianca that Antonella had spent her summers there with her paternal grandma, with beautiful hydrangeas plucked from the garden. A large weaving – with ancient red and black embroidery from Abu Dhabi, where Antonella lived with her late husband for a period of time – hangs over the four-poster bed. With each room, Antonella lets out a contented sigh.

'Saf. Murad. This is genius. You've done a splendid job,' Antonella interlocks her arms with her younger brother, who keeps her steady. 'You make perfect partners.'

I smile benignly, ignoring the inevitable hurt such a remark causes. Safiya refuses to make eye contact with me, instead smiling at Antonella before she moves out towards the hallway. 'And now, for our favourite room.' She opens the door to the newly refurbished kitchen, which she had deliberately bypassed earlier, and steps back, allowing Antonella and then Gianfranco to precede here, pausing at the threshold next to me.

The sun is shining into the kitchen as though we're outdoors. A third of the wall up from the ground is bricked and the rest is glass, including the ceiling and, as a result, the light in here is spectacular. The cabinets are all wooden base units, adding to the rustic feel of the room, with an island in the middle. Pots, pans and utensils hang from suspended beams and there's some faux ivy cleverly entwined around them, adding to the kitchen's charm. It looks like something out of a magazine and it's stunning.

When I first saw Safiya's plans for making this room into the kitchen, I had my doubts. I thought it would be better suited to be something else, but she insisted that it would work, and she wasn't wrong.

Antonella has turned to face me and Safiya and I can see she's got tears in her eyes. 'Would you believe my nonna always thought this room would work as a kitchen but none of us agreed with her, so she used it for her plants and to sit here when she wanted to be outside but couldn't be. Your vision is just . . . I have no words. *Grazie mille*, Safiya and Murad. You have done an absolutely glorious job.' Antonella hugs Safiya before coming towards me and holding her hands out. 'You are an absolute gem, you know that, don't you?'

'So you say.' I grin at her. 'I'm just glad you're happy with the villa, Antonella. It was a big responsibility.'

'I love it. Any buyer will be thrilled to have such a place.'

'Buyer? I thought you might be tempted to keep it because of its history in your family.' Safiya's eyebrows are lowered in a frown, clearly confused about Antonella's desire to still sell the property she has such fond memories attached to. A sale I had told her I would make happen.

237

'In all my years, there are many lessons I've learnt, and one very important one has been not to attach sentimental value to material things. They can get damaged, taken from you or need to be sold and sometimes it can be against one's wishes. Imagine if we kept every single thing we attached some meaning to? The weight of it would be too much to carry, and that's saying nothing of the physical weight of all those things. *Sì*?' Antonella smiles kindly at Safiya, who nods, before she says something to Gianfranco and leads him out towards the courtyard from the kitchen, leaving me and Safiya alone.

I watch her crestfallen expression. 'Don't take it to heart, Saf. Antonella's a businesswoman and knows what she wants. But the good news is, she loved your work. Didn't I say she would?' She nods but her expression doesn't change much. 'Then why aren't you looking very happy?'

She looks at me closely, before a smile slowly emerges on her face. 'I am. I am happy. Are you happy?'

I look at her for a long moment, seeing a lot more than she's willing to say, but I let it go and nod. 'Yeah, I'm happy too. I want you to remember this project whenever you doubt yourself. I want you to be happy all the time . . . Saf.' I was so close to calling her Fiya but I want to, need to be proactive in keeping things between us as friends.

Her smile dims slightly, but doesn't disappear as she closes the distance between us. She rests her hand against my chest and I'm pretty sure my heart skips a beat.

'This project, this feeling, this . . . sense of success and accomplishment has only been possible because of you, Murad. Sometimes I feel like you were born in the wrong era. You remind me of the knights of bygone times, full of valour and honour. You're just missing the armour and sword.'

That makes me chuckle and she gives me a cheeky smile, all earlier signs of sadness gone.

'Thank you. You paint a very gallant picture of me.'

'But, seriously, anyone else would have left me high and dry, told me to finish the job myself and moved on or had me taken off the job. But not only have you stuck around after . . . everything, you've supported and encouraged me every step of the way. You've lifted me up and reassured me whenever I've doubted myself. You're the best, Murad, and I pray that you can find the same happiness you wish for me.'

She wraps her arms around me and hugs me around the waist, resting her head against my shoulder, and it takes me no more than a few milliseconds to return her embrace, even though my brain is screaming at me that this is a bad idea. My soul wants to make the most of it, because it knows that this is the last time we'll ever be this close again.

32

Murad

'Mumu!' Sumaira shrieks as I walk through the door. I had hoped to surprise her but her beady eyes miss nothing. She launches herself into my arms and I hold her close, inhaling the smell of butter and sugar off her. She holds my face in her two baby hands and smacks a big wet kiss on my cheek. 'I missed you, Mumu.'

'I missed you too, Sumi. Where is your brother?'

She sighs and rolls her eyes. 'Irfan's gone swimming.'

'And why didn't you go swimming?'

'Because Zubair refuses to take more than one child with him. Apparently only I get the pleasure of taking two children swimming. He'll take them in turns,' Meerab grumbles beside me as she ruffles her daughter's hair, her expression full of love.

I spend a good hour with Sumaira as we eat home-made cupcakes with a little too many sprinkles and icing. She fills me in on what I've missed since I last saw her, as though we didn't have regular telephone conversations, and by the time Meerab is ready to put her to bed, I'm ready to crash too, but, of course, Meerab's having none of that. She gives the children's bedtime gig to Zubair and then the two of us sit in her cosy sitting room with tea and biscuits.

'So?' She eyes me over the rim of her mug.

'So what?' I know exactly what she means and her answering expression tells me as much. She knows how things stand between me and Safiya. 'Nothing's changed really,' I say, the rehearsed line flows out. 'We'll just treat the last few months as a moment out of time and move on.'

Meerab frowns. 'But it has changed, Murad. Only an idiot would pretend it hasn't. How can you still want to stay and work in London? Move to Birmingham and make a fresh start closer to your family. I can introduce you to—'

I get up and my sister holds my hand to stop me.

'OK, fine. I won't introduce you to anyone. Happy?' She tugs on my hand and I sit back down. 'I just want to see you happy, is that too much to ask?'

I heave a heavy sigh. 'In one word? Yes. It is. Because, right now, as it stands, I'll only be happy with one woman and she doesn't want me, so . . .' I've been back from Perla Rosa for about three weeks now but it feels like it's only been a couple of days. My emotions are still all over the place.

'That's not what she said, is it?' Meerab questions, her eyes narrowed. 'I mean, I'll be the first to say she's persona non grata for breaking your heart not once, but twice, but did she say she doesn't *want* you?'

'No. She thinks she's not good enough for me and that I deserve better.' I rub my temples.

'And she's absolutely right,' Meerab retorts cheekily, except her words lack any heat. Her harsh expression falls. 'When I met Zubair—'

'Are you about to be lovey-dovey? Because if that's the case, then I'll leave.'

'Can you just listen for once?' she asks, firmly. 'I never thought I'd have a love like Mum and Dad. Until I met Zubair. God knows he wasn't my usual type,' she says, adoringly. 'But I love that ridiculous man. So much. I

241

can't even imagine letting him go because I think I'm not good enough for him, or vice versa. I just can't help but feel sorry for Safiya. Her ex must have really put her through the wringer.'

I grunt in agreement. 'A bit of a change of tune for you.'

'I always liked Safiya. I just hated what she did to you,' Meerab says with a shrug. 'Perhaps I've been a bit unfair on her though, what with me not knowing all the facts until now.'

'God, am I dreaming? Did you admit you were unfair on Safiya?' Zubair walks in, looking like he's been put through his paces, and flops onto the sofa beside his wife, plucking her teacup out of her hand and taking a long, loud sip. 'Why did we decide to have kids again?'

'Because being a dentist wasn't challenge enough for you.'

Zubair rolls his eyes as Meerab retrieves her tea. He wraps his arms around her and Meerab settles into him, a soft smile on her face as he pecks her on the cheek.

'Right, I'm going to bed,' I say. I can't deal with these two. They'll play bicker and then become nauseatingly romantic in the next moment and I'm not sure I can handle that right now, though I love that for my sister.

I bid my sister and brother-in-law a goodnight and head up to the room Meerab keeps for my visits. My head hits the pillow and inevitably my thoughts go to the one place I wish they wouldn't but not wholeheartedly.

Despite the pain of her rejection at the end of it, my time with Safiya in Perla Rosa was some of the happiest in my life. It made me fall in love with her a little bit more, prize idiot that I am. I wish my heart, brain and body would get onto the same page when it comes to her, maybe then I might feel a tad more optimistic about moving forward.

Maybe Meerab's right and I should consider moving. Maybe a fresh start is what I need and being closer to the children would be ideal. It's not like I'm ever going to have my own, so I want to make the most of Meerab's.

I'll spend at least two weeks here before heading back and hopefully, by then, I'll have some idea about where my head is and what my next steps need to be.

'One, two, six, eleven, eleventy-two, seventy-two, ninety-nine, one hundred. Ready or not, here I come,' Sumaira shouts just as I close the pantry doors behind me. Meerab's standing at the worktop putting finishing touches on the hundredth batch of goodies I baked with my niece earlier, the smell of them making my mouth water.

'You need to work on your daughter's counting skills. There are four numbers that come after six and before eleven and don't get me started on the whole seventy-two to ninety-nine thing she's just pulled,' I whisper through the tiny gap between the two closed doors in the floor-to-ceiling walk-in cupboard. It even has overhead lights which go on when the doors are opened. Fancy. Safiya would love this.

And there I go again. Idiot.

'You forgot about the eleventy-two,' Meerab says sardonically, before adding, 'She's only three, Murad.'

'Shh. Quiet. She's got the hearing of a bat. I forget she's only three. She acts like a—'

'I'm coming, Mumu!'

'What did I say? Didn't I say she's got the ears of a bat.' I spot a basket of crisp packets on one of the shelves and I pull out a packet of pickled onion crisps, the first bite so sour, my jaw nearly locks.

'She gets that from her father.' There's amusement in Meerab's tone.

243

'I heard that, Meebs,' Zubair responds affectionately from the kitchen table, where he's tapping away on his laptop.

'Found you.' The doors to the pantry swing open and the lights above my head flicker to life. Sumaira is standing in front of me looking thoroughly pleased with herself before opening her mouth in an O and eyeing the packet of crisps in my hand, her tiny eyebrows launching into her hairline. 'Is it snack time?'

'Not just yet, munchkin. Mumu's being naughty.' Meerab comes forward and snatches the packet of crisps out of my hand, glaring at me.

I swoop down, grabbing Sumaira by her tiny body and toss her up in the air, eliciting the sweet sound of her joyous shrieks and giggles. 'More, more, more!' I blow raspberries on her tummy and then nuzzle her neck as she giggles, the sound making me laugh.

Meerab looks at me and smiles. 'It's good to see you laugh.' Before I can respond, the doorbell rings. 'Let me see who that is. Might be Mum and Dad.'

'Right, is it your turn to hide, Missy?' I put Sumaira down and she races towards the front door to investigate, the nosy little thing. I'm about to pilfer a cupcake when I hear Meerab's voice. 'Don't even think about it, Murad.' How does she even do that?

Two minutes later, my parents walk into the room, and ten minutes later, we're all sitting around the kitchen table, catching up on each other's news.

'So, are you done in Italy? No more return trips?' Mum asks as she pulls the plate of cupcakes out of Dad's reach.

'For now. I might have to go back to finalise the sale if I can't manage it remotely.' Something I'm ardently hoping doesn't happen. I'm not ready to go back to Perla Rosa any time soon.

'What are you working on next, son?' Dad asks.

'I'm doing a project with Zafar, a country house in Surrey, and Antonella got some good deals at an auction which I'll take over when I get back to London.'

'Will you be here this weekend?' I narrow my eyes at Mum's not-so-innocent tone.

'Depends. Why?'

'You don't have to look at me accusingly like that. I'm having a friend over and I thought you could join us. Meerab will be there too, won't you?' She looks to Meerab for support and I glare at my sister, forcing her to choose a side. We both know Mum's up to her usual, unwanted and unnecessary matchmaking tricks.

Meerab rolls her eyes. 'He'll come, on the proviso you don't try to set him up.' She glares at us in turn, trying to find a happy balance, and Dad and Zubair both scoff, knowing that's impossible.

Mum looks at Meerab and then me and then her face falls as she drops her hands on the surface of the table. 'All I want is to see you settled. Is that too much to ask? I don't think there's any mother who doesn't want that for her children. Have I got it wrong? Do you not want a partner or a family of your own?' Mum's genuine confusion gets me and I can see it's got Meerab too.

'No, Mum.' I sigh, knowing that I need to tell my parents the truth, otherwise they'll be left waiting and wondering why things are how they are. 'You haven't got it wrong. I know you love me and you care and you want to see me happy. I get that. But the truth is, I'm not going to feel that way with anyone except one person, and the sad thing is, I can't be with her.'

I give my parents an abridged version of my history with Safiya, omitting the nastier threats her grandfather made and telling them that he had simply arranged her match elsewhere. By the end of it, Mum's openly crying, while my dad looks like he's on the verge of tears. 'Oh Murad. Why didn't you say anything in all these years?'

I shrug my shoulders at her question as I catch Meerab brush away her tears. *Great.* Way to spend a pleasant afternoon with the family.

'What about the relationships you've had since then? Surely there was someone you connected with?' Dad asks, his expression filled with concern.

'It never happened and it's not likely to. Besides, it's not fair on the other person if I keep trying to find a connection which I know, deep down, I won't find with anyone else. At least not in the immediate future,' I add in an effort to try to placate them somewhat.

There's silence around the table, the only sound coming from Sumi's playroom where she's watching TV. Mum and Dad share a mournful look and Dad shakes his head. I get up and make my way to Mum, hugging her from behind and bending to rest my head on top of hers. 'I'll come this weekend and be there with you, as charming as I always am. OK?' I feel her nod her head. 'Just . . . just don't ask for more than that, please. That's all I can give.'

33

Safiya

I put my key in the front door of my parents' house and push it open, fatigue making me drag my feet. It's become the story of my life really. I'm tired all the time and nothing I do makes me feel a sense of energy or enthusiasm. It's been six weeks since I've been back from Perla Rosa, but it might as well have been six years given how time has dragged.

Going into the Saeed office has been depressing in the extreme. Nothing seems to hold my interest enough to stop my thoughts from wandering Murad's way. He's not been in the office since we've been back, working remotely from wherever he is – Birmingham, I presume. I've not braved asking Zaf and he's said nothing to me. I've been tempted to message Murad, but I've not given into the urge. It's not fair for me to say no to him but then contact him just because I'm missing him like crazy.

I've not heard his voice or laid eyes on him for six weeks and in every moment of every day, I ask myself how I managed to survive seven years without him. It's been an agonising six weeks and not a millisecond has gone by in which I haven't missed him with my whole heart and soul. Love is supposed to be freeing, isn't it? So why do I not feel free? I said no to him because I want more for him – but in doing that, I've sentenced myself to a lifetime of soul deep sadness which I don't think will ever diminish.

I take in a shuddering breath as I make my way into the front room, coming to an abrupt stop when I see my grandmother sitting there with my parents.

'Hello, my angel.'

'Daadi? What are you doing here? Mum didn't say you'd be over.' I make my way towards her and she pulls me in for a tight hug, her floral perfume reminding me of my childhood. She reluctantly lets me go to greet my parents before she insists I sit beside her, my hand squeezed between hers.

'Haroon dropped me off not ten minutes ago. I hadn't seen you all in a while and when I found out you were coming today, I thought it was a perfect day to drop by.' She looks at me intently, her aged eyes missing nothing, just as sharp as they've always been.

She smiles at me before turning her attention to Mum and Dad, catching up with each other before Mum heads to the kitchen and, two minutes later, Dad joins her.

'I'm just going to go and see if Mum needs a hand with the lunch.' I'm about to get up, but Daadi tightens her grip on my hand.

'Sit with me for a bit. Tell me, how are you? Your mother was telling me that you did a project in Italy and it went brilliantly well.'

'It did. It was a really beautiful villa which we restored and modernised in parts and the finished project looked pretty good. Let me show you the pictures.'

I pull my phone out and show Daadi the Perla Rosa album. She flicks through the photographs, pausing on some and zooming in on others, being pretty vocal about what she sees.

A picture of me and Murad comes up and my heart jerks painfully. Of course, there were pictures of the both of us there, I should have remembered that. In this one, I'm holding a paint tray in one hand and a paintbrush in the other, wearing my splattered overalls as I test colours on the wall. Murad is in the frame, his arm held out as he takes the picture, both of us smiling at the camera cheesily.

Daadi swipes across the phone and the second picture of us comes up, where he's on a ladder, bent over till his head is upside down and I'm laughing as I'm taking the picture, standing just in front of him. Daadi looks at me sharply and I realise I must have made a noise. I can feel the corners of my eyes prickle and I blink hard to stop the tears from forming. Daadi watches me keenly but doesn't say anything until she finishes looking through the pictures and hands me my phone back, a soft smile on her lips.

'I've always known that boy is a treasure,' she says softly before hastily carrying on. 'Beautiful photographs, sweetheart. You and Murad did a fantastic job on that villa. The before and after photos are amazing.'

I can do nothing more than nod and force a smile I'm not feeling, but it doesn't seem to bother Daadi as she carries on.

'I was clearing out the drawers in the sideboard in my room yesterday. I've been putting the job off for quite some time now, but when I found myself at a loose end, I thought I might as well eat that frog and get it over and done with. I've not touched it in years.'

She moves back a bit to rest her back against the sofa. I have no idea what she's talking about, but I'm quite happy for her to say whatever she wants if it means I don't have to say or do anything. My emotions are far too close to the surface at the moment.

'I found this.' I turn my head her way as she pulls an envelope out of her cardigan pocket with my name on it.

For a moment, I'm dumbstruck. It's not the sight of the envelope or my name being on it that shocks me, it's the penmanship. It's my grandfather's handwriting.

Daadi smooths her hand over the envelope. 'He gave this to me for safekeeping towards the end. He never told me what's in it and I've never opened it, what with it not being addressed to me. All he said was that whenever you come home, I should give it to you. I'm sorry, sweetheart. I completely forgot about it. I only remembered yesterday because I found it when I cleared that drawer out by chance. I should have given it to you after you came home.'

I shake my head as I look away from the envelope, not daring to touch it. I bite down on my lip, the emotions within me threatening to boil over. What is with me today?

I feel Daadi's hand rest on my knee. 'Talk to me, my darling. Maybe I can help.'

Her eyes are awash with tears and she's looking closer to her age than she usually does. A wave of affection for her comes over me and I scoot forward and hug her tight, my emotions breaking through their barrier and pouring forth from my eyes. I hear her sniffling too.

I don't know how long we hold each other like that for and I don't really care. I didn't realise how much I needed this. When I pull away from her, I can see tears rolling down her cheeks unchecked and her expression is one of utter sadness. I shimmy down the sofa a bit and swing my legs up as I lower my head onto her lap, her hand landing on my head and smoothing my hair away from my face, like she used to when I was a child. Inevitably, when I think of my childhood, my thoughts go to my grandfather as well.

'I don't want to see what's in there,' I whisper.

'I can understand that, sweetheart. It's a fear of the unknown, you don't know what to expect. And Zafar Senior hardly filled any of you children with confidence in him or his choices and decisions.' Daadi's voice sounds tart.

'I told him I'd never speak to him and I didn't break my promise. Even at the end. He called me, but I never responded.'

'I know, love.' Daadi sighs and it contains so much, I can't pick out a single feeling from it.

I lift my head and sit up. Her expression is pensive.

'I never forgave him either.'

'What?' Throughout my childhood, I'd never heard Daadi say something contrary to anything Daada said, let alone speak like this about him, so this comes as a shock.

Daadi nods sadly. 'He broke up our family because of his pride. He kept secrets from me and he drove my children away. I told him as much, but he wouldn't listen. Not until it was too late. He thought he was always right; he knew best because he was the patriarch of the family and he had to make the tough decisions. I had never called him out on any of those decisions and that's my weakness and something I have to accept. I should have challenged him a lot early on in our relationship. Maybe I could have done something. If I had spoken up, opposed him even, maybe my family wouldn't have fragmented the way it did.'

I shake my head. I've never heard my stalwart grandmother, the fiercest woman I know, talk with so much defeat in her voice.

'No, Daadi.' I grab her hand and hold it tightly between both of mine. 'You're one of the strongest people I know. Please don't blame yourself.' I feel guilt swamp me because before meeting up with Daadi and clearing the air like we did when she came to Mombasa with Zafar and Reshma,

I had believed the same about her and put her in the same boat as my grandfather. Ejaz had relished seeing me isolated from my family and often used it as ammunition whenever he was in the mood to fire shots at me, telling me that I was of no importance to anyone.

Daadi shakes her head as a fresh tear rolls down her cheek. 'No, Safiya. I let you down. I let Qais down. I let my own son and daughter-in-law down when I should have stood up to my husband on their behalf, not just made a short protest and then backed off when he didn't listen to me the first time. It's something I don't think I'll ever be able to forgive myself for.'

I shake my head even more vigorously. 'No, Daadi. Please don't say that.'

'Why not, Safiya? It's the truth, isn't it?' Her voice is crestfallen and full of sadness.

My conversation with Murad goes through my head in that moment and I reiterate the words to Daadi. 'We always do the best we can, but after an event we often feel like we could have done better when that's not the case. Your relationship with Daada wasn't exactly a partnership of two equals, he never allowed that. If you had stood up to him any more than you did, how would things have ended up between you two? And can you say for sure that things wouldn't have worked out in the same way they did anyway? Maybe *I* should have stood up to him more strongly.'

Daadi huffs, 'And how would *that* have looked?' She shakes her head before her expression clears a bit and she looks at me. 'It's entirely up to you whether you open that letter or not. Whether you read it or throw it away without reading it. I won't suggest one thing over the other. It's about time my children took charge of their own lives and made their own decisions and mistakes – which I hope aren't too costly and they learn from them. That's what life is. And as long as I'm able to, I'll be here to guide you, should you ever need it, but I want you all to make your own choices and thrive, rather than listen to someone who doesn't necessarily know better but just happens to be in a certain position where he can control everyone to do his bidding.' Daadi's voice has a defiance in it I've not heard before.

'Promise me something, my darling. Promise me you'll make a conscious effort to move away from all of that. Take the reins of your life in your own hands and steer it in the direction you want it to go in. If you happen across a dead end, then I trust you enough to know you'll figure out a way to get back onto the right track. But being stationary will lead you nowhere. Put the past seven years behind you and, like you did with that villa, bring yourself into the here and now. Your experiences will stay with you, but that doesn't preclude you from living a fulfilling life on your own terms from here onwards.'

I swipe at the tears on my cheeks. 'How did you know I needed to hear that?'

Daadi chuckles heartily, before quirking an eyebrow, her signature sass making an appearance. 'I didn't. I took a chance, something you should consider doing.' She winks at me and then gets up and toddles towards the kitchen to join my parents, leaving me staring after her.

'Dinner time, Biccie. Eat up please or your mum will have my head.' I put Biscuit's bowl in its place and, after giving it a sniff, she starts eating. I then go about warming up my own dinner. Vaz is at an event this evening – some engagement party – so it's just Biscuit, me and my miserable thoughts at home. I pull out the lamb korma and pilau rice Mum packed for me earlier today and go through the process of warming it all up on the cooker.

Since leaving my parents' house, I've been feeling restless. The letter Daadi gave me was burning a hole in my pocket, so I've left it on the side table in the front room, still in two minds whether or not I want to know what's inside. The things she said to me won't leave my mind, sticking at the forefront of it like a pinned post.

Take the reins of your life in your own hands and steer it in the direction you want it to go in.

She made it sound so simple. As though I can click my fingers and make it happen.

I shake my head and take a seat at the small table in our kitchen, the aroma of the food making my mouth water. At least I've got my appetite. I tuck into the meal, hoovering it up pretty swiftly before I clean up after myself and make my way to the front room with a cup of tea, biscuits and Biscuit in tow. I can't help but smile at the thought and Biscuit yips.

'I know, I know. It's a sign I'm going bonkers. But maybe you can help me out, Biccie.'

Biscuit trots to her bed and circles it a few times before lowering herself onto it.

'Or not.'

I open the packet of shortbread and a vision of me and Murad, sitting in the cottage in Perla Rosa with tea and biscotti, flashes through my mind. I bite into the biscuit, but rather than tasting the buttery, sugary flavour of it, I feel like I've got sand in my mouth.

I rest my head back against the sofa and close my eyes as a fresh wave of emotion comes over me, Daadi's and then Murad's questions echoing in my mind, and not for the first time. Tears break through my closed eyelids and stream down my cheeks. After a moment, I hear shuffling and then feel a little wet nose press against my hand before a fluffy bundle drops itself in my lap. I rest my hand on Biscuit's head as I open my eyes.

'What should I do, Biccie? Do I deserve to wallow for the rest of my life because of my grandfather's short-sightedness? Am I being just as cruel to Murad now as I was seven years ago? At least last time I was trying to save him from my grandfather, but what am I doing this time? Am I pushing him away because of my own fears and insecurities? That's not really fair on him, is it?'

Biscuit whines softly before resting her little face on my knee.

The loud admission of my thoughts has the impact of a cannonball hitting me square in the gut. I brush away my tears, and swallow down the threatening wave of more, but they come anyway.

'I'm lying to myself if I believe that Murad's future will look any different from mine. It'll be just as lonely and devoid of love. He won't find someone else and get married and have children and live happily ever after. He hasn't in the seven years we've been apart and someone like him would have had no trouble finding a partner, if he had made the effort. But he won't, I know that, deep down. If we're not together, then he won't move forward with any relationship.' Pain washes through me at the thought of Murad spending the rest of his life alone when he's so full of love and light and deserves nothing less in return.

My heart sinks to my toes as I voice and face my thoughts, showing me my selfishness. In trying to appease my own conscience, I've completely ignored Murad's feelings and it's not like he didn't tell me what they were. But can I give him that?

I remember my grandmother's words from many years ago. Strangely, I had forgotten her words until sitting with her today prompted my memory.

You are Safiya Saeed. Mumtaz Saeed's granddaughter. We make mistakes, we fall over, but we never, ever, stay down. We get up, brush off the dust, adjust our crown, raise our chin and we march forward with purpose. We don't let mistakes – our own or those of others – hold us back from going after the future we want and which is right for us. Understood?

She said I should take a chance. But I can only do that if I put the past firmly behind me and *march forward with purpose*. And that purpose has to be not letting a diamond like Murad Aziz slip through my fingers a second time.

I brush away my tears and take a deep breath, eyeing the envelope on the side table.

I know what I have to do.

'I know what I have to do.' Saying the words out loud cements my thoughts and feels so liberating, I can't help but smile. Biscuit lifts her head and turns her shining brown eyes on me. 'I know what I have to do, Biccie.' She lowers her head once more and I bend down and kiss the top of her head.

34

Murad

'Mumu, you have to come down. I want to show you something.' Sumaira charges through the door I'd stupidly left ajar.

'Sumi, sweetheart, I'm working. What did we decide? When I'm working, I can't play. I'll come afterwards, OK?'

Sumaira folds her arms across her chest and scowls at me in a way that would make her mother proud. 'I want to show you my new friend.'

Shit. Meerab did say she was having friends over, but I'd hoped to keep away and get some work done. Judging by my niece's determined expression, that's now going to be impossible.

'OK. Give me five minutes. Let me finish what I'm doing and then I'll come, OK?' I'm such a sucker when it comes to this kid.

Being a three-year-old means she has no concept how long five minutes should be and demands we go after one. I manage to stall her for three, consider it a win and then she's dragging me behind her as we leave my room and go downstairs.

It's strangely quiet downstairs and Sumaira takes me past the front room, past the dining room, through the kitchen and into her playroom. It's a room I would have loved to

257

have as a child, with toys, a little desk, bookshelves, a wall-mounted TV and a door that leads out to the garden. But I see none of those things. I see the woman of my dreams sitting on a kiddie-sized pink chair looking jittery as she smiles at me nervously. My heart swoops and then soars.

'Here he is.' My niece presents me like I'm her favourite stuffed toy. 'I brought Mumu.'

'Thank you, Sumi. You're the best.' Safiya gives Sumaira a brilliant smile, while the little one looks up at me proudly.

'This is my friend. Her name is Auntie Saf.'

I crouch and hold my niece around her tiny body. 'This is your new friend?'

She nods enthusiastically. 'Yeah. She's really nice. She got me a new unicorn and special Lego. You can be friends with her too.'

'Gee, thanks, Sumi.' I ruffle her hair and she giggles.

'Mummy said to bring you down and show you to Auntie Saf and then I could have my treat.' In the blink of an eye, she darts off and it's just me and Safiya in the room.

I have no idea what's going on or what to expect. It's been nearly three months since I've seen Safiya and it's just as hard as it was the first time around – except this time, I don't have the crutch of hating her. Just the dull ache of loving her, which surged when I walked into the room and saw her.

I stand and make my way towards the window, leaning against the sill with my legs stretched in front of me and my arms folded across my chest, unsure about what to do with myself or what to say.

Since we got back from Perla Rosa, I've not heard anything from her or about her from Zaf – our conversations have been limited to work or much about nothing. I've not dared to get in touch with her myself, wanting her to initiate any conversation because I don't want her to think I'm trying to push her towards anything. I want any friendship we decide to pursue to be completely organic rather than obligatory. I can't bring myself to hope for anything more and then for that hope to be lost. It would kill me, and even now, when a small part of me wants more, a greater part of me is content to sit behind a barricade, avoiding putting myself out there.

She gets up and walks towards the door, closing it softly before leaning against it. She's wearing a traditional salwar kameez the colour of dusky roses and her hair is resting in loose waves on her shoulders, half of it pulled back with a clip. Long earrings dangle from her ears and the bangles on her wrists jingle whenever she moves her hands. She looks stunning, but then there's no version of Safiya which I don't find stunning.

Seeing her unexpectedly has thrown me for a loop. My heart is pulling me in one direction – hers – while my head wants to go the opposite way.

'I like your niece,' she says softly and that makes me laugh.

'It's kind of you to say so, but she can be a little nightmare when she wants.'

An awkward silence descends and she fidgets with the end of her dupatta and I can't help myself. 'Can I ask what prompted this visit?'

She nods. 'You.'

'Me? You could have called.' As soon as I say it, I know I don't mean it. I'd always rather see her and speak to her than just hear her voice, knowing she's miles away from me, literally and figuratively. Despite that persistent ache, I'm gladly soaking in the sight of her.

She shakes her head at that. 'This conversation has to be had in person.'

259

I raise my eyebrows at that.

She rolls her lips between her teeth before wiping her hands down her kameez and then she steps forward, while my pulse feels like it's working on a jerky rhythm as I wonder what this is about. 'There are a few things I need to say, but I'll start with the most important.' She takes a deep, audible breath in and I find myself holding mine. 'I love you, Murad.'

My heart screeches to a halt before it kick-starts again at twice its usual speed, the whooshing in my ears making me feel like I won't be able to hear her speak above it, but I do.

'I never stopped loving you. You've been the only man I've ever loved and you will always be the only man I'll ever love. I should have said that to you when you put yourself out there in Italy and suggested we give our relationship a fresh start. But, instead, I hid behind my fears and insecurities.'

I drop my arms by my sides and straighten a bit, but I keep myself against the window frame, afraid that if I try to stand on my own two feet right now, I'll be unsteady because of the strength of emotions rushing through me. Words clog in my throat but not a single sound emerges from my lips and then Safiya's speaking again.

'I'm punishing us both when I use my insecurities as an excuse not to try to move forward in the direction you want us to and which, deep down, I want to as well but I'm afraid of. But the truth is that neither of us is ever going to move on with anyone else, are we?'

I manage to shake my head in answer to her, even though her earlier declaration is still booming through my head. *I love you, Murad.*

'I'm sorry I didn't answer you honestly in Perla Rosa when you asked me if I love you. I lied when I said I didn't, because I do. In fact, that's the only thing I know for sure with every fibre of my being and every part of my soul.' The conviction in Safiya's voice tells me that she's speaking the absolute truth, her voice hasn't wavered even once, but she takes a shuddering breath now and I can hear the tremor in her voice when she continues. 'It's everything else I'm unsure about. Since coming back after the divorce, and even before then, I've found myself in a dark place, uncertain and insecure about everything, and I didn't want that for you. I was thinking about how I would drag you down when I should have looked at the fact that being with you will pull me up. It'll take me out of those depths. When I think about you, I see you as the sun in my universe and your love as its rays and I want to bask in that sunshine and soak up its warmth. But then I think that perhaps that's selfish of me. You bring so much to us while I—'

'It's not selfish.' I manage to croak out the three words, then I clear my throat, knowing how important it is for me to speak now and not let her believe any of the negative things she's saying about herself. 'People who love each other lift each other up, Fiya. Sometimes I'll lift you up and at other times you'll lift me up. And selfish is a word I can't associate with you when it comes to me. You gave me up for my own sake, that's not selfish, Fiya. It's love. I just couldn't see it. And choosing to be with who you love and who makes you feel good is a good kind of selfish. You have nothing to apologise for, and as far as bringing something to the relationship goes, I want nothing more than you and that really important thing you said to me at the start.'

A corner of her lips lifts and she raises an eyebrow at me. 'And what might that be?'

I can't help but chuckle, as gradually, a sense of lightness begins to fill me both in feeling and brightness. 'Nice to see the sass is back.'

She grins and then slowly begins to close the distance between us, while my feet remain rooted to the spot, as my feelings overwhelm me and I simply watch her.

She's no more than an arm's length away from me when she stops and says the words I've been wanting to hear again since she first uttered them. 'I love you, Murad. More than I can even articulate and more than I ever have before. Being with you fills me with a zest for life nothing else can compare with and I want to live that life with you, with your brightness and your warmth, with your energy and your serenity. All of you. Will you give me – us – another chance?'

A feeling of calmness washes over me and all other noise recedes into nothingness as I take in the sight of the woman standing in front of me. I want to savour this, soak in every moment and emotion. I feel a prickling in the corners of my eyes and my vision of Safiya slowly blurs before I blink the moisture away, only to have her erase the distance between us and cup my cheeks in her hands, her thumbs moving across them and wiping away my tears.

I lower my head as she moves closer and when I rest my forehead against hers, peace fills my body and I feel like I'm taking a full breath of air after a long time. Joy blossoms from within and I can't help the soft laugh that escapes through my lips. 'I've only ever allowed myself this moment in my dreams, not believing it can ever happen in reality. Please tell me I'm not dreaming. You're really here, aren't you? I've not just imagined all this.' My words are little more than a whisper, full of hope and uncertainty.

'No. You're not dreaming this. We get to live our dream now, Murad. We get to finally live the life we wanted to and which was denied us the first time round.' Her hands land on my shoulders, and I move my hands to her hips, relishing the contact with her.

'I love you, Safiya. With everything I am. Nothing would give me greater joy than living our dream together and having the chance of spending every day of the rest of my life with you. You make every day beautiful and I want that beauty in my life.'

She pulls away and I can see her eyes are awash with tears, but there's a broad smile on her face. A glow which takes me back seven years makes her face shine and I find myself falling in love with her all over again as she wraps her arms around my neck and squeezes me close to herself. I wrap my own arms around her body and hold her as close as possible, a part of me hoping that this moment never ends and another part of me ready to start living our dream already.

I slowly pull away from Safiya and hold her face in my hands, my eyes roving over every beloved feature of her face. Her bright, shining eyes look back at me, full of love and hope. Her cheeks are flushed and her glossy lips are lifted in a smile full of joy. 'You're gorgeous.' I can't help but tell her and before I can do anything, she reaches up and presses her lips against one of my cheeks and then the other, making my heart sing.

'I could look like a scary garden gnome and you'll still be stuck with me because I am never, ever letting go of you again.'

'I'm going to hold you to that, Fiya.'

She edges forward and I close the remaining distance between us, our lips touching softly, tentatively at first as she moves her hands to grip my T-shirt, pressing herself forward as I push my hands through her hair, the silky strands running through my fingers as I angle my head to press deeper into the kiss.

Kissing Safiya feels like having access to a well of fresh water after having traversed a desert with an empty water bottle for days and I drink like the parched man I am. She meets me stroke for stroke as she boldly takes control, pushing her tongue past the seam of my lips. A moan punctuates the silence around us and I don't know if it's her or me.

When I begin to feel lightheaded, I reluctantly pull away, though my hands stay where they are and I touch my forehead to hers once more, needing as much contact as I can get as our ragged breathing slowly begins to calm.

'Thank you for coming and doing this. I don't know how I would have gone through life if you hadn't—'

She moves back, pressing a finger against my lips to stop me from speaking. 'I had to. And there's no room for those thoughts in our lives anymore. Only good things from here onwards. And right now, I only want to hear three magic words from you. On repeat.'

'I love you, Fiya. I love you. I love you.' Her mouth drops open momentarily and I swoop down and kiss her on the cheek. 'I love you.'

'I love you too.' She hugs me around the waist and I hug her back, revelling in this moment and savouring the feeling of her finally being in my arms. Echoes of my rule about not falling for Safiya again go through my head and I can't help but smile. Breaking a rule has never felt so glorious.

'Mumu!' I hear Sumi seconds before the door swings open and she tears into the room, a stuffed unicorn clutched under one arm and smudges of chocolate on her gorgeous little face. She pauses a few feet away as she looks at me and Safiya. 'Are you and Auntie Saf friends now? Mummy said that if you are, you can come to the front room.'

Safiya and I look at each other before we both chuckle and make our way out of the playroom as Sumi runs ahead of us.

35

Safiya

'Safiya! It's so good to see you.' Antonella pulls me in for a tight hug. 'Murad gave me the good news and I couldn't be happier for both of you. I knew there was some chemistry brewing, but Giancarlo told me not to meddle.'

I smile at her as we both take a seat in her front room. 'It's only been six months since we've been together officially, but you're right, there's always been chemistry between us.' I don't tell her how long that chemistry's been there for.

The last six months have been like something out of a fairy tale and there have been moments when Murad has had to reassure me that this is really happening. Not that I've not done the same with him on the odd occasion. It's been a whirlwind, but only in the best way.

That day, when I had decided to firmly put the past behind me and move forward had marked a huge turning point for me. I hadn't rushed to declare my feelings to Murad. I had first gone to my parents and Qais and told them *everything*. Of course, they'd been heartbroken, but seeing my new resolve and determination to now live life on my own terms went a long way to reassure them that I was fine and that I'd be fine. Qais had been furious at the whole thing and what our grandfather had done, but, over time, he's calmed down. Just like I had my demons to slay, Qais has his and only he can decide how and when he wants to do so and come out from the shadows of the past, and I'll be with him every step of the way when he does.

I then spoke to Zafar about everything. I didn't think he would be up in arms about it, that's not like him, and I was right. Though of course he hadn't liked the fact that he'd been none the wiser about what had happened seven years ago. He warmed up to the idea of me and Murad pretty quickly and was more than happy to help put me in touch with Meerab – something I had been dreading, but I knew I had to do it.

It was one of the most difficult things I'd had to do in a long time – and I've done a lot of difficult things. She really put me through my paces when I told her how I felt about her brother, but once she was convinced I was serious about my feelings for Murad, she was fully committed to helping me see my plan through.

I arranged to be at her place when Murad would be there. My family were all onside with my plans, but I had insisted on carrying them out alone, making my way to Birmingham by myself and getting only little Miss Sumi to help me by bringing her uncle down to her playroom. Even Meerab had stayed out of the way after helping me plan everything and it had all worked out perfectly. Murad's reaction and response had been everything I'd hoped for. Seeing him as happy as he'd been had filled me with a deep sense of joy and satisfaction. I couldn't believe that I had come so close to forgoing all that because of my own hang-ups, sentencing us both to a life of isolation and misery, though that was soon forgotten when I finally – *finally* – got to kiss him. It had been everything I remembered of our connection and yet so much more. Pleasure had infused me and I had felt like I was floating amongst the clouds. And since then, it's only got better.

After that, we had taken it in turns to meet each other's families anew – though, of course, everybody already knew each other – before getting the families together. Our mothers were strictly warned about using the 'M' word. Murad and I had decided to wait before taking our relationship any further, just wanting to savour being with each other and discovering who we were, seven years later.

Murad began dividing his time more equally between London and Birmingham for work and I continued working on design projects on a part-time basis whilst doing additional courses to brush up on my knowledge on the side.

And now, six months after that incredible day, I'm pleased to say that I couldn't be happier. Sometimes, my heart feels so full, I don't know how to handle it. When I see him, my tummy does a somersault and I wonder if I'll always have that reaction. I don't think I used to, but I don't want it to stop. I hope I don't get used to the sight of him, because whenever I see him, I appreciate anew that this man is all mine. He loves me and I love him and we're blessed enough to get a second chance and finally be able to be together.

We meet up a non-negotiable minimum of twice a week for dates, during which we've talked, laughed, cried and reconnected in a way I never thought we would. The thought makes me smile until Antonella's voice pulls me out of my thoughts.

'I'm sure Murad told you that we made a staggering sale on the villa.'

I nod. 'He did. I'm glad it went to a family who want to make a home there. It needs to be lived in, it's too beautiful to sit empty.'

'*Sì*, you're right. Are you working on anything at the moment?' I've not kept much in touch with Antonella after we finished at the villa in Perla Rosa, aside from the odd catch up when she and Murad are working together. I was surprised when she called me out of the blue last week and asked to meet up, though I guessed it must have something to do with a design project.

'I'm working on a small project of a garden office for someone which should wrap up in three or four weeks, but alongside that, I'm doing a course on advanced colour theory and helping my parents do up their place.'

'Have you got anything lined up after the office? I mean, are you taking on any new projects?'

'That depends on the project.' I smile at Antonella and she smiles back.

'How about one in Switzerland?' I get butterflies in my stomach. 'It's not as lengthy a project as the villa in Perla Rosa, but I have a friend who has a chalet that needs your magic touch. He saw the villa and insisted I reach out to you on his behalf. So, if you're willing, the project is yours.'

'Oh. Wow. I . . . I don't know what to say.' I hadn't been expecting that. Maybe an enquiry but certainly not an outright offer.

'Say nothing for now. Let me email you all the details. Have a think about it and let me know what you decide when you're ready. And if you have any questions, just ask. If you like, I can even set up a meeting with him.'

While I'm surprised by Antonella's offer, it fills me with pride that she has. It makes me believe in myself in a way I never thought I would when I first met her and my confidence in myself has come a long way since then.

We catch up for a while longer before I take my leave and head outside, making my way towards my car and reaching for my phone as soon as I get inside.

'Fiya?' Goosebumps skitter over my arms and a pleasurable shiver goes through me at that name and the voice it's said in when Murad answers.

'Guess what?'

'Antonella had an offer for you?'

My face falls. 'Has she already told you?'

Murad chuckles. 'She told me she had an offer, but not what it was. What is it? Another villa near collapse?'

'Not quite. A chalet in Switzerland.'

Murad whistles.

'I know, right?! Crazy.'

'Not really. It only makes sense that if your work on the villa was so successful, you should get offers from others who want to work with you. Word of mouth like that beats all other forms of marketing. You can't create that, it's purely organic. And this sounds like a great opportunity.'

'Yeah, but Switzerland, Murad?'

'What about it? You did brilliantly in Italy, so why not Switzerland?'

'You think I should go?' I've not really gone anywhere since Perla Rosa so the idea of working by myself in Switzerland is daunting. Moreso because this time Murad wouldn't be with me.

'Only if you want to. I think it's a great opportunity and a chance to really build your portfolio, but if you don't feel comfortable, then don't do it. But whatever you decide, I want you to be sure of your decision. Either way, you'll be right and I'll support you.'

I take in a deep breath. The things this man says sometimes really get me. I can't help but say, 'I love you. You're the best. I'll think about it and see what I want to do. Antonella said she'd send me the details, so I'll look over those before coming to a decision.'

'Sounds like a good plan. And I love you too.'

We end the call and I start the car, knowing that whatever I decide to do, I know it'll be right because Murad will be by my side.

Karl Cella's expression gives nothing away. Not once, as he moved from one part of the chalet to the next, did his expression change, not even a twitch of his moustache, which makes him look kind of severe.

We circle back to the front door and he turns and faces me. 'I'm happy with this. Quite happy.'

Something tells me that this is a huge amount of praise from Karl.

He gives me a nod and I breathe a silent sigh of relief. I'm not going to lie, he kind of scares me a bit.

I've been working on Karl's chalet for just over three months now. He's been in and out a few times, largely leaving me to get on with the job while he stayed with a friend and I stayed at a nearby hotel. Since there wasn't much structural work to take care of, the project wrapped up pretty swiftly. The construction team were arranged through a contact of Zaf's and they've done a spectacular job of bringing my vision to life. The finish is better than I had imagined with a beautiful harmony of wood, metal and glass throughout the chalet. Karl preferred a minimal finish so the furnishings, while luxurious, are simple. If I had the chance I would love to spend a cosy weekend here with Murad and he agreed with me when I did a little video tour with him yesterday. And while I've really enjoyed working on this project by myself and seeing it come together so beautifully, I've missed Murad so much. I can't wait to get back to him.

With that thought in mind, I conclude the meeting with Karl and then make my way to the hotel I'm staying at.

I've enjoyed my time here in Switzerland, but I'm looking forward to going back home.

I step into the foyer of the hotel and walk towards the bank of lifts at the other end. 'Hello, Ms Saeed.' A deep voice rumbles behind me and a full smile is on my face before I turn around and launch myself into Murad's arms.

'What are you doing here?' My arms are wrapped around his neck as I look up at him. His hands rest on my hips as he ignores my question and lowers his head towards mine. I don't need to even think about it before I reach up to meet him, our lips unerringly finding each other. My body immediately melts towards Murad, savouring every brush of his lips and stroke of his tongue against mine. Too soon, he pulls back and rests his forehead against mine, something I find us doing a lot.

'I was missing you. Thought I'd drop by and say hello. I've heard such romantic gestures are much appreciated and amply rewarded.'

'You have, have you?' I nuzzle my nose against him before turning and leaning forward to push the button to call the lift.

We get out on the fifth floor and I lead the way to my room.

'So, how did the meeting with Mr Cella go? Is he happy with the chalet?'

'He was quite happy with it,' I say as I shrug out of my coat and make my way towards Murad, who's also taken his coat off and looks delicious in a jumper and jeans.

'Yeah, but what did he say?' He snakes his arms around my waist as I glide my hands up his chest.

'Just that. He said he was happy. Quite happy. He shook my hand and said it was nice to meet me, and that's it. Mr Cella's rather economical with his words.'

'Watching the guided video tour, I thought the chalet looked amazing. I think you're amazing too.' He lowers his head and I lift mine, only for him to bypass my face and nuzzle my neck, eliciting a rush of sparks along every nerve ending in my body. 'You're smart and sassy.' His hands move up my torso, stopping just short of the underside of my breasts before coming back down. 'You're fierce and funny.' I spear my hands through his hair, trying to urge him to bring his lips closer to mine. 'You're hard-working and—'

My stomach rumbles and both Murad and I freeze, his fingers paused on my waist.

'—Hungry?' he says and I can hear the mirth in his voice.

I lower my head against his shoulder as I groan and he chuckles.

'Stop laughing at me. I've not eaten anything since breakfast and it's nearly dinner time.' I try to pull away, but he tightens his grip on me.

'I'm not laughing at you, I wouldn't dare.' His lips twitch as he looks down at me and then he lowers his head and kisses the tip of my nose. 'Let's go and have dinner. What's the hotel restaurant like?'

I let him pull away but grip his hand at the last minute. He turns and looks at me questioningly. There's such a vast difference in the Murad I saw in that conference room over a year ago and the Murad of now and my heart overflows with my feelings for him.

'Fiya?'

'I love you.'

He smiles, the joy of it reflected in his eyes as he moves back towards me and cups my face in his hands.

'I love you too. My life is incomplete without you, Fiya. I'm not going to say I feel like the luckiest man in the world because that would mean quantifying how lucky I feel. But I feel blessed beyond compare that I have you in my life and that I get to make this extraordinary journey with you by my side.' Tears pool in my eyes with the depth of emotion in Murad's words and he lovingly wipes them away when they fall. 'We have loved and lost and found love again and that tells me that there is no one else for you or me. Whichever direction we choose to go in, we will always come back to each other.' He presses a kiss to my forehead and then we both make our way out of the room.

36

Murad

Two Years Later

'What do we get for moving the partition, Aziz?' Zafar asks me with a smirk on his face, as he and Qais stand at each end of the partition that's between me and Safiya, refusing to move it, even though the ceremony was done five minutes ago and I'm supposed to be seeing my wife for the first time without any morons coming in my way. Except her bastard brothers are very much standing in my way – all six of them.

'I can tell you what *I'll* give the lot of you if you don't move that partition in the next five seconds.' Safiya's voice comes from the other side and I grin at the six men standing in front of me.

'At the very least, you get to avoid a blistering from your sister, gentlemen. Now, if you please.' I wave my arm, and after some urging from the parents and some theatrical groaning of their own, they finally move the flower-bedecked frame that stood between me and Safiya while the imam conducted our nikah.

My eyes unerringly go straight to her. She looks absolutely magnificent in a rich burgundy lehenga with gold embroidery on it. She's wearing gold jewellery and her hands are adorned with henna all the way to her elbows, with bangles on both wrists. But the most striking thing about her right now is the radiant smile on her face as her eyes meet mine.

We close the distance between us and I hold her face in my hands, lowering a little to brush a kiss on her forehead before holding her close as everyone around us cheers and applauds.

'Congratulations. You've bagged yourself a wife,' she says to me cheekily as her hands rest on my chest.

'And I'm the happiest man for it.'

We make our way towards a beautiful two-tier cake and cut it together as our family and gathered guests look on. I feed Safiya a small piece, despite her brothers urging me to smash cake onto her face, and she reciprocates.

After an exquisite dinner, I hold her in my arms as we sway to the music on the dance floor, soaking in the magic of the day.

'How are you feeling?' My cheek is resting against the side of her head and she turns towards me as I ask her the question.

'Lucky.'

'Lucky?'

She nods just before I twirl her around and then pull her close again, facing her this time.

'Why lucky?' I ask.

'I get to call you my husband and myself your wife. We've waited a long time for this and in between I had thought it would never happen. And now that it has, I feel extremely lucky. But I'm content too. And I'm happy.' She scrunches her nose a little, making her faux nose ring lift and drop. 'Actually, I'm not sure how to articulate what I'm feeling. It's like a mixture of emotions, but they're all good. You?'

'Same, I guess. I'm just over the moon that we've overcome every obstacle that came our way and get to be together. Forever. It took some time and tears, but we're finally here.'

'I'll make a poet out of you still,' she says with a sunny smile.

The music changes tempo and everyone gathers on the dance floor.

Safiya's dad steps towards us and twirls his daughter into his arms before she moves to Qais, Zafar and then her other cousins in turn. Sumi dances with Dad while Zubair and Meerab join the dance floor together. Me, Mum and Irfan dance together until he decides he'd rather head towards the trolley bearing sweets. I'm about to go after him but Mum does as Daadi intercepts me and demands her dance with the groom. She dances with me for all of five minutes before she manoeuvres us towards Safiya and Harry and swaps places with her and Fiya is back in my arms, her face shining with joy. I enjoy every moment of our day as I'm certain Safiya does, knowing how hard won and precious it is for us.

The party carries on for another few hours and it's nearly midnight by the time Safiya and I make it to my – *our* – penthouse.

Safiya's done away with her bridal finery, with some assistance from me, and is now standing in front of the floor-to-ceiling windows in her jogging bottoms and over-sized T-shirt, her face bare of make-up and her hair in a knot on top of her head, clutching a mug of hot tea. I come and stand beside her, heaving a soft, satisfied sigh.

'This view is amazing.'

I turn to face her. 'I agree.'

'You're so cheesy. I'm talking about the skyline.'

'You can talk about whatever you like. I'm talking about you.'

She rolls her eyes, but there's a wide smile on her face.

I pluck the half-finished mug out of her hands and place it on the table before I stand directly behind her, my arms closing around her waist as she leans back against me. I move my lips to the side of her face and drop two kisses there before making my way down to her neck and then her shoulder, moving her T-shirt down so I can feel the warm velvet of her skin. My other hand is resting against her abdomen, but I move it upwards, grazing my thumb against the underside of her breast and she rewards me with a soft groan.

'Murad.'

'I don't know about you, but I'm keen to carry this on in our bedroom.'

She nods her head and then swallows loud enough for me to hear. 'Yes. God, yes.'

She turns in my arms and reaches up, holding my face in her hands and pulling it down towards herself. I barely get a chance to take a step back before she pulls me against herself. Her lips move over mine in a sensual rhythm and all thoughts flees my mind, except the thought of Safiya. Her tongue brushes against my lips and I open to allow her entry, sliding my hands around her back and then down to her bottom, lifting her up as she pushes her tongue into my mouth. Her hands have moved to circle my neck and she's wrapped her legs around my waist. Without breaking contact with her lips, I make my way to the bedroom.

Safiya

I could lie here for the rest of my life and you'll not hear a peep out of me. OK, maybe I'm being fanciful and exaggerating, but I'm allowed to. It's the morning after my wedding and I'm lying in my husband's arms – the husband I chose for myself and who I love with my heart and soul and who I know loves me back – and I'm warm and content and very much satisfied. As I lie cocooned under the covers, I can see the sky begin to gradually brighten through the floor-to-ceiling windows in the bedroom. It looks like it'll be a clear, sunny day.

I feel Murad's arms around me tighten and I look at his face, only to find him gazing back at me with a content smile on his face. 'Morning.'

'Morning.' A wave of shyness comes over me and I turn my face, but not before I hear a sigh from him and he squeezes me close.

'I forgot to give you your wedding present last night?'

That has me scooting back and sitting up. He sits up himself and grabs an envelope from the bedside table. He settles against the headboard as he hands it to me.

I waste no time in opening it, gasping when I see the contents. 'What?'

He shrugs, but his smile is full of satisfaction at a gift well given. 'I called in some favours. Better get your reds ready – we're going to Silverstone for the Grand Prix.'

'You bet.' I reach up and kiss the side of his jaw. 'How did you know?'

'You mentioned it once in Perla Rosa.'

'You remembered?'

'Is that a question?' His eyes are full of affection as he looks at me and I shake my head in wonder.

Feeling pangs of hunger gnaw at me, I decide it's time to haul myself out of bed and when I make it to the kitchen after my shower, I see that Murad's already warmed up the breakfast his mum had stocked in the fridge for us. There's a spicy chickpea curry and a creamy semolina pudding and Murad's buttering toast. Murad's family have been both warm and welcoming, something I found hard to accept initially given mine and Murad's history but my nervousness around them was soon overpowered by their affection for me. I make us both some tea and we sit down to our mini feast at the breakfast bar overlooking the river.

After breakfast, Murad moves to the sofa with fresh cups of tea for us and I decide to grab my phone and catch up with any messages. I take it out of my bag and spot the corner of the envelope I had stuffed in there when I packed. I pull it out and look at my name on the front. It's the letter Daadi gave to me over two years ago which I still haven't opened.

I've often pulled it out but always stopped short of opening it and reading it. I didn't chuck it away without reading, having decided that I will read it eventually, when I feel the time is right. I do want to know what's written.

I look around the room. What used to be Murad's room but is now *our* room after we decided to move into his place together after our wedding.

We've come such a long way from our past. None of that stuff has a bearing on our here and now. All the choices and decisions we've made have been our own.

I carry the letter to the front room and place it on the coffee table as I pick up my tea and sit on the opposite end of the sofa Murad's sitting on. He spots the envelope and quirks an eyebrow. 'Another present?'

I can't help but scoff. 'Not quite. It's a letter from my grandfather.' He doesn't say anything, but his expression becomes one of curiosity and concern. 'Daadi gave it to me after I came back from Perla Rosa, before we got back together. I've not opened it.'

'And now?' he asks softly as he watches me and I look between him and the letter.

I shrug my shoulders. 'It won't change anything. What's done is done. We've both moved forward and put the past behind us. But I'd be lying if I said I wasn't curious to see what's in it. When Daadi first gave me the letter, it was such a shock, I didn't feel ready to read it, so I put it away. I've been focusing on moving forward and a part of me is scared that reading this letter will push me back. I've pulled it out a couple of times but put it back without opening it.'

Murad doesn't say anything, but just having him there, listening and knowing that no matter what, he will support me with whatever I choose, helps settle my agitated nerves. I also know that he'll never say or do anything which he thinks will trouble me in any way or cause me detriment.

'I think you might be ready to read it,' he says softly after we've both sat in silence for a few minutes. 'It's like you said, we've come a long way and the contents of that letter can't change that. He was your grandfather and it's natural for you to be curious about what he wants to say to you. There's no right or wrong time to open it, Fiya. Go with your gut. I'm here with you, either way.'

I put my empty cup on the table and pick up the envelope before making my way towards Murad and settling in close to him. 'Will you read it with me?'

He nods, that serene smile that centres me directed my way. 'Open it. Let's lay this final piece of the past to rest.'

Unable to stop myself, I reach up and kiss the underside of Murad's jaw and settle back against him, feeling him put his arms around me.

I run my thumb across the cursive writing on the front of the envelope, the loops on the S, F and Y and the flourish with which it ends with the A. All I ever wanted was my grandfather's approval. Oh well. I can't change what's happened, but at least I'm now content with the decisions I've made since and which I will continue to do going forward, with the man I've chosen by my side.

I slip my finger under the seal and slide it to open the envelope, pulling out a handwritten letter.

My dearest Safiya,

I know I've likely lost the right to say anything to you, but if I don't take this opportunity to share a few things with you and apologise, then I'll never get the chance. It would serve me right but . . . I'd like to meet my maker knowing I made some effort to right my wrongs in this world, though I'm well aware that some of my wrongs can't be made right, no matter what.

You are my only granddaughter. I should have cherished you and held you close to my heart like the precious flower you are, but I made the gravest of errors when I moved you even further away from me than you already were. I hope you can find it in your heart to forgive your grandfather because, the truth is, and I've realised this far too late in my life, that I do love you. I was just too prejudiced, blinkered and full of my own consequence to see anything beyond it.

Qais and you are as much my grandchildren as Zafar, Ashar, Ibrahim, Rayyan and Haroon. I was wrong in treating all seven of you so differently and I'm more sorry for that than you'll ever know. I'm not going to get into a discussion about the era or my time or circumstances being different. I was wrong, end of story. The words 'tough' and 'love' shouldn't be in the same sentence.

282

Love is complete by itself, it needs nothing more added before it or after it.

But I think my greatest mistake when it comes to you was to separate you from the boy you loved and who loved you in return. I let my prejudice towards what I believed success meant dictate a matter which should always be handled without prejudice or negative bias like mine. You both had something perfect and I ruined that for you and him. No apology I make will ever be good enough for that failure of mine – I can't even call it a mistake.

I can't change what I've done and you're right in refusing to speak with me. I don't deserve easy forgiveness. But from the bottom of my heart, I pray that both you and Murad find happiness in your futures. I hope and pray that my mistakes don't cause you a lifetime of misery and that you find peace, happiness and love, because that is what's important and what you deserve.

I love you, my darling, and hope that one day, you'll be able to bring yourself to forgive your old Daada. May you always shine like the sun and fill everyone's life with brightness and warmth.

Lots of love,

Daada xoxoxo

P.S. Haroon showed me what 'xo' means recently. Sadly, I've run out of time and paper but imagine an infinite number of xos for you.

I slowly fold the letter and put it back in the envelope. Murad takes it from my unresisting fingers and places it on the side table. He settles back, his head resting on the top of mine.

'How do you feel?' Murad's voice rumbles against my back after a few moments of silence.

'I don't know. Is it bad to say I feel nothing?' Having had such strong feelings about my grandfather all this time, and with the weight of this letter with me for two years, not knowing what it might reveal, I now just feel nothing, maybe even empty.

'No, not at all.'

'I don't really know what to feel. It's been so long since I've held this fixed idea about him in my head and then along comes this letter.' I shrug.

'It's OK to feel like that, love. There's no right or wrong feeling here. And there's no deadline either. Your feelings may change over time and that's perfectly fine. For what it's worth, reading that letter's given me a small sense of closure right now. At least where he's concerned.'

'It has?'

I feel him nod. 'It has. Maybe it's because we're sitting here together, married and content. I do find it amazing how the same person can be different things for different people. I always looked at your grandfather through Zaf's lens, but after you told me what he did, I saw him in a different light. And now it's changed once more. I used to look up to him and think he wasn't a bad role model to have and I still stand by that to a certain extent. You can't take away the fact that he built what he did from very little, but I think he lost himself along the way. The way he behaved with you was . . . But he's apologised and he realised his mistake, and it's important to remember that.'

Murad's words resonate with me. I've felt a mixture of feelings and various thoughts have gone through my head since I received the letter, but Murad's right. Maybe it's because we're sitting here together after everything and so we can afford to look upon Daada with a little kindness than we might have if the situation had been different.

'You know he called me but I never responded? Maybe that's what he had wanted to say to me.'

'Don't beat yourself up about it, Fiya. I think it's great that he left a message for you and you've finally got it. I'm sure it's more than you ever expected.'

I nod and Murad kisses the top of my head.

'Just take that then and let's put all our other thoughts and feelings that have no place in our present into a box and lay it to rest. When he wrote you that letter, he probably had no idea that, despite what he did, we would still end up together. But after reading this letter, I'd like to think that he'd have been OK with it.'

'Yeah, me too.'

'What's meant to be will always be, Fiya. Nothing and no one can stop it from happening. You and I were always meant to be together. We just took time to get there and at times even we didn't know or believe we would be together, but we got there in the end, didn't we?'

I smile at that, even though he can't see my smile. He can probably hear it in my voice. 'Yeah, our love found its way seven summers later via Perla Rosa.'

Murad's arms tighten around me. 'That place is pretty special, but now it'll be more so for us. It's where we finally found each other again.'

'Yeah, there and in Sumi's playroom.'

That has him laughing and I luxuriate in the rich sound and the feeling of Murad's arms holding me, hoping and praying that from here onwards our lives are filled with laughter and love, forever more.

And if there are any more obstacles to face . . . well, we'll face them together.

Epilogue

To: *Murad Aziz*
From: *Safiya Saeed*
Subject: *Items for our List*

Husband,
I've got some new items I'd like to add to our list.
- The trip to Silverstone was incredible – as I knew it would be – so I propose making that a yearly thing if we can. I'm also open to going to other circuits around the world.
- There's a new adaptation of Twelfth Night at the Globe.
- I want to try a new steak place in Fitzrovia – Vaz said it's amazing.
- Should we plan a trip to the Highlands?

Feel free to add to the list.
S x

To: *Safiya Saeed*
From: *Murad Aziz*
Subject: *Re: Items for our List*

- Yes to Silverstone.
- Movie night at home
- Quality time with the Mrs at home
- Something else – anything else – that I can do at home

P.S. Saw Baz today. I told him about us. He silently
patted my shoulder and left the room.

To: Murad Aziz
From: Safiya Saeed
Subject: Re: Items for our List

That's so boring, Murad. Where's your sense of
adventure?
And Baz needs to retire.
S x
P.S. Even though you're boring, I still love you 🖤

To: Safiya Saeed
From: Murad Aziz
Subject: Re: Items for our List

Please find attached booking confirmation for our trip to
the Highlands.
P.S. Love you too, Fiya 🖤

Acknowledgements

I always thought that the more books I write, the easier I'll begin to find it. Ha!

Anyway, now that *Seven Summers Later* is done, I'm trying to remember what it was actually like. There were dead-lines, dead-ends and days of staring at the screen without blinking, wondering what I was thinking when I decided to write a book. Well, I wanted to tell stories and to do that, I have to go through the above every single time and while it feels insurmountable in the moment, the reward is just as sweet each time. Readers, I've done it – I've written another book!

However, none of this would have been accomplished without some very important people. I'd like to thank my champion of an editor, Sanah. You are an absolute treasure and I'm so lucky to have you in my corner.

Thank you to all the readers who have reached out to me. Writing is a pretty solitary job (despite me thanking a team of people right now) and hearing from people who are interested in my books, want to check them out and those who have already checked them out and loved them is a pick-me-up every author needs and loves. Keep them coming!

Lastly, a big of a thank you to my family. You lot are the only thing that keep me going on most days.

Until next time folks... LR x

Credits

Laila Rafi and Orion Fiction would like to thank everyone at Orion who worked on the publication of *Seven Summers Later*.

Editorial
Sanah Ahmed

Copy-Editor
Jade Craddock

Proofreader
Laura Gerrard

Audio
Paul Stark
Louise Richardson

Contracts
Rachel Monte
Ellie Bowker

Design
Rachael Lancaster
Loveday May
Nick Shah

Editorial Management
Charlie Panayiotou
Jane Hughes
Bartley Shaw

Finance
Jasdip Nandra
Nick Gibson
Sue Baker

Marketing
Javerya Iqbal

Publicity
Alisha Javaid

Production
Ruth Sharvell

Sales
Dave Murphy
Esther Waters

Victoria Laws
Rachael Hum
Ellie Kyrke-Smith
Frances Doyle
Georgina Cutler

Operations
Jo Jacobs

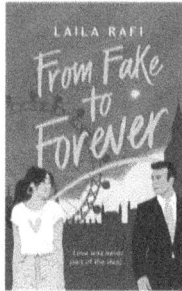

**One fake relationship. Two complete strangers.
And a love that was definitely not
part of the plan . . .**

Jiya and Ibrahim are a perfect couple. Except they're not
actually together, just faking it to get their families off
their backs.

Jiya wants to complete her MBA and get her dream job
in the city. So being perfect wife material and finding
the right guy is the last thing on her mind . . .

And Ibrahim certainly doesn't want to end up like his
older, dutiful brother by being pressured into a marriage
not of his choosing!

Their plan is perfect, until the attraction they're faking
starts to feel all too real . . .

They might be married.
But now it's time to fall in love . . .

Zafar is the perfect son. After all, he does keep his head buried in the family business and sets the right example for his younger brothers. But being the perfect husband doesn't come so easily to him . . .

Reshma didn't expect romance when she agreed to marry Zafar. And definitely not love. But there's something about Zafar Saeed that makes her long for the romance she reads in her books, so falling for him was easy. The only issue is that he barely acknowledges her!

And when Zafar and Reshma are reluctantly swept away to beautiful Mombasa for a family wedding, avoiding each other becomes even trickier. Forced to be in close proximity, Zafar and Reshma are about to discover that sometimes falling in love comes after saying 'I do'.